What the Readers Are Saying

"I love the Orange Stone because not only is its magic system and plot intriguing and unique, but is relatable to the younger generation of people. The Orange Stone is one of my favorite books and I highly recommend it to all readers." -Maryam Szigethy age 12

I loved this book. The story was highly relatable & filled with important life lessons.
I enjoyed being part of Someisa's adventures& her journey of self discovery. I was fully engaged & entertained from start to end. HIGHLY RECOM-MEND IT. Erika Toler

In this exciting new series, The Wasaru Stones, *The Orange Stone* being second in the series, engages your PEMS (physical, emotional, mental and spiritual) levels. Each stone's color gives new approaches to age old threats by celebrating non-violence through personal intention and the power of positive love by illustrating energy work. It shows how the real and tangible power of love overcomes the love of power. I've read it three times and learn something new each time. So.... I am impatiently waiting (like a kid asking for a pony for Christmas) for the next book, *The Yellow Stone*. Janet Parsons

Within my first sitting, I couldn't wait to dive in again to her vibrantly real characters, enticing story line, and transformative concepts. Though fantasy, I feel our world is so ready for the intriguing practices and often wise perspectives of the Cheschenaki people. I enjoyed every moment engaged in the world of Someisa, her community, and her intriguing companions. Linnie's skilled approach to revealing aspects of characters, cultural practices, and interwoven events ,made me feel at home and deeply connected with the community, their journeys, and the mysteries they must resolve. Jeanine Dubois

Other Books by Linnie Thomas

Fiction

The Red Stone

Non-fiction

The Encyclopedia of Energy Medicine: a Comprehensive Reference to
Healing Modalities from Acupressure to Zero Balancing
Pioneers in Healing Touch
Laws Governing Energy Medicine Practitioners
There Is No Hell

The Orange Stone

The Wasaru Stones Book 2

Linnie Thomas

Copyright © October 2024 by Linnie Thomas

Cover design by Tessa Guzman

A cozy fantasy book / published by arrangement with the author

Published by Ellinwood Publishing

Wilsonville Oregon

Library of Congress-in-Publication data

Thomas, Linnie 1946 –

ISBN: 978-0-9967776-6-7

Dedicated to

Joyce Strahn
Oreg & AMAG

What happens when people who have never known violence or war come face to face with a people who kill, but cannot be killed?

Prologue

The tree people welcomed the fog people, who came to say good morning. All was as it should be until something created a disturbance in a little glen not far from a path that wound through the forest. A shimmering took form at the edge of the trees. All movement stopped, and the forest went silent, watching the something foreign that had just arrived.

An odd creature stepped through the shimmering. Shaped somewhat like a man, it appeared to be made of metal. The energy around the thing did not mingle with the surroundings. Instead, it clung to the creature, venturing no further out than an inch. The metal man looked around to get a bearing on its location. Then it waited.

The plant people sent their consciousness into their roots and waited for the thing to go away. The animal people shied away from the area and silently made their way to places of observation where they felt safe.

The creature never noticed them. Its attention remained on the shimmering in front of it. Presently a man came rushing through the shimmering, nearly fell as he emerged, but stayed on his feet. He oriented himself, took note of the creature in front of him, and nodded as a way of greeting.

The creature pointed at the man, and a projectile flew from a finger like appendage. A hole bored into the man's forehead, and he twisted and fell. The odd creature looked down at the dead man, now lying at his feet, with no sign of emotion. It entered the shimmering and disappeared.

The forest stayed quiet. The animal people left the area. No songs were sung that day.

Chapter One

Curiosity may have killed a cat, but satisfaction brought it back to life.

Something didn't feel right. The forest noises were quiet, which was not unusual, although it seemed odd for so early in the morning. The cat couldn't put her paw on what was bothering her. Rising to her feet, she scouted around the area where she had been napping, making no sound. Nothing caught her attention. Soonak moved her search a little farther out.

It wasn't long before she found the source of the unease. On top of a little knoll stood a man made of metal talking to another man wearing a hooded cape. The metal man had a round head on top of a much bigger round body, two arms and two legs. The second man appeared to be Cheschenaki, although Soonak knew better than to judge a man's heritage by his clothing. The hood covered the man's face, making positive identification difficult.

The Cheschenaki threw his arms out in angry gestures while the metal man stood without moving. There was something about the Cheschenaki's energy that seemed familiar and at the same time alien, but the two were too far away for a detailed inspection. Soonak wanted to creep closer, but the Cheschenaki shook his fist at the metal man and stomped off through a grove of trees. Soonak lost sight of him just as it began to rain.

The metal man stayed behind and appeared to be observing the village of Chehalem about a mile downhill from where it stood. Soonak had met this kind of thing before. She covered the ground between them in silence. Drawing near, the panther stalked the metal man, her tail twitching. Coming up behind him, she gave a mighty swat with her paw and knocked the thing's head clear off its shoulders. The head rolled over some ground and came to rest at the foot of a small boulder. Soonak nodded approval at the boulder, which returned the nod with a smirk.

Curious about the other, Soonak searched the area for any lingering hints of the man and found nothing. The rain came down in torrents, dispersing scents to her disappointment. Still, she had a great sense of smell and even with the rain, she expected to pick up something, but nothing came to her senses. With a sigh, the big cat turned her back on the remains of the metal man and went in search of Reisander, one of the rangers, often called wanderers, who roamed the Cheschenaki territory and helped keep the peace.

She found him at The Eldest Grandmother's house, located on an island a short distance from the shore of a lake. The panther crossed the stone bridge leading to the house. Being in a hurry, she ignored the beautiful gardens surrounding the house, the dogs sleeping on the porch, and rushed through the door to be greeted by an old woman.

The Eldest Grandmother, known to close friends as Esther, and for her young friends, she preferred to be called Grandma Tea. As the oldest and wisest of her people, it was her job to be advisor to all the Cheschenaki tribes and keep them together. Each individual tribe is ruled by an elder grandmother, which causes some confusion at times with the young ones. They don't always see the difference between an elder grandmother and The Eldest Grandmother, but they know enough to be polite to all of them. To avoid confusion, the young ones liked to refer to The Eldest Grandmother as "The Old One" when she came up in private conversation among themselves, and thought they were clever doing so, not knowing their parents and grandparents did the same thing.

Of all the rangers, Reisander was the only one to have visited every village in the tribal lands within a five-year period. He knew each village's character and the feel of the combined energy of the people who lived there. He not only kept a close connection to the people, but to all living things, as well as the rocks and soils. If something was amiss with anything connected to the ground or the people living on it, he was usually the first to know. Reisander knew all the traders and tinkerers who also wandered from tribe to tribe. In addition, dragons guarding the planet kept Reisander informed of activities in the other nations and, on rare occasions, things going on off-planet.

Someone sent Reisander a message that morning, saying some men from Chehalem found the body of a metal man about a mile from the Chehalem village. The head was missing. Reisander had no doubt as to whom the culprit was that had removed the head. It was this last event that caused him to stop what he was doing and head to The Eldest Grandmother's house.

The ranger arrived at Esther's house to discuss this and three other sightings of metal men. She greeted him with a hot cup of tea, as though she expected him to arrive at that moment.

Happy to see Esther and Reisander in the same place, Soonak invited herself into Esther's home and sat down in front of the fireplace. "Encountered a strange being again today," she said by way of a greeting, knowing she was interrupting their conversation. The cat had no patience for good manners.

"And what did you see today?" asked Esther.

"A man made of metal. I have seen others on rare occasions. The sightings have become more frequent. They look very much like the metal men Someisa describes in her dreams."

"When did you first see one of these creatures?"

"Locally, about fifty years ago."

Reisander's head jerked up. "Why didn't you tell us about it, then?"

"Needed to confer with my people. It was of some concern, but as there was only one and nothing came of it, we let it go. We chose not to warn you, as we felt it wasn't dangerous at that time. Much later, we noticed activity elsewhere was escalating. It concerned us enough for Dragonis to call a meeting of the elder grandmothers fifteen years ago.

"After the first local sighting, we heard nothing about the metal men in these parts until Someisa began seeing them in her dreams. That was when we decided I should come here in the form of a black panther and be her power animal. I could talk with her mind to mind and also be visible to the two of you."

"What were the other occasions?" asked Esther.

"Those sightings were not on this planet, which is what led us off track. At first, we thought the one sighting here was merely a waypoint, or perhaps a lookout for observing the territory, not finding it to its liking, and leaving. Someisa's dreams have changed all that, and we have become more alert.

"Then there was the finding of Bromo's body. We have suspicions that one of the metal men killed Bromo, but don't know why. That metal man ignored the Accords and performed a violent act on this planet. I think they believe they have nothing to lose, as they don't recognize death as anything more than a defective unit."

"It sounds to me like you know a lot more about these metal men than you let on," observed Reisander.

"Yes," said Esther." Tell us more. Where do they come from? What do they want from us?

"They come from another universe. Don't know why or how. Someone in this universe invited them here or they could not have come. We have traced a communication with the metal men to somebody, we don't know who, on this planet. We have no knowledge of anyone here having that much technology or telepathic power. Whoever it is, has kept himself well hidden."

"This scares me," said Esther. "To have such a dangerous person in our midst and not know about it is unthinkable. And yet it has happened."

"We don't know where on the planet this person lives. It could be a sprite, or dolphin, or even a whale, although I doubt that. More likely, it is a person living here within this nation."

"I have not felt the presence of such a person, have you, Reisander?" asked Esther.

"No, but then I haven't been looking for someone like that. I'll pass this information on to the rangers as soon as possible. What else do you know about these metal men, Soonak?"

"Because they are made of metal and are a different type of soul than us, they don't acknowledge our Accords, which is another reason they may think they have nothing to lose. They have no understanding of how a biological universe works. Birth and death may be meaningless to them. Apparently, though, we have something they want, and want it badly enough to break the laws of our planet."

"Do you know something about the head being knocked off a metal man found on Finnegan's Knoll? It looks like some of your work," said Reisander, frowning at Soonak.

Soonak yawned and began washing a spot near the base of her tail.

"That is disgusting," said Esther. "Do that somewhere else."

"I am merely making a point," the cat replied. "By physically expressing what I feel about these metal men."

"You don't have to be rude about it," said Esther.

"I think you're going to lose this argument, Soonak," observed Reisander. "She's right. That's no way to act at a lady's house."

Soonak moved on to washing her hind foot.

Reisander began pacing. "But enough. We've far more important things to talk about. I'm thinkin' the metal men have a way of tracking each other. Possibly the head contains the tracking mechanism." Reisander finished some lukewarm tea and gently set his cup down on a nearby table.

"Do you suppose it has a brain, then?" asked Esther.

"Don't know," said Reisander.

Esther reached for the teapot and poured herself some fresh tea. "Do you want some more tea?" she said, having noticed Reisander had set down an empty cup.

"Thank you. I'll have another cup." He breathed in the woodsy aroma of freshly made breakfast tea and sighed with pleasure. He reached down, removed his boots, and rubbed a sore spot on his foot where there was a hole in his sock.

"You are welcome. Please put your boots back on. Your feet smell to high heaven," said Esther, wrinkling her nose. "I have something for you." She left the room and returned with a dozen pairs of new socks.

Reisander face reddened as he accepted the socks. "Thank you very much," he muttered.

"So now, what do we do with the rest of the body?" said Esther, settling back down on a couch. "I don't think it is safe in Chehalem and I do not want it here. While this place is well protected, I don't want unwelcomed visitors prowling around looking for a headless body"

"I agree." Reisander sighed, took off his old socks, donned a new pair and put his boots back on. He carefully tucked the new socks in a pocket and the old ones in a separate pocket. "Any ideas Soonak? How about the Grand Library?"

"Not good," said the cat while scratching an ear. "Might lead the metal men to our most sacred treasure."

"True. I hadn't thought of that." He gave another tired sigh.

"I think Gobha might know of a place," interjected Esther. "Is he anywhere nearby?"

"Last I heard, he was over at the Kewoyuspan camp learnin' more about their dietary needs."

A knock at the door interrupted their discussion. Reisander went to open the door.

"Somethin' told me I had otta be a headin' this way. What can I do for ya?" announced Gobha as he entered the house.

Gobha, a ranger, and instrumental in aiding the capture of the Kewoyuspans, loved the plant and animal people. A few were known to be seen in his hair and beard. He towered over Reisander, who was taller than most Cheschenakis. Gobha, seldom seen by the villagers, loved the rain forest in which he lived. He also loved the wide open spaces of the high mountain desert east of the mountains. The variety of plants and animals, their differences and similarities, were his favorite field of study, especially for medicinal purposes. He spent much of his time working with the healing arts for plants and animals. He frequently visited with Zoenka, Someisa's mother, and a master healer for the Cheschenaki nation. Although not well known, Gobha was The Master Healer for the Cheschenaki nation and had mentored Zoenka.

Reisander hugged the man and ushered him into the room. Esther left the room to get a mug. Her tea cups were too small and fragile for Gobha's tremendous appetite and size.

"Thank ya, Ma'am," said Gobha. "I'm mighty obliged". He completely filled the largest chair in the room and his knees rose above his waist when he sat down.

"You're just in time," said Reisander. "We've a problem that we think you've an answer for."

"Lemme at it. Love a good challenge." Gobha spied a plate of oatmeal raisin cookies ,his favorites, on the coffee table and promptly helped himself to six of them.

Reisander grinned when he saw Gobha go for the cookies and then got serious again. "The body of a metal man turned up on Finnegan's Knoll outside of Chehalem. The head is missing. We need a place to hide the body that has enough light so we can study it without exposing it to the elements or unwanted eyes. Do you know of such a place?"

"Yup. I knows just the place. Tis in wood sprite territory. About as safe as can be had in these parts. Hole in the roof for light. On the downside of yon mountain where protected from rain fall so stays dry inside. Wood sprite village nearby to stand guard, too." Gobha reached for more cookies.

"I know the mountain," mused Reisander. "It has an unusual formation on the eastside. Didn't know about a cave, though."

"Wood sprites know how ta keep thin's hidden. I'll go now and tell 'em we're needin' the cave for a while." With that, the big man grabbed another handful of cookies, which emptied the plate and rose, preparing to leave the house."

"Soonak," said Esther. "Bring Someisa here and we will learn more about these dreams she has been having." The panther disappeared.

"Wait a minute, Gobha" called Esther. She was on her way to refill the plate of cookies. "I think you should wait to hear Someisa's stories about her dreams with the metal men before you leave."

"I'll be back afore she gits here," he said.

Chapter Two

Patience may be a virtue, but who cares?

S omeisa sat in front of an entry way framed by red curtains. A flame burned in the upper center. Her assignment was to make the flame grow until it reached a leafless branch hanging from the top of the frame. Attached to the branch was a small candle. The goal was to raise the flame to where it would light the candle without burning the curtains or the branch. The whole thing had to be done through the use of her mind as a tool.

It was a tricky assignment. Not only did she have to raise the flame, but she also had to bend it in order to light the candle. Someisa had been working on this assignment for months. She had figured out how to grow the flame straight up without setting fire to the curtains, but when it came to bending the flame, the curtains or the branch caught fire every time. The rules given to her by The Eldest Grandmother stated she was not to move the container holding the flame either.

This was one of the many trainings set for her by Grandma Tea. Two years had passed since the girl's Wasaru, a coming of age ceremony each teenage Cheschenaki had to go through. When her turn came, she drew the rare white stone from the ceremonial basket. Hers was the most difficult life training. All the other stones were colors of the rainbow and each color designated the type of lifework to be studied by the person who chose it.

Because Someisa drew the white stone, she needed to learn all the colors' offerings before she could work on the white stone topics.

Most all of her mentorship training with The Eldest Grandmother involved the use of her mind. This exercise frustrated her. She was sure there had to be a trick to accomplishing the goal. A thought passed through her mind. She was not allowed to touch anything surrounding the flame, but what if she was to touch the flame itself?

She closed her eyes and set an intention to surround her hand with a protective barrier so she wouldn't get burned. Once done, she grew the flame to the height of the candle, and visualized her hand reaching into the flame, bending it, and lighting the candle. It worked. Pleased with herself, she sat back and watched the candle burn.

"I'm not sure if that is cheating," said Soonak. "But it is one way to light the flame."

Someisa jumped. "Don't sneak up on me like that. I thought you were Elder Grandmother." Toshu, the elder grandmother of the Chehalem village where Someisa lived, served as the official leader of the village in a role similar to a mayor. Toshu frequently stopped by to see how Someisa's training was going.

"Nope, not me," said Soonak. "Knowing Toshu and Grandma Tea, they'll congratulate you on your first solution and then ask you to try another. By the way, your sleeve has caught fire."

"What?!" Someisa hurriedly pushed her sleeve into some dirt to stop the flames from reaching further up her tunic. "Shuckey darn. Now I'll have to make another new sleeve."

"Cut it off and make your tunic short sleeved."

"Yeah, I could do that, except I've already shortened the sleeves on all my other tunics. Mother isn't happy about it and insists I make new sleeves. Shuckey darn. This is the last long-sleeved tunic I own. I guess I'll have to sew some new sleeves. I hate sewing."

Soonak did her best not to laugh at the unhappy girl. Fortunately, she had a message to give to Someisa.

"The sewing will have to wait. Reisander wants to see you. You are to run up to The Eldest Grandmother's house immediately." Reisander was another one of Someisa's mentors.

"Honestly, everything is always immediately with him. And when I get there, he makes me wait until he is ready to see me."

The cat showed no sympathy for the girl and faded from sight. Someisa sighed, put out the flame, and went into the house to let her mother know about the summoning from Reisander.

"Couldn't Reisander give us some warning, a little time for preparations at least, before he summons you hither and yon," complained Zoenka, Someisa's mother.

"You know I haven't any say in the way he does things. You'd think in the two years I have been serving as his foghlamach, he would get the message that I need a little time before I can go rushing off to meet him somewhere."

"I wouldn't have allowed my mentor to treat me the way Reisander treats you."

Someisa sighed. "I know, Mother. We have been over this before. You got to choose your mentor. I didn't. The Eldest Grandmother chose him, at least I think she did. So let's leave it at that. I'll grab my backpack. I gotta go."

"You'll find a long-sleeved tunic on the bed. I replaced the sleeve for you."

"Thanks, Mama," Someisa grinned in delight and ran to her room to change tunics and pick up the backpack and a cloak that were waiting for occasions such as this. She stopped long enough to kiss her mother good-by and headed out of the village to the path that led to The Eldest Grandmother's house.

Chapter Three

No matter how learned we may think we are, there is so much more that we do not know.

Tonguetied called all the rangers to be present at The Eldest Grandmother's house to hear Someisa's stories about her dreams. One by one, they each arrived in the hours before Someisa came. Toolan sat quietly, smoking a pipe filled with cherry flavored tobacco. He breathed in deeply, enjoying the flavor and aroma of the smoke, while listening to the quiet chatter of others in the room. As he waited, Toolan mused over the sightings of metal men.

Most people thought of Toolan as a foolish old man and tolerated his presence out of kindness. As a result, he collected information from unsuspecting Cheschenakis. People weren't afraid of talking in front of a fool and often teased him for living in stories rather than real life.

What they didn't know was that he had a perfect memory. Words he heard, he often recorded in his mind and later put on scrolls of parchment to be stored in the Grand Library, a huge underground building that housed the history of the Cheschenaki people.

Hara, picking up on Toolan's thoughts, said, "What strange creatures these things are." Hara said little up to this point. He was a small man, thin, and only a couple of inches taller than Someisa. As a creator of new life species and the observer of older species leaving the planet, he was quite curious about the metal men. "Sentient they might be, but I can't bring meself to decide if they are life beings or some sort of mechanical construction that somehow has attained intelligence. Could we even call them sentient?"

Langor entered the conversation. "I can see no way of communicating with them," he commented. "If they have no language, I do not see a way of acknowledging their existence as sentient beings. I think they are something else entirely." Langor was tall, thin, and a little pale. He spent much of his time in libraries, especially the Grand Library, trying to decipher ancient languages.

"You may have a p-point." Tonguetied, the official leader of the rangers, got up from his chair and began pacing. His mentor gave Tonguetied his nickname because he stuttered. He meant it as a compliment, as Tonguetied thinks faster than he can speak, thus the stuttering. No one knew his Wasaru name, and it's possible even he didn't remember what it was. "We need to m-meet with one of these things in real t-time. The d-dream time, coming through Someisa may tell us much, but I think what she says will b-barely scratch the surface of what we face. Let's hear from Soonak."

The black panther stretched out in front of the fireplace, enjoying its warmth. Not wanting to leave it, she stayed put. Originally, when Soonak came to the planet, she intended to remain invisible to all but Someisa, Reisander, and Esther. Times changed and the need for her to converse with others became evident. Until that moment, Reisander and Gobha were the only rangers who noticed she was even there.

Langor crossed the room to reach for some cookies and saw Soonak. "Who's pet is the panther?" he asked.

All he got for an answer was laughter and the sound of purring. "That's Soonak," said Reisander.

"Oh ,really?" Langor looked from the cat to the other ranger. "Why is a black panther sitting here in Esther's living room?"

Before Soonak could say anything, Reisander replied, "She came to this planet as a volunteer to be Someisa's power animal. Who or what she really is, is not important right now, so don't ask."

Soonak, annoyed that Reisander was answering questions meant for her, changed the subject. "We are deeply concerned about these metal men. They are not from our universe. They run by a different set of universal laws that make up their accords, if we can call their laws, accords. We think they are so alien to us, as to who and what they are, that we have no way of finding an understanding between our people and them.

"I would like to know how they discovered our universe and how they crossed into it. I know of no way to create a portal that enables the crossing between two universes. It would require technology as yet unknown in our universe. Did the metal men build it, or was it done by one of us?"

"I have found something," interrupted Seefar, who could project his consciousness anywhere on the planet. He was as big around as he was tall. The man had to sit on a sofa because the only chair big enough for him was taken up by Gobha. Seefar's hair had never been cut. Tied and braided at the back of his neck, it hung down almost to his ankles. He took great care to make sure he didn't sit on it.

Seefar had been in a trance for some time. "It was very difficult to find any trace of these metal men. They leave nothing behind of where they have been or where they are stationed on this planet. I think it is because they have no fluid energy fields and no emotions.

"So, I needed to look for something else to find their where-a-bouts. I began by looking for differences in frequencies. That proved fruitful, as

I found one. I compared its frequency with that of the plant and animal people surrounding it. There is a big difference.

"I recorded my findings and again searched our nation's territory for signs of that frequency or one like it. I found none which disappointed me and I thought I was on the wrong track. Then it dawned on me they might not exist in our dimension, being from another universe. That's when I found them shifting in and out of our dimensions with apparent ease. The base of their entrance and exit to our world is on the southeast edge of the dead lands.

"What worries me is the possibility they don't travel via a portal. They shift dimensions and go wherever they please. They may be using portals for other beings or they are teleporting them somehow."

"Interesting," said Reisander. "Can it be that they know we can't go near the dead lands because of the wasting sickness that comes upon anyone who goes near it? I don't like the thought that they know so much about us."

Chapter Four

If you are the cause of a problem, then you are also the solution to the problem.

While the men talked, Seefar checked on Someisa's progress up the trail several times. "I am uncomfortable with Someisa traveling alone right now. I sense something in the energy fields surrounding a small meadow near the path from Chehalem to here." Concerned, he had interrupted the conversation. He started to say something to Soonak about guarding the girl for the rest of her journey, but the cat had already left.

Half a mile from Grandma Tea's house, Soonak sensed a presence that disturbed her. It was cold, hard, and lacking in the energetic fluidity natural to the natives of the planet. Someisa was still a short way down the path from where the cat stood. The fur on the cat's back stood on end and her tail fluffed to three times its size. Yet, no strange smells reached her nostrils. The surrounding countryside was unusually quiet, though. Unable to figure it out for herself, the black panther immediately contacted Seefar to check the surrounding area again, as she didn't want to venture far from Someisa and, at the same time, alarm her.

At first, Seefar found nothing. He was about to leave when he noticed movement at the far end of a meadow a little way from the path to Grandma Tea's. What he saw frightened him.

The thing was smaller than the other metal men he previously observed. This metal man was intent on something and didn't notice Seefar's presence, which gave the ranger a better chance to observe the thing more closely. It looked like a small ball on top of a much larger, round ball with long arms and short legs in appropriate places. It didn't have the usual organs of an animal. He doubted it was breathing, as there seemed to be no structure within its body that could serve as lungs. Thin metal ropes and doodads of all kinds dangled from its body. Seefar couldn't tell if it was male or female or asexual, or something else entirely. A sense of foreboding came over the ranger. Even though the thing gave off no emotions, Seefar felt it was a threat of some kind. Whether or not it was a life form, he really couldn't tell.

The thing seemed to have some intelligence as it peered at its surroundings. After watching it for a while, it dawned on Seefar that the thing was looking, or possibly waiting, for something. It stayed in the shadows at the edge of the meadow, looking in all directions. When Soonak approached the turnoff to the meadow, it disappeared.

Reisander shook Seefar out of his trance. Apparently, the far seeing ranger had been screaming. All the rangers and Esther looked at him with concern.

"What did you see?" asked Esther, kneeling down to look into his eyes. "Send me and each of the others a picture of what you saw."

Seefar obliged by putting a picture of the thing he had seen in the window of his mind and sent it first to Grandma Tea, and then to each of the others. "What is it?" he asked once he was done.

"I think we are seeing a face of our true enemy come to invade us," said Reisander. "The other metal men we have observed up to this point do not display an ability to make decisions for themselves. This one does." Turning to Toolan, he asked, "Will you read to us the prophesy that you found in the old records?"

"Yes," answered Toolan. "You had suggested that I look through the records of the prophets from long ago. It turns out about eight hundred years ago several seers from all over the planet made the same prophesy. I brought along a copy for each of you." Toolan reached into a bag he carried with and pulled out seven scrolls and handed them around.

"The messages are short. Each one says the same thing in a little different way. I don't understand all of it myself. From what I can make out, they are saying stone cold beings will invade our world."

"What does that have to do with us?" Langor asked as he reached for a warm oatmeal cookie not long out of the oven. He sniffed it, savoring the enticing smell of cinnamon that Esther had added to the recipe. The cookies were not exactly small, more like the size of a salad plate.

"We don't know," said Toolan. He, too, reached for a cookie and continued talking around mouthfuls. "We don't know what they plan to get from us or why they picked us to study. We do think they pose a threat of some kind."

"Do any of the prophesies predict what we need to do?" asked Reisander.

Toolan frowned. "It isn't clear. Only one of the prophesies addresses that subject and it doesn't make any sense."

Esther had quickly skimmed over her scroll and missed what Toolan was talking about. "What does it say?'

Toolan shifted uncomfortably in his chair and cleared his throat. "Love will find away," he said.

Chapter Five

Use your fear. It can take you to the place where you store your courage.

The forest grew totally silent as Someisa made her way up the trail. It reminded her of a time with Thistle, just before they found Bromo's body. Thistle was a wood sprite, about five inches tall. Her wings rarely stopped moving, which made her hard to see at times. Someisa had rescued her from a large spider web and the two became lifelong friends. She wondered where the little wood sprite was. Just then Thistle landed on Someisa's shoulder, highly agitated.

"Waiting."

"What? Who's waiting?"

"Waiting," Thistle repeated.

"What would you like me to do about it?

"Run!" cried Thistle, suddenly.

"Why?"

Highly agitated, Thistle fluttered around Someisa's face. Looking the girl straight in the eye, the wood sprite yelled, "Run, now!"

Someisa ran as fast as she could. She missed the sneaky rock that had caught her unawares so long ago, and caused her to fall just before she went off the trail.

"Faster!" cried Thistle.

Scared, Someisa ran as if her life depended upon it, which wasn't far wrong. A stitch formed in her side, but in her panic, she ignored it and kept running. Finally, she made it to the gate at Grandma Tea's place. Reisander was waiting for her.

He held the gate open for her and she ducked in. They ran together past the uncomfortable place which protected The Eldest Grandmother's territory to a little bridge that crossed over part of the lake to the island where the old woman lived.

Someisa stopped before crossing the bridge to catch her breath. She doubled over, close to tossing her cookies. Reisander pushed her gently down to the ground, letting her get control of herself.

"You're safe now, gal," he said. "Breathe in slowly and deeply through your nose, then let it all out through your mouth in a whoosh."

Someisa did as she was told and soon found she could talk.

"What is going on?" she demanded. "First Soonak comes and tells me I must hurry to Grandma Tea's house, and she leaves me. Then Thistle appears out of nowhere and tells me to run. And scolds me for not running fast enough. I thought I would never get here."

"You up to walking the rest of the way, gal?" said Reisander.

"Yeah .I want to know what is going on."

"All in good time."

"That man can be so infuriating," she thought as she got to her feet.

Chapter Six

In times of trouble, it is wise to unburden yourself to kind listeners.

S omeisa arrived at The Eldest Grandmother's house, still a little out of breath. Grandma Tea stood in front of the open front door, waiting for their arrival. "You made good time getting here," she said to the panting girl as she came closer. "We have need of you. Come, sit down, and I'll get you some tea."

***

Quietly, Soonak entered the house by the back door and settled herself in front of the fire.

***

"Thistle made me hurry. She kept telling me to run. I felt like something was chasing us, although I didn't see anything," said Someisa.

Grandma Tea handed Someisa a cup of steaming tea and a tiny thimble sized cup to Thistle. Speaking to the little wood sprite, she asked, "What was the big hurry?"

"Weird energy,"

"What do you mean by that?"

"Different."

"Was it just energy or something more tangible?"

"Different."

Realizing she wouldn't get more out of the little wood sprite, The Eldest Grandmother called over to Langor and asked him to come talk with Thistle. She knew her knowledge of the wood sprite language wasn't sufficient to interpret all of Thistle's trills. Reisander had some knowledge, much the same as hers, but Langor was the real expert. The others waited while Langor and Thistle trilled to one another.

Finally, they stopped talking, and Langor interpreted. "She says whatever it was, it wasn't visible to her eyes. More that she felt it, and it was very uncomfortable. She didn't want to go near it and feared for Someisa's safety."

Esther, who noticed the panther's arrival, turned to Soonak and said. "Do you have anything to add to this?"

"What Thistle described is correct," said the big cat. "It wasn't something tangible, more like a projection."

What do you mean by a projection?" asked Tonguetied.

"Like a three-dimensional picture," answered the cat.

"We'll talk of this later," interrupted The Eldest Grandmother. "Make yourself comfortable, Someisa. Have a cookie. We have a few serious questions to ask you. Please answer them as best you can. It sounds like your arrival has brought even more questions. Not that we expect you to answer them."

Some of the men seated around the room Someisa didn't know, except for Gobha and Langor. Someisa found her favorite chair waiting for her and sat, wondering what she could possibly know that these men didn't. She decided not to eat a cookie until she knew where she stood. The embarrassment of having a bit of cookie get caught in her throat, because a question caught her off guard, did not appeal to her.

Soonak sat up and faced Someisa. "They want to know about your dreams."

"What dreams?"

The cat sighed. "The ones about the metal men, of course." Soonak playfully poked at Thistle.

"Bad cat," retorted Thistle, and moved to the other side of Someisa, away from the cat's paws.

Someisa frowned at both of them and took a deep breath. She could smell the aroma of oatmeal and raisin cookies, and her mouth watered. But she decided she was right in resisting the temptation of eating a cookie just then.

"Why now? It's been almost two years since the dreams happened," she said.

Reisander spoke up. "It's been quiet as far as the metal men are concerned. Only recently have we had reports of them."

"Who are all these people?" Someisa asked, looking around the room.

"Oh, sorry. I forgot you might not know some of these men," said Grandma Tea. "You know Reisander and Gobha, of course."

Someisa nodded, wishing she dared eat a cookie.

"Someisa, I would like you to meet Tonguetied, the ranger leader, Hara, creator of new life, and Seefar, who can do just that, see far distances. Toolan you may have met before as he is the keeper of the Grand Library, and Langor you have also met while working with him to learn the Kewoyuspan language," said Grandma Tea, pointing to each man as she spoke his name.

The girl swallowed and began her tale about her dreams. "I haven't had a dream in along time. It is strange that you would ask about them now. I thought I sensed one starting last week and blocked it out by forcing myself awake."

"This is important. You were able to stop the dream just by coming awake?" asked Soonak.

"Yes. It was the only way I could think of to get out of it. I've given it much thought since the last one. I thought I would try it, should I have another, and it worked."

"Amazing," said Grandma Tea.

"This is good news," Soonak said. She took some time to think by washing a paw.

Reisander decided not to wait until Soonak finished her wash and asked, "Let's start with the very first dream. What happened in that one?"

Someisa swallowed some of her favorite tea that Grandma Tea had thoughtfully made for her. It was nice and hot and had bergamot in it. The flavor and fragrance helped her to compose her thoughts while thinking back to the first dream.

"It began with me standing in an empty room. There was a deadness to my surroundings. The walls were made of some kind of stone that looked more like the grey walls in the haunted ruins. There were no seams in the walls, yet they had a rock like energy. The only light came from two small windows forming the upper corner of the room. Away from the windows, it was dark.

"I walked around for a while. I really had no desire to move, but it was something to do. I sensed someone was watching me, but it was hard to discover. I can always tell when one of my friends is looking at me. This felt different. My friends are warm and fuzzy. This felt cold and uncaring. I don't know how else to describe it. It was kind of like when someone gives you a cold shoulder, uncaring, yet there. Then I came awake. It was a long time before I went back to sleep. There were no dreams of any kind for the rest of that night. I remember it clearly, as it was the first, and I thought it very odd. I passed it off as just a strange dream."

"Can you describe this feeling of being watched in more detail?" said Reisander.

"Not really. There wasn't that much to it. In fact, for a while, I thought it was my imagination. I pondered over the dream for several days and came to the conclusion it wasn't my imagination. The best I can say is that it was like touching something made of metal with my mind."

Soonak and Reisander looked at each other and then at Esther. Someisa didn't notice. Her mind was still on the dream.

"Did you try to get out of the dream?' asked Grandma Tea.

"It didn't occur to me to try. I thought it was a strange dream, but nothing to be afraid of."

Soonak quit washing her paw. Satisfied it was clean, she started on another one, but not before she asked a question. "When did the next dream occur?"

"The next dream was a few weeks, maybe a month later. I can't remember for sure about the dates. I found myself in what looked like the same room. The lighting was the same. It seemed a little colder, although I don't remember noticing the room temperature in the first dream. Is it all right if I jump back and forth when I remember something from another dream?"

"Good comments on the details, gal. It's okay if you find you remember somethin' about other dreams that occurred before the one you're describing." Reisander smiled at her, which was a very rare event. Someisa felt encouraged to tell all she remembered, even the tiniest detail.

"Like I say, the room felt colder. I think I shivered after a bit. I am not sure if the shivering came from the cold, or the sense that someone was behind me. In this dream, I sat in a chair. It was that sense of someone there that caused me to move, or, I should say, try to move. I could turn my head, but I couldn't move anything else.

"My legs and arms were bound to the chair by metal straps. A large piece of metal went around my waist and lower chest. The one around my neck was most uncomfortable. The metal straps felt cold and had no give to them.

"I decided to ground myself to enable clearer thinking and waited. I could sense movement behind me. It felt like someone was studying my back. I don't know why it felt like that, but it did. So, I sat there. I got sleepy, which makes no sense in a dream, and then the dream ended and I was back in my room. It was a long time before I went back to sleep.

"I told Pokela about the two dreams. She laughed them off as the result of something I ate. Not wanting to be teased, I dropped the subject and decided not to tell anyone else.

"The third dream began just like the others, only there was a big change. It was like I was strapped to the chair, only there wasn't anything I could see that held me in place. I felt no bindings like the metal wrappings I experienced in the previous dream. I couldn't move anything except my head. Being held in place by some invisible force scared me. I didn't know what to do. The invisible watcher was creepy, and I didn't like it. I began to panic a little. I struggled to get free, but whatever it was that held me in place had no give to it.

"It seemed like I sat there for a very long time. I decided I would wait out whoever or whatever was watching. I began to think if it as a what rather than a who, although I cannot tell you why.

"Eventually I grew bored. I thought about trying to wake myself up. Then, out of the corner of my right eye, I saw movement. This thing, for lack of a better word, came around from behind me. I might have dosed off, and the thing came through a door that materialized out of the dark in the wall to my right, but I doubt it. It might have been in the room before I got there and stayed where I couldn't see it, but I don't think so. It gave off a little heat, yet had no more energy surrounding it than a stone has. I am sure I would have noticed it earlier, having sat there for so long."

"What'd it look like?" said Gobha, ready with paper and pencil to draw or write down what she said.

"It's hard to describe, because I have never seen anything like it before. I would say it was about seven feet tall. It had arms and legs, hands and feet. Its torso was long and thin. Its head reminded me of a clock face except that it didn't have numbers. Instead, it had two big, round eyes, no nose or mouth."

"That's interesting," interrupted Seefar. The thing I saw was short, maybe four and a half feet tall and it had a mouth. Or something in place of one."

"Two varieties, for lack of a better word," said Esther. "Please continue, Someisa."

"There was a hole on each side of the head, but I don't know if those were ears or something else. I thought it rather ugly. I know we aren't supposed to be judgmental about another's looks, but that's what I thought."

She stopped talking and took a long sip of the now warm tea. Normally she liked it hot, but right then, it tasted just fine. A cookie beckoned to her, but she ignored it.

"It's okay, gal," said Reisander. "We all get thoughts like that at times. It's normal. Let it go and tell us more."

"All this thing did was look at me. It walked around me. Its movements were jerky ,like a toy puppet propelled by strings. It had none of the fluency of a Cheschenaki. There was no grace to it. I began to think of it as a toy with away of moving on its own. I thought it was going to touch me, but the metal man never touched me in this dream."

"Were you touched in other dreams?" interrupted Grandma Tea.

"Yes."

"I suggest we wait to hear about that as the gal tells her story," put in Reisander.

"You are right. I'm sorry I interrupted. Please continue, Someisa." Grandma Tea didn't look happy. "So what did the metal man do in this dream?"

"He just looked at me, like he was studying everything about me that he could see. I felt uncomfortable, but not really frightened. To have someone stand and stare at you for a long time is a bit wearying. I wanted to say something, do something. But I just sat there and stared back. And suddenly I found myself in my bed again."

"In the next dream, it did the same thing, only this time I thought it was going to touch me. I screamed, and that ended the dream."

"Were there more dreams after that?" asked Toolan.

"Yes. I wish there weren't. It got worse from that point on."

"What do you mean?" said Grandma Tea.

"A week later, I had another dream. This time, the metal man held a small piece of some kind of small metal machinery in its hand. It held the thing about ten inches away from my feet and moved it slowly up my body. I felt tingling sensations in my major energy centers. I didn't like it. I felt like I was being violated somehow. From time to time, it looked at the little machine as if studying some information there, and then returned to aiming it at my body. It reached my head and stayed there for a few minutes. It was then I woke up in my bed.

"Things got more complicated in the next dream. The metal man was there with his little machine, but other metal men had joined him. I don't know how many as I couldn't see them all at once. The metal man with the small machine ran it up and down my body. The others crowded around to see the results, or whatever, and seemed to confer with each other, although I never heard a word.

"After that dream where the metal men approached me, I was never alone in the room. Sometimes there were several of the metal men looking at me. They were studying me. They weren't very nice about it. But they weren't nasty either. It is hard to explain, but up to that point, I had not been physically touched.

"In each succeeding dream, it was as if they probed more deeply into my body. I don't know what they did to do it, but I felt like my body was being invaded. Like I wasn't alone in my body and yet alone at the same time. I know I am not making any sense. I don't have words that can describe the experience.

"It was the dream when Reisander and I were traveling together that I first felt touched. Everything was the same except that two metal men were watching another one move its little thing over my body. The little thing connected to a gray box by a metal string. Knobs and levers and round things that looked like clocks only weren't, covered the box that sat on a small table beside my chair. I've been calling it a machine, although it's nothing like the ones used in the quarry. The word has come into my mind as the correct terminology.

"It started at my ankles, then moved up to my knees and hips. I felt like fighting back, only I didn't know what to do. When it got to the root, I felt acute discomfort. It wasn't pain exactly, more like a sense of loss. I begged him to stop what he was doing. It was as if he never heard me. Finally, he left the root energy center, and I felt a sense of relief. He fiddled with some knobs and small levers and moved on to my sacral energy center. The sense of loss was replaced by a feeling of invasion to my body. I began screaming.

"The three metal men seemed to have a conference, although, again, I heard nothing. I don't know if they were communicating with each other or with others not in the room. They just stopped moving for a few minutes. Then one of them, I can't tell them apart, pressed a button and pushed the little thing into my root energy center again, but didn't touch my skin. The tingling became intense, almost unbearable. It felt like the little gray box was pulling energy out of the root energy center. I felt violated. I remember screaming and Reisander shaking me awake. He told me to ask my guardian angel to protect me from the dreams at night. That worked until the night we were in the long cave and the huge moving wagon puller came roaring through it."

Grandma Tea turned to the black panther. "What I want to know is why the metal man pulled energy from Someisa's root chakra. What was it hoping to get?"

"I agree," said Reisander. "That is the important question of the day. Although another important question is, how did they do it?"

"Were there any other dreams that you haven't mentioned?" said Toolan, not wanting to miss anything about the dreams before the conversations took another turn.

"Yes. I forgot. There was one other, just before the Wasaru. In this dream, they brought in machines and attached metal ropes to different places on my body. I felt like they were measuring something. I don't know why I thought that, yet it seems right. I haven't had one until two weeks ago when they attempted another. It has been two years in between. I don't know why they've come back. So far of late, there has only been one dream."

"Was there any feeling of life in these metal men, as you call them?" asked Esther.

"No."

."Did you get a sense of leadership among these metal men?"

"Not that I noticed. That is one of the things that was so strange. It was as if they all worked together as one unit. I never saw any of them give directions to the others by way of pointing or other gestures. I never heard them speak to each other. Up to that point, they never spoke to me. The room was always silent. Even their movements, while disjointed, made little or no noise."

Someisa, realizing she had been sitting upright in her chair gripping the arms so tightly her knuckles were white, let go and sank back in the chair. She felt thoroughly spent from the effort to tell the others about her experiences.

"I feel like I have betrayed a trust or broken a vow," she said. "It is as though the metal men commanded me not to reveal any of the dreams to others of my kind. Or theirs for that matter. I don't know why this feeling is so strong. It has been hard to tell you what I have. I'm sure I've left out important details for you to know. Suddenly, I'm so terribly tired."

Grandma Tea got up and asked Someisa to follow her out of the room. Someisa found herself being led to a bedroom. "Take your shoes off, Someisa, and lay down on the bed. I'll wake you after you have had a nap."

Someisa did as she was told and was asleep before her head hit the pillow. Grandma Tea gently covered her with a down comforter and left the room.

Chapter Seven

*Love the light, for it shows you the way, yet endure the darkness, because it
shows you the stars.*

Awakened by the aroma of elk and vegetable stew, Someisa wandered
toward the living room by way of the dining room. Two large pots of
stew, platters full of sandwiches, and more cookies sat on the dining table.
Nine place settings filled the remaining spaces. Someisa heard Grandma
Tea call to the others to come to dinner. Someisa seated herself and waited
for them. There was much scurrying as the men went about the business
of washing up before the meal.

Gobha sat across the table from her. To her astonishment, a little titmouse emerged from the depths of his beard, grabbed a cookie crumb, and
ducked back out of sight. The man didn't seem to notice.

All were silent, waiting for Langor to say grace. "We give thanks to the
four-legged who gave up his life that we might eat today. We also give
thanks to the plant people who have provided their nourishment for our
enjoyment and good health. We give thanks to the cook who prepared our
meal. And we give thanks for the friendship that binds us all together. Let's
eat." With that said, he sat down and everyone dug in.

Toolan was the first to speak to Someisa. Not wanting to wait until the meal was over, he addressed the girl. "Ah, welcome back. Relate to us a little more about the moving machine. This intrigues me."

Encouraged, Someisa began, "I forgot all about the tunnel dream. Only I am not so sure it was a dream. It was more like a vision, because I was awake at the time. I could feel it long before I saw it. The ground shook. The noise was deafening. None of the others seemed the least concerned and kept on sleeping. Then, at the far end of the long cave, I saw a light that was moving in circles. It came from a lantern at the front of an enormous machine. At least I think that's what it was. It doesn't look like any of our machines. But then, neither do the ones the metal men use in my dreams. The light swept around the top, bottom, and sides of the tunnel. The closer the thing got, the bigger it appeared. It seemed to fill most of the tunnel. It smelled awful. Smoke came from a round tubular thing on top of the machine toward the front. I could taste grit in my mouth thrown up by the huge metal wheels."

"I wanted to scream to warn everyone it was coming, but, for some reason, I couldn't. I moved back against the wall as the thing drew near. It roared past me, belching thick black smoke. I began coughing. The front puller machine was huge. It had wheels that were twice as high as I am tall. The wheels followed the lines imbedded in the ground. Behind the machine was a wagon full of shiny black rocks, followed by an assortment of wagons with closed doors. I have no idea what they carried.

"The next thing I knew, I was awake and Reisander and Kag were there to comfort me. I told them a little about the dream and how real it seemed. Once I calmed down, I went to sleep thinking I wouldn't have another strange dream.

"But I had a second dream that night. I was bound in the same metal chair and a metal man walked up to me and actually spoke to me in a monotone. The thing had a raspy, grating voice that was unpleasant to the ear. It asked me if I liked his gift. It said something about a thing of the past. He touched my forehead just above my nose. I screamed and Reisander was there, shaking me awake. That was the last dream I had before I was captured and taken to the Kewoyuspan camp."

'Pass me a sandwich please," said Toolan, while holding out a bowl for Grandma Tea to fill with stew. "That machine and the wagons it was pulling may have been a train. They were used to haul goods long distances. I wonder why the metal man would pick a train." The old man paused and rubbed his chin with his hand. Then he said, "I think it is a message to let us know how long they have been observing our planet."

"That's not possible," said Esther, filling other bowls with stew as they came to her." We know from what Soonak has told us, the metal men have only been here a few years and someone from this planet invited them here."

"The first sightings of the metal men in this neighborhood began about forty or fifty years ago," put in Soonak, who had moved to sit beside Someisa. Although Grandma Tea offered the cat food, she refused to eat. "We knew of none here until just recently, but that doesn't mean they weren't here many thousands of years ago."

Esther spoke up, "To know about trains could mean they have been studying this planet's history. But how did they get the information, is the question."

"An easy answer," said Soonak. "This planet's history has been studied by other peoples for thousands of years. Your race and its evolution is a fascinating study. And perhaps they did it by personal observation."

"I am not so convinced that what you relate, Soonak, is of significance right now. I don't see the relevance of a train in our present circumstances. However, for the sake of history in the making, do you think you could draw a picture of it, Someisa?" Toolan could hardly sit still in his chair. This would be a great coo to add to the library."

"I am not very good at drawing things." Someisa pushed some hair out of her eyes with her fingers.

Toolan wasn't going to let go of this. "Do you have paper and a marking stick, Esther?"

"Couldn't this wait until after dinner?" asked Esther while looking at Someisa..

"I don't mind, Grandma Tea. I just as soon get it over with and I'll need the table to work anyway."

The Eldest Grandmother went to a desk in a corner of another room and produced both items plus a piece of rubber to be used as an eraser.

Someisa set aside her bowl of stew and left a sandwich sitting on a plate. Even though she was hungry, she concentrated, closing her eyes as she did so. She brought up the train in the window of her mind, taking in all its details as best as she could remember them. Picking up the marking stick, she began to draw. The others watched in anticipation. Everyone stopped eating. No one dared to breathe loudly or make some other noise that might distract her.

Slowly, with lots of erasures, Someisa drew a reasonable likeness of what she had seen. As an afterthought, she drew a little stick man beside the thing to give Toolan an idea of how big it was. Before they could ask her to do anything else, she grabbed her bowl of stew and began shoveling the food into her mouth.

"Would yer look at that," said Hara, his mouth hanging open. "Anybody ever seen something like that before?"

"Yes," said Toolan. I found something like that in a very old text in the back of the Grand Library. It's in a volume that is crumbling with age and rarely opened for fear of further damage. The language is unfamiliar to me. I'll find it and make a copy to preserve what it says. Perhaps Langor can translate it."

"I would be most willing to be of service in this way," said Langor. "I agree with Toolan. I don't quite see the relevance of this enormous wagon pulling machine to the metal men."

"Perhaps it is a means of t-transportation," offered Tonguetied.

Reisander noted the way the wheels overlapped rails in Someisa's picture. "That makes sense. It also gives a reason for the sunken lines in the tunnel and perhaps the reason the tunnel itself was built. There's nothing natural about the tunnel. It's definitely made by something other than nature."

Why would them metal men be sendin' such a vision ta Someisa?" Gobha got up from his place at the table and began to pace around the room. "If this's somethin' from our planet's past, how'd the metal men even know about the durn thin'?"

"I have a feeling t-t-time is not an element that rules their existence," said Tonguetied

"Are you talking time travel?" Reisander said.

"No. I am saying m-maybe-time is-different for them. Their universe m-may not use it the same way we d-do."

Hara frowned. "I don't understand this business of using time in a different way than we do. Please explain."

"I c-can't. It's just something that occurred to me. I am no scholar. I'll leave that to the historians. Any c-comments, Toolan?"

Toolan ran his fingers through his hair. "You got me," he sighed.

Tonguetied reached for the last sandwich on the platter. Esther got up and left for the kitchen to refill a cookie plate from her larder.

"I think we are getting off the m-main road. This may be f-f-fascinating, at least it is to m-me, but it hasn't given us any clues about the m-metal men," Tonguetied said.

"I disagree," said Reisander. "This is important. It's one thing for the metal men to invade Someisa's dreams. It is another to give her such a realistic vision that includes all five senses. What I would like to know is why just her? Why not show it to all of us? Why show it at all? And how did they do it? Reaching into someone's mind like that is against the Accords."

"I be thinkin' they don't give a tinker's darn about them Accords. Probably don't even know about 'em" drawled Gobha.

"Yer're right. They have already broken several of our laws," said Hara.

Frowning, Gobha grabbed a large handful of cookies and began stuffing them into his mouth. "S'not natural, no matter how ya look at it." Cookie crumbs went everywhere. The little tit mouse poked its head out of Gobha's beard again and grabbed one.

Someisa had been quiet through all of this discussion. She had an idea of why they showed her the vision, but felt shy about bringing it up, until Reisander turned to her and said, "What are your ideas on this, gal?"

"I think they were trying to compare themselves to the machine in the tunnel. It moved without help of any kind, just as they do. Maybe they don't use time the way we do. Being able to move through time made it easy for them to reach back into our history. Somehow they brought up what would be a memory of the thing and showed it to me. The machine was made of metal, just as they are. Didn't you say something about shifting dimensions, Seefar?"

"Yes, and that might help explain the differences in time. There is no time between dimensions." Seefar adjusted his weight. The dining room chair was too small for him.

"It's an idea," admitted Tonguetied. "But I think we n-need to move on. All of you, increase your wandering time. Report back to both Esther and me, anything you notice that seems unusual. I don't care how t-trivial it may be."

Once the meal was over, the men prepared to leave. It started to rain while they were eating, so there was much rustling and fussing about as they pulled rain gear out of backpacks that had been left by the front door when they came in. Gobha filled his pockets with cookies before he went out the door.

Chapter Eight

Accepting a decision, once it is made, is the first step in revealing the obstacles.

S omeisa was preparing to leave, too, when Grandma Tea pulled her aside. "I want to talk to you," she said. "As soon as all of our visitors have gone. Start the cleanup while I see the men out."

Someisa sighed and began clearing the table and putting all the dirty dishes in the kitchen. The china with its bouquet of roses in the center and roses around the rim fascinated her. There was nothing like this at home.

It was the first time she had an opportunity to explore the kitchen, and it surprised her. It was huge. Someisa's entire house could fit in a kitchen this size, yet from the outside, Grandma Tea's house didn't look big enough to include a large kitchen, much less one of this size.

She counted three large ovens, four sinks, several ice boxes or what she thought were ice boxes, loads of counter space, and cupboards everywhere. An island in the middle seemed to be the central point of the room, with easy access to everything. After placing all the dishes on the island, she sorted them and began washing the glassware first, followed by all the eating utensils.

She was elbow deep in suds and washing plates when Grandma Tea returned to the kitchen. "They have all left," announced her mentor as she picked up a towel and began drying the glasses and putting them away.

They worked together in comfortable silence until the last pot was washed, dried, and put in its place. "Thank you for helping," said Grandma Tea. "Very few people think about the amount of work involved to feed a large group like this one. Especially a group of hungry men who could eat me out of house and home if I let them. They would help with the cleanup if I asked them to. But it takes me a long time to find where they put everything." She laughed and put down the dish towel. "Come, let us make some tea, and settle ourselves in the living room."

Someisa filled a kettle with water and set it on a wood stove that still contained burning wood. Grandma Tea got out two mugs and the tea. A few minutes later, they were sitting in front of the fire with their feet up. It was evening, and the air had grown chilly. It felt good to relax with warmth on their feet. Soonak curled up in front of the fire and appeared to go to sleep.

"It is time to talk about your learning objectives for the orange stone," announced Grandma Tea as a way of opening the discussion.

"I have been wondering when you would get around to it," admitted Someisa.

Grandma Tea laughed. "I thought you might. Do you remember your list for the red stone?

"No."

"I am not surprised. The list for the orange stone is an expansion of the list for the red stone. These are the things you will be studying.

Someisa interrupted, "Why so long since Kanshisha gave me the red one? It's been over two years."

Soonak raised her head at the rude interruption and gave a clipped growl. Someisa heard her, ignored the cat, and gave The Eldest Grandmother her full attention.

Grandma Tea noticed the interaction, smiled to herself, and decided the girl needed no further reprimand. She took a sip of the tea, enjoying the aroma of the bergamot blended with black tea leaves, and said, "You needed time to practice what you learned with the red stone. Now it is time to move on."

"Oh," was all Someisa could think of to say.

"So, here is the list. I suggest you write it down and keep it with you. There is a writing stick and some paper in the drawer under that blue vase, if you need it."

Someisa found both and settled herself in her comfy chair to hear what The Eldest Grandmother had to say.

"Receiving of the White Stone is the first on the list, although like all the lists, there is no particular order to them. You will be working with all of them off and on until you master the list, sometimes two or more at the same time."

"What do you mean by receiving of the white stone? I'm wearing the darn thing around my neck, aren't I?"

"Just by the attitude that you have displayed in that comment, tells me you have not accepted receptance of it. You are wearing it because it is expected of you, not because you want to. You are not in a state of receptance."

Someisa fingered the stone that hung underneath her tunic on a leather cord around her neck. "I suppose you are right," she said. "I'm very uncomfortable with it and would rather leave it in a drawer in my bedroom."

"Again, I am not surprised," chuckled Grandma Tea. She paused for a moment, enjoying the fragrance of the tea and the warmth coming from the mug she held in her hands. "I see you have not written down the first learning objective."

"Oh, sorry." Someisa hastened to write it down. "Receptance of the White Stone, right?"

"Very good, but not quite right. All you need to do is be willing to receive the responsibilities required of the bearer of the white stone. That doesn't mean you have to like them," Grandma Tea smiled at the troubled girl and continued. "The rest of the list includes creativity; receptivity, acknowledging and receiving what you ask for; to start choosing your own set of standards for living; acknowledging responsibility for maintaining your personal integrity; seek independence from outside influences; understand that giving to yourself is the same as giving to others; and lastly, enjoying the beauty all around you and within you."

Someisa sighed. "No explanations, just like the last list?"

Grandma Tea laughed. "Of course," she said.

Chapter Nine

Waiting takes so much longer than action.

Someisa's training with Reisander had come to a stop for several weeks. She spent more time with the Elder Grandmother and Grandma Tea. She assumed Reisander was roaming the countryside, looking for traces of the metal men. He'd talk to her when he had something to share.

Pokela's arm was taking shape. It had been a very slow process. Someisa took time either in the early morning or after her lessons to do energy work on her friend's arm. The appendage had grown a good eight inches. An elbow was forming. Two small fingers took shape at the end of the new arm. The two girls sat on a bench at the side of Zoenka's garden, enjoying the infrequent sun shining through spots of blue in between clouds.

"Zoenka says I can start using my new arm. There wasn't much I could do with it until the fingers started to grow." said Pokela. "I'm excited. Apparently, using the arm from now on will encourage it to grow faster. Who would have thought?"

Someisa smiled at her friend. Raising her hands, she began the process of the energy work she had been doing whenever the girls could find time to be together. While doing the work, a thought occurred to her. "How's it going with Kag?" she asked.

Pokela blushed. "What makes you ask that?"

"Well, it's obvious something is going on. First Kag makes you a bracelet which got broken during your time with the Kewoyuspans. So, he made you a new one. He has made three more since that time. Seems to me like something is going on here."

Pokela blushed even redder. "He comes by to check on me once in a while when you are gone. Says he doesn't want me to get lonely. We talk a lot. It's comfortable to be with him. That's all."

"Sounds like a lot to me."

"Maybe. I don't want to make it into something it isn't. After all, I have several more years of being a foghlamach. That doesn't leave much time for courting," Pokela sighed and stared out at the garden.

Concerned, Someisa asked, "Are you okay? You don't seem like your usual bouncy self, even with the good news for using your arm."

"I don't know. Maybe it's hormones."

"Or maybe it's Kag being gone for a month and you miss him."

"I haven't heard from him in all the time he has been gone. Not even a letter." A tear escaped Pokela's eyes and ran down her cheek.

"Kag, write a letter? He's never written a letter in his entire life." Someisa chuckled. "Don't worry. If there were someone else in his life, he would let you know. So, do you have exercises you are to do with your new arm?'

"Just slowly wiggling my fingers whenever I think of it. Oh, and moving my arm up and down a little. I am to move it until it starts to hurt and then back off a bit. Zoenka says it isn't ready for side to side movement yet. The elbow hasn't developed enough for me to bend my arm yet."

Someisa finished the energy work, and let the Kag discussion go. The two girls sat quietly enjoying a nice day together. It was wonderful to sit with a good friend and not be concerned about talking all the time. They both had changed a lot in the past two years. There were lots of days now when they enjoyed each other's presence without words. Today was one of them.

Someisa nearly dozed off when their pleasant interlude came to an abrupt end. "You haven't finished weeding the garden," said Zoenka, pointing to a row of carrots. She stood in front of the two girls, grinning.

"That will have to wait," announced Reisander, coming around a corner of the house. "Someisa needs to come with me. Gal, go inside and pack for a journey. Prepare for several days." Reisander turned and headed for Toshu's house across town.

"Well, how do you like that? Not so much as a hello or anything. That man can be incredibly rude. Well, daughter, I guess you have to do as he says." Zoenka sighed and stalked off to her root cellar, where she had been going when she spied the two girls.

"I guess I have to say goodbye again. I'm sorry I won't be able to work on your arm like I have been doing. I'll pretend to work on it while I am gone. That way, I won't miss you so much." Someisa stood up and brushed off some small leaves that were floating on a slight breeze and landed on her tunic.

"We have so little time together as it is," complained Pokela. Now you have to go off on another adventure and I have to stay home. I spend a lot of time worrying about you."

"Don't worry so much. I'll be fine." She smiled at her friend and gave her a long, embracing hug. "I expect to see another finger when I get back."

Pokela scratched the end of the growing arm. "I wish it didn't itch so much."

They both laughed and Pokela took off for home.

Reisander arrived just as Someisa was throwing the last of her things into a pack. Quickly, she slipped it over her shoulders and went to greet him.

"Did you pack any food?" he asked.

"Not yet." Chagrined, she took off the pack and headed for the kitchen. Her mother frowned as she handed her daughter some packages of travel bread, dried fruit, and jerky. She gave Someisa a quick hug and went back to work packaging dried herbs.

"Wait a minute," she called to the retreating girl. Zoenka tucked some bundles of herbs into Someisa's pack. "You might need these." She turned her back on her daughter so the girl wouldn't see the tears on her mother's cheeks.

"Where are we going?" Someisa asked Reisander.

"To meet with Hara," said Reisander.

Chapter Ten

If you know what you're looking for, that's all you will get,
what's previously known.
But when you're open to what's possible, you may get something new.

Reisander led her to Hara's house and left her there without a word to either one of them.

He comes, and he goes," chuckled Hara. "He didn't tell yer, yer would be spending sometime with each of us rangers, did he now?

"No. He hardly said anything during the three days it took for us to get here. Whenever I asked a question or made a comment, he either grunted or ignored me."

"Well, at one time or another, each of us rangers will serve as mentors for yer. As for Reisander, he's got a lot on his mind right now with this metal men business. So, welcome ter me humble home. Come see where yer'll be staying for a while."

Someisa remembered Hara as a slender, small man from her meeting with the rangers at The Eldest Grandmother's house. Now, he didn't seem so small. There was something about his presence that made him stand out from his surroundings. Smudges of dirt and growing things covered his tattered clothes. His ears came to a sharper point than most Cheschenakis did. He had a nicely trimmed beard and dark curly hair that stopped a little below his ears. It looked a bit ragged and Someisa suspected he cut it himself.

The ranger lived in a magical place. He had built his home from living plants and trees, grown to form the walls and roof of his one-room home. The plants formed a protective layer of greenery consisting of branches, twigs, leaves, and moss. The one large window had no glass, but opened to the outdoors. During times of heavy rain or a rare snowfall, he could lower a living film of lichen and moss that let in some light, but kept out the rain and cold. The house had a high arched ceiling. Flowers decorated both the inside and outside of the house. The place smelled of rich earth and happy growing things.

Many of the trees forming Hara's house bore fruit and always seemed in season. Plants and trees that normally lived in warmer climates flourished. A stone fireplace, framing a fire that never went out, helped keep the tropical trees and plants happy and content. Apples, peaches, cherries, plums and pears hung from the ceiling waiting for him to pick them. In one corner by the fireplace, three varieties of citrus fruit: kumquats, oranges, and lemons created not only food for him to eat, but framed a pleasant, living picture of strawberries growing around the trunk of a grapefruit tree. Berry vines framed the windows. He carefully saved the seeds from all the fruits and planted them whenever he found a suitable place for them.

The house had no plumbing. Someisa didn't like the necessary room being outside of the house and a little way down the hill. She made a note to herself to be sure to take care of herself before she went to bed, so she wouldn't have to get up in the middle of a cold night to go use it.

A little stream ran under a corner of the house away from the fireplace. It never changed size, no matter how heavy the rain might be. It was always crystal clear, and the water tasted wonderfully sweet.

Hara pointed to a pile of heavy fabric that lay on the ground at one side of the house. "That there is the means ter build yerself a tent ter live in while yer're here buildin' yer own house," he said.

Someisa blinked in dismay, although she tried to hide it. She had imagined she'd be sleeping in cozy comfort on a soft down mattress near a warm fire.

Hara caught her feeling and chuckled. "Yer can have those things yer expected, but yer have ter build 'em for yerself," he said.

"I what?"

"Yer'll be sleeping in that there tent until yer builds yerself yer own house. Just like I said. Always wanted a guest house, but never got around ter building it. Put up the tent anywhere yer like. I'll fix us some supper." Hara turned his back on Someisa and entered the house.

Someisa sighed. The life of a foghlamach was never easy, but she hadn't expected to be treated like this. The fabric of the tent smelled old and musty. It took her awhile to figure out its shape and size. No matter how she arranged it, there always seemed to be something in the way, leaving her no sleeping room. The loops for the grounding pegs were in strange places. The more she tried to set it up, the worse the whole mess became.

Hara looked out his window and chuckled. "If yer start with the floor and peg it smooth, yer will have more luck with that pole yer holding to make a ceiling," he called to the struggling girl. "I'd start with a corner. It's easier that way. And a storm is brewing, so I would get a move on iffen I were yer."

Someisa glanced at the perfectly blue sky and wondered why her mentor thought a storm was brewing. She wanted to ask where to find a corner, but Hara had disappeared from view. She sighed again. Starting with one loop, she followed a fold from one to another until she found three that formed a corner. From there, she found what looked like it might be an entranceway. Looking for a place to put the entrance, she decided she would enjoy looking at the little stream that tumbled down the hill from the corner of Hara's house. Once she got going with the tent pegs on one side, the rest fell into place. She placed her bedroll so that she could see out the entrance. There were still a couple of poles leftover. Not knowing what to do with them, she set them aside thinking they were spares. Picking through her pack, she took out the food she brought for Hara.

Not knowing what to do next, she knocked on a tree trunk marking a corner of Hara's house." Come on in," he called to her. She handed him her food package. He opened it and found a carefully wrapped bunch of sausage links, some spices, and a few loaves of bread. "Ah, the kindness of yer mutter," he said. "She knows how much I likes her sausages and fresh bread, not that I can't make my own, mind yer. But somehow, yer mutter's always tastes better than mine."

The old man set the sausages in a tin box nestled next to the stream and closed the lid. The fragrance of the spices filled the room as he poured them into their respective jars. It made Someisa hungry, and she wondered what was for supper.

A pot hung from a tripod over the fire. The girl breathed deeply of the fumes coming from it. Hara added a few bits of an herb. "We'll let the essence of a little thyme mingle with that venison stew. While we wait, do yer have any questions?"

Disappointed they weren't going to eat right away, Someisa sighed. She was ravenously hungry. Hara plucked an apple from the ceiling and handed it to her. She bit into it and the juices ran down her chin. It was sweeter than any other apple she had ever tasted. It didn't take long for her to eat the whole thing.

"I ferget yer young folks are always hungry. Until yer can grow yer own trees that will feed yer, yer'll have ter eat some of mine."

Dismayed, she said, "What do you mean, grow my own trees? How long am I going to stay here?"

"As long as it takes ter build me a guest house," he answered.

"But it takes years for a tree to grow," she cried.

"That's what yer think now. Yer'll know better when yer done. I'll help yer plant yer first tree right after supper cleanup, to get yer started. Yer'll need a strong corner one. If yer look yonder in that corner, yer'll see an oak for my foundation of this house. I suggest a maple for yer's. Maples is a might more flexible than oaks and easier for yer ter work with. I have a couple set aside for this purpose. Yer can choose which one yer want and get it growing, so's yer can begin a wall tomorrow."

Someisa looked at the old man, thinking he had lost his mind, and wondered if she should sneak out during the night to head back home. It wasn't in the rules, but neither was what this man was proposing.

"Yer won't find yer way home in the dark through these woods. They's very protective and know yer would be lost if they didn't cause yer to turn back no matter which way yer chose ter head away from here."

His smile was kindly even though his words sent a chill down Someisa's back. "Am I a prisoner then?"

"Oh no. I just don't think traveling alone at night around here is a good idea. Perhaps by the time yer pick out yer maple tree, yer'll feel a little better about staying here."

She sat quietly, mulling over what he said while Hara stirred the stew. It smelled of venison, potatoes, carrots, celery, and, of course, thyme. Waiting until after supper seemed a good idea, so she began asking questions. "This bit about growing a foundation tree. How long does it take to grow one?"

"As long as yer wants it ter. I suggest a day or so. Otherwise, the other trees and supportive plants get impatient and may grow out of turn. Then yer've got a mess on yer hands that requires a lot of pruning. Takes a lot of patience, pruning does," he said.

"But trees are slow growers. It takes years to grow a tree the size of the one in the corner," she said.

"Does it now?" replied Hara, grinning at her. "If that's what yer believe, that's what'll happen. If yer can grow a flame high enough to light a candle perched near the top of a doorframe, yer can surely speed up the growth of a living thing."

"Doesn't that interfere with the tree's free will?"

"Not at all. Yer never thought about interfering with a tree's free will when you transplanted it, now did yer?"

"No," said Someisa. "It never occurred to me."

"So, why would speeding up its growth be any different than moving it from one place ter another?"

Thoroughly confused, she fought for another question to change the subject. Finding one, she asked, "Do you have a garden? I didn't see one when I was outside."

"It's down around the bend a bit," nodding his head in the direction of the fireplace. Taking off the stewpot lid ,he sniffed the savory odor drifting up. "I think the stew's about done. Yer'll find bowls, spoons, and such in that cupboard over there."

Someisa looked where he was pointing and saw nothing but a thickening of the plants and moss in one corner. It didn't look like anything resembling a cupboard, so she glanced right past it.

"Back up there, little miss," he said, watching her. If yer reaches through the right of that thick patch thereon the wall, yer'll find a handle. Pull on that, and yer'll find that yer opening the door ter the cupboard.

Someisa did as she was told. It felt quite odd to be grabbing a small branch of a living plant to open a cupboard she couldn't see through the thick foliage. Once opened, she discovered a deep cupboard that held all manner of wooden dishes and tableware. The girl thought it clever to have the cupboard extend outward instead of taking up space inside the small house.

With her hands full, she looked around the room in dismay. No chairs or tables were present anywhere in the room. It was quite empty of any kind of furniture.

"Do you eat sitting on the floor?' she asked.

Hara laughed and said, "Sometimes. But not today." He reached down and tugged on a small branch in the floor. Immediately, a table and two chairs made entirely of living plants and shrubs rose out of the floor. "You can put those things here."

Dumbfounded, Someisa stood where she was with her mouth open.

"Yer keep yer mouth open like that long enough, a fly is sure ter take interest and amble in," commented Hara as he picked up a tangle of dried vines and placed it on the table. Grabbing a small mat of soft vines and moss, he folded it over the handle of the stew pot, picked up the aromatic pot, and placed it on the tangle of vines.

Closing her mouth, Someisa set the dishes down, placing a plate in front of Hara and another across from him for her.

"Sit down, girl. Let's eat," said Hara.

"We give thanks ter the plant people and the four-leggeds what offered themselves ter us, that we might eat," said Hara before he served Someisa a helping of stew and then spooned out some for himself.

They ate in silence. Someisa washed the dishes in the little stream when they finished, all the while wondering what came next. A few hours of daylight remained in the day.

"Time to pick out yer maple tree," announced Hara when all the kitchen chores were done. He led the way down a path and around a bend. To Someisa's surprise, a large garden full of all types of fruits and vegetables filled a meadow with the little stream winding through it. Not a weed was in sight within the garden, although all kinds of weeds grew around the perimeter.

"You suggested a maple tree to start with. I'm okay with that. I like their smell. What should I look for when picking out a tree?" said Someisa.

"Well, yer wants a variety that grows strong, but not too tall. They's lots of pretty maples that smells good, but they don't have the strength ter support a building. I suggest yer might want ter look at these ones here," said Hara, indicating a small group of maple trees with thick trunks for their size.

Someisa had never seen that variety before. Not knowing what to look for, she decided on one that looked like it would be easier to dig up from the tangle of branches and roots. It was slightly shorter than the others, coming up to her shoulders. Its trunk looked strong and not too thick.

"Good choice," said Hara. "Now let's each take a spade and make a circle around the roots, cutting them as we dig. Then we'll let them set overnight so they can heal themselves." He produced a spade from a condensed pile of bushes that turned out to be a storage shed for tools and such. The tang in the shed smelled of rich compost, so over powering she nearly choked on it.

Following Hara's example of how and where to dig, the two of them soon had the job done.

"Now we need ter prepare the ground for yer new house."

They walked back up the trail to Hara's house and Hara told her what he had in mind. "I think we need ter spread apart the houses for plenty of privacy, yer being a girl and all. Besides, who knows who'll come ter visit me once yer moves on down the trail. So, I picked this little clearing over yonder."

The spot was across the creek and a short way around a bend in the trail leading away from Hara's house. It was a lovely setting with the aroma of fresh flowers that grew all around the edges. The trees parted to let in enough light, yet provided some protection from the rain.

"It's beautiful," exclaimed Someisa.

"Glad yer likes it."

"I think the house should go here. There's a little branch of the creek that runs across this space and could make a waterway like you have at your house," she said.

Hara smiled. "Good idea. I see yer have some good thinking in that head of yers."

The discussion about the house went on until sundown. The two of them cleared a space where the house was to be built and then went their separate ways for bed.

Someisa found the tent lying on the ground and called for Hara to help her put it up. The floor was still in place. When it came to putting in the tent poles, Hara laughed and asked her to put it up the way she did originally.

"Yer've got it all wrong, youngun'. This pole goes here and this one yer've got sideways. It's late. I'll help yer."

It was done in minutes.

***

It didn't take long to dig up the young maple tree and replant it in the little cleared area. Hara was very instructive about the right amount of compost and water needed for the project. Someisa spent the entire morning picking out all the trees that made up the walls of the house. To her surprise, Hara knew all about the work she had been doing to get the flame to light a candle. He admitted the exercise was his idea. He suggested she use the same technique for growing the flame on the trees.

"What yer needs ter be doing right now," said Hara, once all the trees were planted. "Is ter train the trees ter grow the way yer wants them ter be when the framework for the house is done. I suggest at least eight feet tall. We have some pretty tall characters coming here from time to time."

Mystified, Someisa asked, "How does that relate to the flame exercise?"

"Yer grew the flame, didn't yer?"

"Yes, but that's not a living thing."

"Who told yer fire isn't a living thing?"

"No one. I just assumed it isn't. How can it be alive?"

"That's for a discussion at a later time. Right now, I want you to start with the backwall. Make it eight feet tall with a little opening at the bottom to bridge over the stream in the left-hand corner."

Someisa's first mistake was to train one tree at a time using the techniques that worked with the flame. The first tree grew all over the place, crowding out the other trees and protruding into where the room would be.

"I don't think that's what yer had in mind," commented Hara rather dryly, and doing his best not to laugh. Let's do some pruning and then grow the whole wall at the same time."

The smell of freshly cut trees filled the meadow. Once the tree was back to its original size, Hara asked the girl to try again.

"I have never done two things at the same time, much less an entire wall of trees."

"Nothin' ter it," replied Hara. "Just remember how we're all connected, and you'll get the idea."

"Yeah, right," said Someisa sarcastically, which Hara ignored.

Two days passed before Someisa finished the back wall. She completed the other three in a single afternoon. The window provided the most difficulty. For some reason, picturing a window in her mind and having the trees frame it just didn't happen.

"I see yer havin' difficulty with that there winder," he said on the morning of the third day. He had come to see how things were progressing.

"I keep picturing a window, but the trees keep covering it up. The walls went up easily enough, once I got the hang of it. What am I doing wrong?"

Hara surveyed the wall where Someisa had wanted to put the window. "Well, have yer noticed from which direction the wind comes? That might give yer a clue. Perhaps the solution to the problem is ter pick a different wall."

"I don't understand. What does the wind direction have to do with the window?"Someisa licked her finger and held it up to the air. The wind seemed to come from the southwest.

"Winders can be a bit tricky when it comes ter keepin' out the rain, especially when a storm's a blowin'. The back wall is up against the forest. But the east wall is opposite where you had planned the window. Try one on there, and see how it goes. What were yer using for a picture of a window?"

"My bedroom window."

"What does it look like?"

She sat down and pictured the window in her mind. "Well, it's round, about two feet across, has glass to see through, and shutters for when it storms."

"Are yer seein' it from the inside or the outside?"

"The inside. Does that matter?"

"When yer looking at it from the inside, where are the shutters?"

"I switched my view to the outside for the shutters."

"Do you see the shutters open or closed?"

Someisa saw then where she had made her mistake. Giving Hara a kiss on the cheek, she ran back outside and finished the job of framing the window. This time it worked. Without a fireplace to keep the house warm enough for tropical trees and plants, she had settled on an apple and a pear tree for framing the roof.

Hara came from his garden to check over her work. He pushed on the southwest corner and the whole building sagged, nearly falling over. "This here needs some more work before you go filling in all the holes," he said and went back to working in his garden.

Feeling discouraged, Someisa sat down and studied her design from the inside. It looked alright to her. She got up and walked around the perimeter. Three sides had supporting trees to help carry the load. The tree in the fourth corner where Hara had pushed was a bit spindly and had nothing to support it. Once she made the corrections, Hara again came to look at what she had created.

"It's a bit crooked here and there," he said while running his eyes over the sides of each wall. "But it's sturdy enough. Yer can fill in the holes now and yer'll have yerself a house. Be wise to add a door, though." He meandered down the garden path and never looked back.

It was exciting to sleep in a house she had built herself, she thought. It rained that night. Someisa woke, wet and cold. The roof leaked in several places. Holes in the walls let in more rain. The floor was a sea of mud. Fortunately, she hadn't taken down the tent. Grabbing a damp blanket, she crawled into the tent and found a dry quilt waiting for her. Gratefully, she snuggled into it and went back to sleep.

***

A full week passed before the little house pleased both Hara and Someisa. The ranger taught her how to encourage the growth of fruit on the apple and pear trees, so she had her own source of food for breakfast waiting for her each morning.

While Someisa was busy growing her house, a species of insects that ate white flies and tiny red spiders, the scourges of many plant varieties, planned to leave the planet. Hara worked with another type of insect to teach it to eat the flies and spiders.

"Why are these insects dying off?" she asked Hara.

"They're ready to advance in their development," he explained. "There is another planet they want to explore. So they will be reborn there."

"I didn't know they could do that."

"Why not? All living things want to grow and learn in their own ways. Once they have learned all they can from one way of life, they move on to another. Then we create a new species to replace it so that the balance of nature on this planet can continue."

"Huh," said Someisa.

Chapter Eleven

It is far easier to point out what is harmful than what is good.

While the two of them were working in the garden with some young insects, Someisa felt uneasy. Glancing at Hara, she saw him rise and look around.

"What is it?" she asked.

"Don't know. I feel something is wrong."

"Me, too."

The ground shook, and a roaring sound filled the air. At first, Someisa thought it was an earthquake.

"It's not an earthquake, Someisa," said Hara. "Something very bad has happened."

A white wolf the size of a small horse stepped out of the woods and approached Hara. The ranger reached up and scratched behind the wolf's ears. "What is it, my dear friend?" he asked. "What has happened?"

"This here wolf was sent ter us by Seefar," he said to Someisa.

The wolf began to bark and growl. Hara listened intently and then translated for Someisa. "There's been an explosion at the wood sprite village. There's a cave nearby where we put the metal man's body. Most of the wood sprite homes have been destroyed or badly damaged. Many of the little fellers are badly hurt and I'm afraid some may have died. Our help has been requested to come repair homes if we can. Maybe even build some new homes for the little ones."

"How did Seefar know about this so quickly?" asked Someisa and, as an after thought, added, "Is the metal man's body still there?"

"Don't know, don't know," replied Hara.

The white wolf bounded off, leaving the two of them behind.

"Gather what you have in the way of medical supplies. We must hurry," called Hara as he ran to his house.

Someisa grabbed her backpack, which still had the packages of herbs in it, and ran to Hara's house to add some food and more medical supplies. Hara filled his pack with small gardening tools, and strapped a shovel and an ax onto his belt. The two of them ran to the small kingdom of the wood sprites. Fortunately, Hara's home was only a few miles from the wood spites' village. Hara would have easily outdistanced Someisa if she hadn't caught hold of his sleeve to tell him she didn't know where they were going. He held her hand, and together they ran as fast as Someisa could go. Foliage of all kinds seemed to move out of the way as Hara approached, making the way easier for both of them.

A wood sprite village would not be noticed by a casual observer. Community gatherings and a safe place for eating and sleeping were its primary functions. They don't build or make things. They use what they can find. In the case of this wood sprite village, large cedar tree branches formed the roofs of their homes, often one branch forming the roof of several homes. Intertwining small vines made up the walls, and the door was nothing more than a large leaf that needed frequent replacing.

They used their hands to eat and mostly ate raw food, rarely bothering with cooking. They wove their clothing out of moss and lichen, using only their hands.

Signs of damage to plants and trees appeared as Hara and Someisa drew closer to the homes of the wood sprites. Broken branches and scattered debris made the going more difficult. Suddenly Hara stopped. Someisa was a step behind him and nearly ran into him. She stumbled to avoid him. Once stable on her feet, she looked around to see what had stopped the ranger.

It was a nightmare. Everywhere was wanton destruction. What was once a small clearing atop a knoll at the side of a mountain, and surrounded by a wood sprite village, was now a mass of confusion and pain. Trees were downed, blown away from the mountain, plants uprooted or totally smashed, with dirt in piles here and there. Most of the homes of the little wood sprites were demolished by the falling trees and flying debris. The smell of blood and vomit filled the air, along with a sharp tang that Someisa didn't recognize.

Someisa sobbed as she observed all the destruction and heard the cries of pain and anguish coming from the little wood sprites. Realizing crying wasn't going to help, she gulped down her feelings. It was all she could do to follow Hara as they crossed the clearing, even though it was only a few steps. He showed Someisa where to step to avoid any further harm. Wood sprites fluttering everywhere made the way more treacherous.

Hara beckoned to one of the wood sprites. "Where would we find Chester Oak?"

The little wood sprite twittered. Hara listened and then said, "We're to follow the wee one."

It got worse when the little one brought them to the wood sprite version of a place of healing. Normally, wood sprites' homes and healing places abounded in trees or large shrubs. Here, the ground around the former healing place was strewn with little tiny beings, many of them chittering out in pain. Off to one side lay four small wrapped bundles that Someisa guessed contained dead wood sprites. The smell of blood and bodily fluids was everywhere. Someisa was somewhat used to it, having helped her mother in the infirmary off and on when needed, but she was unprepared to encounter it here.

"Stay here, while I talk ter the king," said Hara, indicating a stump nearby.

Someisa did as she was told, making sure no one was on a stump before she sat down on it. Everything was such a chaotic shambles, she felt a need to watch her every step and especially where she sat. The horror of what she was seeing took hold of her. The girl closed her eyes, trying to shut away the carnage, but it didn't help. Pictures of shattered little bodies, wrecked homes, families trying to find each other, swept in front of her vision, regardless of whether or not she closed her eyes. She cried until exhaustion took over and she could weep no more.

Finding Hara beside her when she opened her eyes, she took a deep breath, gathered herself together, and asked, "What do we need to do first?"

"Yer needs ter set up a place where the wee folks can gather ter reconnect and find out about information concerning missing family members, friends, and such. I'll be doin' repair on some of the least damaged houses to get things started for the wee folks to have places to stay. There's the equivalent of a town hall over yonder among them trees. I'll be starting there."

Thistle broke away from a cluster of wood sprites and landed at her customary place on Someisa's shoulder. "Hurting," announced Thistle.

"Oh, no!" cried Someisa. "Where are you hurt?"

"Hurting heart, hurting mind."

Someisa wanted to hug the little sprite, but there was no way she could that. So she said, "Hara and I were talking about setting up a command post where your people could come for information about family and friends, or to use as a meeting place so that they could reconnect with each other. Is there a place where we could do that?"

Hara added, "Wee folk're running and flying all over the place, causing confusion and interfering with rescue crews."

"Come," said Thistle, and led the way to an area beside a small rocky cliff. "Talking, father," she added and left them. Hara followed her, leaving Someisa alone, wondering what to do.

After exploring the bit of space, she set about clearing some of the debris that had blown in from the explosion. A tree had fallen over and covered much of the area. Because wood sprites lived in trees, Someisa thought it would be a nice place for them to rest. A faint cry caught her attention. Working toward the source of the sound, she found several wood sprites caught under the tree. There was no one nearby to help move the tree, and she sensed it was imperative that these little sprites be rescued now.

Someisa studied the situation. Using her skills at growing things, she worked with the tree, causing it to grow a branch down two feet into the ground. This lifted the tree up enough that the wood sprites could free themselves. Two wood sprites did not move although they chittered to let Someisa know they were still alive. At first, Someisa didn't know what to do and then it came to her. Concerned that if she picked them up, she might injure them further, she used her skills at moving rocks with her mind, and through thought moved the injured wood sprites slowly and carefully to the healing area. Thistle saw her coming and created a space for the injured ones. Someisa gently set the injured wood sprites down.

To her surprise, she saw Zoenka and Gobha were working side by side, doing what they could for the little folk. The wood sprite healers had been at a meeting taking place where the blast did some of its worst damage. Two of the best healers did not survive. A call went out to Zoenka and Gobha to come help. Within minutes, Gobha arrived at the scene. Zoenka had been visiting with a friend who lived nearby. She called a bear to carry her to the destroyed village and sent an eagle to pick up a mountain of medical supplies and bring them to the destruction site. As a result, Zoenka arrived a few minutes after Gobha.

Chapter Twelve

The only true emotion is love. All else is reactions.

Feeling she was in the way, Someisa returned to the downed tree. Wood sprites began coming in great numbers, chittering in their language. Hara would have understood some of what they said. Someisa had no clue. She stepped back to look for him and nearly knocked him over. He had come up behind her.

"Yer did a nice job with the wee ones," Hara said.

She blushed, not knowing what to say about what she had done and yet feeling smug because she had done something right. "Let's find someone who can serve as a leader and also translate for me," she said to Hara.

No sooner were the words out of her mouth, when a male wood sprite flew up a couple of feet in front of her face.

"Ah," said Hara. "Here's Pippin, Thistle's brother."

"Thistle has a brother?"

"Two of 'em. No sisters, though."

"Greetings," said Pippin and he gave a little bow.

"Pleased to meet you," returned Someisa. Not knowing what was expected of her, she gave a little bow in return. The prince chittered and trilled while Hara listened carefully. He translated as best he could for Someisa.

"The royalty wishes ter thank yer for savin' their young uns."

"I did?"

"Apparently ,the two little uns yer took to the healing place are grand-children of the king and Pippin's niece and nephew. He says they owe yer a debt of gratitude. The way yer transported 'em saved their lives. If you had picked them up with yer hands, they would not have made it. They were both badly damaged in their spines. Gobha says they are going to make it, although one may have trouble walking from now on."

Someisa didn't know what to say to that, so she smiled and gave a small bow to the little wood sprite. He was about to fly off when Someisa said, "We need your help. We want to set up a command post here, where people can come to reconnect with family and friends, a place where parents can reunite with their children, and a temporary place for your people to stay until homes can be built for them."

Hara translated for Someisa. "He is telling his people that mothers with their children are ter go ter that area of trees ter the right over there." He pointed as he spoke. "Male sprites are ter stay with Pippin and be given assignments. Lost children are ter stay with Missmom until a parent is found. The children know her. For now, yer are ter stay here where wood sprites can see yer and learn where ter go."

Pippin finished trilling and flew off to the healing area.

"Pippin is letting the healers and the king know you are at the place ter go for help finding people and ter let their families know they are okay. He's also gathering some wood sprites ter serve as go-betweens for the various families: the wee folks that are with us and those in the healers' area.

Able-bodied wood sprites without children are ter meet here and Pippin will assign work parties to begin reconstruction and clearing debris. Reisander will find yer when it's time for yer to leave. He's on his way here. I need ter start repairing damaged trees and shrubs to support the wee folks' homes. I've had enough interruptions. I need ter get ter work!"

"Can I help with that?"

"I wish yer could, lass. But yer needs ter stand here for a while so the wee folks know where ter go. Yer might cause the tree ter grow a thick branch over the heads of everyone to keep the rain off.

"Once the congestion eases, and it seems like things are under control, I'll find yer. That is, if Reisander doesn't have things for yer ter do. Thistle will stay with yer for a while ter help with telling wee folks what ter do. Missmom is the eldest grandma in the village and will always be nearby should a wee child come for help. Here comes one now."

A tiny wood sprite flew to Someisa's other shoulder. It was crying and very frightened. Missmom saw it land and flew over to guide it to the group of waiting mothers. One of the mothers gave a cry of joy and reached for the little one. With the help of Thistle and Missmom, Someisa kept very busy attracting lost wood sprites by acting as a beacon for them to congregate at the way station. When she got tired of standing, the girl crawled up on a large boulder and sat where she could still be seen.

When things calmed down a bit, she connected with the fallen tree and caused it to grow a branch high enough for even Reisander to stand under without bending over. The tree seemed to understand the situation and without her asking, thickened the foliage enough to keep the area dry.

After some time had passed, the confusion and congestion of flying wood sprites settled down. There were still a few parents fluttering around, looking for lost children. She wished there was something she could do to help the frightened parents. Then she got an idea.

Calling Missmom over, she said, "Assign some teenagers to fly around the area looking for lost children. The older children would know where to look for frightened little ones in hiding."

"Great idea," said Missmom, and hurried off to put the idea into action.

Chapter Thirteen

If everything was perfect you would never learn and you would never grow

R eisander appeared from across the way. "Come with me," he called. Someisa let Missmom know Reisander had summoned her before making her way across the clearing. She was concerned about stepping on something tiny, when Hara appeared and led the way as they crossed the clearing. He showed Someisa where to step to avoid any further harm. Wood sprites were still fluttering everywhere, although with more purpose, making the way more treacherous.

As soon as they reached Reisander, the ranger turned and led them a short way from the destroyed village. More destruction lay ahead of them, and it became difficult to get through, even for Reisander.

"Do you know an easier way to the cave where the metal man's body is stored?" Reisander asked Hara. When Hara nodded yes, Reisander signaled him to lead the way. Shrubbery, downed trees, and piles of debris seemed to move out of Hara's way, making the short journey easier to traverse. At one point the debris became too thick, even for Hara, and he turned to the right, following around an outcropping of rock. On the other side, they encountered more destruction. It looked like dirt, rocks, trees, and plants were all thrown away from the mountain.

The entrance to a cave stood stark by itself on the side of the mountain. The three of them started to enter the cave when Hara stopped them. "Something doesn't feel right," he said.

Someisa felt a disturbance in the energy surrounding where they stood. No one moved. The cave was not a large one from what Someisa could see. It was a little bigger than her parents' living room. A small hole off to one side in the ceiling let in some light. No plant life grew inside, not even mold. Someisa thought that a little strange for rain forest territory. The air had a slight metallic tang to it.

Looking more closely at the rock walls, she thought at first someone had scoured the rocks. The walls and ceiling of the cave looked as though they had been scraped clean. The cleansing was too thorough to have been an act of nature.

Reisander and Hara were quiet, peering at the insides of the cave. Someisa felt like something was missing. It dawned on her there was no sign of the metal man's body, but it wasn't what felt wrong.

Thistle landed on Someisa's shoulder. "No cave," she cried anxiously. "No go."

Someisa, Hara, and Reisander stepped back a little from the entrance to the cave. Someisa stepped on something sharp that passed through her moccasin and cut her foot. She yelped in pain.

"What is it, gal?" said Reisander. Pointing to a log nearby, he helped her to it and made her sit down.

"I stepped on something sharp and it cut me."

Hara carefully removed her moccasin. The coppery smell of Someisa's blood filled everyone's nostrils. Hara reached in to one of his numerous pockets for a clean handkerchief to wipe up the blood and produced a thin piece of metal. He handed it to Reisander and took out some salve from another pocket. After covering the wound with the salve, the bleeding stopped. He fumbled in another pocket for bandages. Finding none, he frowned.

"You'll find clean bandages in my backpack," said Someisa, noticing Hara's frustration at not finding any bandages.

I musta left 'em in my other tunic," said a very embarrassed Hara.

Someisa giggled. "You put the bandages in my backpack as we ran out the door."

Reisander searched through her pack, found the bandages and handed one to the other ranger. While Hara finished with her foot, Reisander put a sticky substance on the inside sole of her moccasin and placed a patch over it. "I need to repair my moccasins a lot," he said. "This will last you for a while."

Hara nodded at the piece of metal. "What do yer think that is?"

"I'd say it is a piece of our 'friend' we came here to meet," Reisander answered drily. "This is the location of the explosion. It explains why the walls of this place are clean of any moss or lichen and all the dirt and debris blew away from the mountain. I put in a call to your brother, Kag, gal. He's the rock expert. I want him to take a look at this cave and its surroundings. It's possibly safe to enter it, but I don't want to risk it. We are picking up the aftershocks to the mountain itself, and so the cave doesn't feel safe. It will be quite a while before the energy of the explosion leaves this area. I'll have Fatidica meet with King Chester Oak to set up a time for a formal clearing ceremony.

"Thistle, would you please send someone to meet with Kag and bring him here? He'll do better if a wood sprite leads him here. Otherwise, he'll end up having to go through the brambles you have surrounding this place."

Thistle flew off.

"Brambles? What brambles? I didn't see any brambles on the way here," said Someisa.

"That's because Hara led you here and held your hand so you wouldn't stray off his path. If you had come alone, you would have found brambles everywhere barring your way."

"Nice during blackberry season, though," interrupted Hara. "Makes mighty good pies." He smacked his lips in memory of hot gooey pies. Feeling a little foolish at his lighthearted remark in the midst of all the destruction, he turned his back on the others and wiped away the tears that had begun to fall with his sleeve.

Another wood sprite approached Reisander. The man bowed to the wood sprite. "We are honored to speak to the king of the wood sprites. How may we be of service to you?"

"Come to thank you for quick help," said Chester Oak.

"We are most honored to help. Would you please tell us what happened?"

"Metal men come."

"Did they threaten you or your people?"

"Ignored us."

"Did you know what they wanted?"

"No say. Go straight to the cave. Take away metal body. They leave. Big boom."

"I wonder why they felt the need to blow up the inside of the cave."

"Not know."

"Did you try to stop them?"

No time. Once here, then gone."

We are in your debt, King Chester Oak." Reisander bowed to the king.

Hara and Someisa followed Reisander's example and the king left.

"We owe the wood sprite people an enormous debt that we have barely begun to pay," said Reisander as he watched the king fly back to the place of healing. "On to what we can do now."

"We need ter clear this cave of the unhealthy energy lingering here before we goin. I don't like the way it smells either. That will be a start. Fatidica can do the formal cleansing when she gets here," said Hara.

"How do we do that?" Someisa sneezed. "I don't like the aroma here. It smells like those bananas the tinker brought up from the south, and some of them were rotten by the time he got here."

"A little bit of wind coming through that hole in the roof and going out the right side of the cave opening away from the wee folk should do the trick," said Hara."How are the two of yer at blowing a wee bit of wind through here?"

"I've never done that," piped up Someisa.

"It's a bit like yer did when yer moved the wee ones, or moving rocks, only this time yer moving bundles of air. It'll work best if the three of us work together. One of us needs ter guide the wind, while another gathers up bunches of air from above the cave, and pushes it through the hole in the roof. The last person guides it out of the cave and away from the wee ones. Someisa, yer are best at moving things, so pushing it through the roof hole will be yer part. Reisander here knows how to call and gather wind. I'll guide it through the cave and swoosh it out over that way," he said, pointing to the left.

It meant that Reisander and Someisa had to climb up the side of the mountain to get to the hole over the cave. Some of the smell rose out of the hole as they got there and caught Someisa by surprise as she took a deep breath after her exertion from the climb. She gagged, followed by a coughing spell. The two men waited until she had control of herself.

"Now, gal, you're goin' to have to be near that hole in order to see where to move the air. Make sure you're upwind. Over here'd be a good place," he said, pointing to a little hollow in some rocks above and upwind of the smell of rotten bananas and a slight hint of metal.

Someisa sat on a rock and waited, not sure of what to do next. She watched Reisander close his eyes and concentrate. Within a minute or so, she felt the pressure of air around her. It got so strong, out of reflex, she pushed it all down the hole.

She heard Hara calling from down below. "Easy does it! Yer nearly blew me out of the cave."

The next time she felt air pressing down on her, she visualized it gently entering the hole and making its way to Hara. At first, she was worried because she couldn't see Hara and it might go the wrong way. So she added him to her visualization, and it worked. Presently he called up, saying all was clear.

Someisa and Reisander climbed back down and entered the cave. To Someisa's delight, the air was clear and fresh. The unpleasant feeling of congested energy was also gone. The cave felt light and cheerful, almost as if nothing traumatic had taken place.

Just as she was about to leave, something in the dirt caught the young foghlamach's eye. She bent over to pick it up. "What's this?" she said, showing it to the two men.

Reisander took it from her and studied it for a moment. "Looks like a screw to me. It's not made of a metal I am familiar with though. What do you think, Hara?" He handed the screw to the other ranger.

"Don't know. Not one of ours," answered Hara as he handed it back to Reisander, who put it in his pocket.

"Folks like Kag can safely explore and study this place now. Maybe they'll find more things like this. Wouldn't be surprised if more pieces weren't pushed into the ground," said Hara. "Right now I had better see what I can do ter help the wee folks with their rebuilding." With that, he left the two of them standing by the entrance.

Chapter Fourteen

The pessimist sees difficulty in every opportunity. The optimist sees the opportunity in every difficulty.

"Soonak," whispered Thistle.

"What about Soonak?" said Someisa.

"Not here."

Someisa took a moment to ground and center herself. She expected the big cat to be waiting for her. Instead, Soonak was nowhere to be found. Someisa closed her eyes and sent out a call, picturing the black panther in her mind. She caught a whiff of the big cat's energy as though it were very far away, and then it faded into nothing.

"Soonak isn't answering my call," said a very dismayed Someisa. "She's never done that before."

"Soonak's temporarily off planet, gal," announced Reisander.

Someisa jumped. She hadn't heard him coming up behind her.

"There's nothing more you can do for the wood spites right now. We've more important things to do. Thistle, we could use your help, what with Soonak bein' busy elsewhere. However, I can see that you're needed here right now to help your father."

Thistle left Someisa's shoulder and headed toward a group of little people surrounding the king.

"Is her father really the king?" Someisa asked, completely forgetting Thistle's brother had been introduced as royalty.

"Yes," Reisander grinned.

"Huh. I had no idea."

"The original plan was for you and Hara to examine the metal man's body and see what you could learn from it. Soonak was to be here too, for the same reason. Obviously, that's not goin' to happen," Reisander gave a big sigh in an effort to pull himself together. We're needed elsewhere. I sense something else is wrong. I find it very strange The Eldest Grandmother isn't here either."

Someisa had been so busy helping the wood sprites, she completely forgot about Grandma Tea. This embarrassed her so much she didn't say anything for some time.

The way out of Thistle's homeland was more difficult to traverse than the way in had been. Brambles were everywhere. Even though Reisander knew the best path, it was still slow going. Someisa had tears in her eyes, which didn't help.

Once they made it through the brambles, Reisander said, "We're to meet with Igni and a few other trackers tomorrow. Seefar found traces of the metal men off beyond Chager's Point. Hopefully, we can get a better idea of what is going on. We'll set up camp in a couple of hours. We both need some rest."

***

The next morning, Reisander and Someisa trudged up and down the path to Chager's Point. The girl pondered over the yesterday's events. Grandma Tea's failure to appear at the remains of the wood sprite village added to her worries.

This was a totally different experience from the time they had stopped the Kewoyuspans from invading their land. At least, Kahn and his people were made of flesh and blood and were sentient beings. The metal men were not, although whether they were sentient or not, remained to be seen. That didn't stop the anger from boiling up inside her.

Because they had yet to find a way to communicate with the things, there seemed to be no way to make peace or to find out what it was they really wanted. Frustration combined with her anger, and she stomped up the path behind Reisander.

You're making a lot of noise back there, gal," said Reisander, a few steps ahead of Someisa.

I don't care," she retorted. "I am angry, and frustrated, and I don't know how to communicate with these—these things. They can reach out to me, but I don't know—know how to reach them."

"Have you ever tried?"

"Uh, no. I wouldn't know how to begin."

"How about putting a picture of one on the window of your mind and see if you can create some connection?"

"Ugh! Do I have to?"

Reisander stopped walking and turned to his foghlamach. "You're the one they sought through dreams. You're the one they played the image of the ghost train to back there in the tunnel two years ago. Somehow, they know you wear the white stone, although I haven't the slightest idea of how they know that or its importance. Your dreams started before your Wasaru. None of this makes any sense. I'm as frustrated and angry as you are, but I choose not to let my anger control my actions. And neither should you."

Someisa sighed and hung her head. "My frustration is in not being able to communicate, in not understanding. My anger is from the cruelty and the lack of compassion. They have no idea of what they have done and they don't care."

"How do you know they don't care, gal?"

"I don't think they feel anything. They do things, it seems to me, without any thought of how their actions might affect others. I am not sure they actually think. It is more like they just do. I can't explain it."

Reisander picked a wooly caterpillar from off of a nearby moss-covered log and held it in his hands. "This little guy doesn't think about his actions either. Because these caterpillars are cute and fuzzy, we tend to think they are friendly. The truth is, they just are what they are. Is that what you mean, gal?"

"No. They're more like some of the movable dolls made by toy makers. The little machines that small children play with have no consciousness. They just go through the maneuvers mechanically programmed into them. The metal men are like that, only on a much grander scale." Someisa scuffed some mud off of one of her moccasins and stared at the ground. She breathed in deeply the damp musty smells of the woods surrounding them. She looked up at Reisander. "Do you understand what I am saying?"

"Yeah, I do, gal. No worries. We're getting close to Chager's Point. It's best if we go very quietly. I've no idea what or who might be in this neighborhood. Later, we'll set a time to see if you can contact the metal men."

Thoughts of what she had seen at the wood sprite village raced through Someisa's mind. Images of wounded and dying sprites brought fear and pain to her heart. Her head ached, and she began to shiver as she trudged behind Reisander. She felt her skin becoming clammy and sweaty. Her breathing grew ragged, and she had trouble taking a deep breath. Nausea caused her to pause. She found it hard to think clearly and wasn't aware Reisander had gone far ahead of her.

***

Noticing the noise usually made by Someisa had suddenly stopped, Reisander looked behind him and didn't see her. He ran down the trail and found her lying on her side, curled in a fetal position.

"This's no time for you to go into shock, gal," he said to her. He laid her gently on the ground and raised her feet up on a nearby rock. He took a thin blanket out of his backpack and covered her with it. To her surprise, he hummed a pleasant melody. The tune wrapped itself around her, bringing warmth and comfort with it. She relaxed into the melody and breathed deeply. Her mind cleared, and she sat up.

"I'm so sorry. I don't know what came over me," she said.

"It's called shock, and it usually occurs when a person has encountered a traumatic experience that is overwhelming. The mind and body can only take in so much and then it shuts down." Before Someisa had a chance to feel embarrassed and ashamed, he said, "You've done well in the short time I've known you. You've been quick to adapt to sudden changes in your life that most folks couldn't do. The White Stone picked well when it chose you." Reisander stood up and held out his hand to his foghlamach. "Feel up to walking again?"

Someisa took hold of his hand and got up off the ground. She handed him back his blanket and said, "Yeah. Let's go."

The warm feeling of his praise stayed with her for a long time.

Chapter Fifteen

You do it even when some might say it's wiser not to.

Someisa cheered up at the thought of seeing Igni, although she didn't want it to show. It had been some time since she had seen him last. He was a good friend, and she enjoyed his company. None of the other boys interested her, but there was something about Igni. Maybe it was because he treated her like an equal, and maybe not.

They reached Chager's Point in the late afternoon. Toolan greeted them. "That's a bad business been done at the wood sprite village. Anything we can do to help?"

"The village hasn't room for many more Cheschenaki. It's pretty small, so stay away from them for now. I've got Kag checking out the cave. He'll be takin' samples of chemicals off the walls and ground to see what they used to create the explosion. He has someone checking out the supplies of explosives we've got stored at the quarry. We want to know if they used some of our stuff or brought their own," said Reisander.

"There's really not a whole lot going on here. We've found some footprints in some mud. Got a fellah making casts. We're also comparing the depth of the footprints with some of our own to get a handle on how much these things weigh." Toolan took them over to a patch of mud and pointed out two sets of footprints. "You'll notice there are two different sizes and shapes here. So, I'm thinking there are at least two different types of metal men roaming around in these woods."

Reisander bent down on one knee and examined a footprint. "That confirms Seefar's sightings," he said." Someisa come here. I want you to look at something."

Someisa moved over beside Reisander and looked down at the mud. "Look down here. What do you see?" he instructed.

Someisa carefully avoided disturbing the mud in front of her as she bent closer to where Reisander was pointing. "I see two different sets of footprints. The smaller one has left some sort of coloration in one of its footprints. The smell of it is much like some of the oil I have seen Kag use when he is working with the rock moving machines."

"Good noticing, gal."

"Well, glory be, I missed that," observed Toolan. "I'll make sure one of the fellahs takes a sample of that, too. Igni, come on over here and take a look at this."

Igni heard Toolan and came running from down the trail. "What can I do for you, Toolan?" he said.

"Take samples of the oil from this footprint and check all the others for possible chemicals before they fill the prints with castings. Reisander, I'd like to converse with you a bit."

The two men turned aside and walked up the trail a short way, and paused at a point where the trail revealed a splendid view of the ocean. Neither one of them paid any attention to the view. They talked quietly, leaving the young people standing on the trail.

"All right, if Someisa gives me a hand with this?" called Igni after Reisander.

"Good idea. Gal, you work with Igni and see what you can learn from him."

Someisa smiled at Igni and asked, "What would you like me to do?'

"Have you got any bandages in that bag of yours/"

"I don't think I gave them all to Hara. Let me look." She rummaged in her bag and produced a handful of bandages.

Igni smiled and said, "Great. Take one of those small ones and lay it on top of that print with the oil in it. The bandage'll soak up the oil and I can take it back to the lab in Chehalem for processing."

"Huh," said Someisa. "I didn't know we had such a thing."

"I'll see to it that Kag or one of the other guys gets it," said Igni as he carefully placed the oil soaked bandage in a leather bag. "Sure, we've got a lab. Not many folks know about it, though. I learned about it when I was helping Kag with something. I forget what."

"Kag is at the wood sprite village, taking samples from the rocks in the cave to determine what caused the explosion."

"Then he'll want this right away. Let's check around and see if there is anything else we might want to give him."

The two young people checked all footprints in the surrounding area. There weren't many because most of the muddy areas were covered with grass and other growing things that made gathering uncontaminated samples difficult. Just when she thought they were all done, Someisa saw something that looked like metal sticking out from under a fern. Reaching down, she picked it up.

"What do you think this is, Igni?"

"Looks like a screw to me," he said. The quarry people use some like that, only bigger in some of their machines that move heavy rocks. I've seen 'em in other machines, too, and even in some toys."

"It looks like one I found in the cave." Someisa wrapped it in her handkerchief, put it in her pocket, and forgot about it.

The men who made the castings finished their work. One of them volunteered to take the oil samples and some samples of water left in the tracks of each sized footprint back to Chehalem. Igni thanked him and gave him their samples, carefully wrapped in waterproof fabrics.

Reisander was still talking with Toolan, which gave the young people sometime to visit with each other, a rare treat.

"Tell me about cave and the village," he said to Someisa.

"It wasn't pleasant. I wouldn't be surprised if I have nightmares about it for years to come. The wood sprites are so little and so many were hurt. A few of them died." Someisa began to cry again and Igni took her in his arms and held her while she cried.

When she calmed down a bit, he asked, "Is Thistle all right?"

Someisa leaned against his comforting shoulder and smelled the manliness of his body. It felt so comforting to be held for a few minutes. She didn't want him to let go. To her delight, he didn't.

"Thistle is okay. I didn't know she has two brothers and her father is the king of the wood sprites in this territory."

"Really? I didn't either. I didn't even know they had a king. Come, let's sit on this log over here that offers a view of the ocean and you can tell me more about it." He led her to the log and saw to it that she got a comfortable place to sit. Then he sat beside her, close but not quite touching.

A cool breeze blew up from the ocean, bringing with it the briny smell of the sea. Someisa shivered. She didn't have her cloak with her as it had been warm that morning and there was no time to look for it when she ran to catch up with Hara for the trip to the wood sprite village.

Igni reached into his pack and brought out a clean tunic. He draped it over her shoulders. "Better?" he said.

"Yeah. Thanks. I hope you don't mind, but I just can't talk about the cave and all just yet."

Igni took her hand and the two of them gazed out at the ocean until Reisander came to take Someisa away. Gobha joined them at that moment.

"Too many big feet was addin' ta the damage at the wee ones' village, so ya Ma and I decided it was time fer us to leave. The little ones know what they're doin' when it comes ta healing. It was the medicine supplies we brought that were most appreciated. So I came ta talk with Reisander here afore I left fer home. Hara'll have all the wee ones' homes finished in about a week. Had no idea there's so many wood sprites livin' there.".

Chapter Sixteen

Success is often achieved by those who don't know that failure is inevitable.

R eisander finished his conversation with Gobha.

Before any of them left, Soonak appeared with her tail twitching rapidly. Thistle came right behind Soonak. Igni jumped in alarm at the sight of the big cat.

Someisa laid a hand on Igni's arm. "It's all right," she said. "This is Soonak, and she's a friend."

"A little big for a pet, don't you think?" he snapped.

"Quiet. Let's listen. Something serious has happened."

Thistle spoke first. "Missing!"

"Who is missing?" said Someisa.

Soonak frowned at Thistle and turned to face Reisander. "The Eldest Grandmother has disappeared. We think the metal men have kidnapped her."

"Where was she when she disappeared? At home or on the road somewhere?" asked Reisander.

"As far as I know, she was at home. I dropped by to talk to her about what I learned about the metal men in my travels off planet, but she wasn't there. I put the word out, asking for her whereabouts. Nothing. There is no sign that says she is anywhere near here."

"Living," said Thistle.

"How do you know she is still alive?" asked Toolan.

"Feeling,"

"Do you have a sense of where she is?"

"Not feeling."

Something in the back of Someisa's mind troubled her so much, she found herself looking for the little screw she had found in the cave. Turning to Soonak, she asked, "Soonak, would this piece of metal enable you to get a better bearing on where Esther might be?"

Soonak took the screw from Someisa, using her mouth. She held it there for several minutes before spitting it out onto the ground, where Reisander picked it up and put it into his pocket.

"Metal men are off planet,' she said. "They have taken Esther with them. Kanshisha has asked for a meeting with Someisa and Reisander early tomorrow morning. There's a glen off the trail to Chehalem that is big enough for her to land and talk with the two of you. Do you know the one I mean, Reisander?"

"I do," said Reisander.

Chapter Seventeen

The spirit and the body carry different loads and require different attentions.

The morning had begun bright and cheerful for The Eldest Grandmother. She drank some tea and enjoyed scrambled eggs, strawberries, and toast for breakfast. The animals had all been fed. She was about to put on her gardening cloak, as the morning was cold, when she heard the dogs sound an alarm. The ground rumbled, and she heard a distant loud roar, somewhat like the blasting the quarry people did when mining for stone. She grabbed her cloak and hurried outside to see what the fuss was about. Two steps out of the door and the world around her ceased to exist.

Esther felt nauseas and lost her balance. For a frightening moment, it seemed there was nowhere to land if she fell. Something pushed her from behind and suddenly she found herself in a place where the sun was so bright, it momentarily blinded her. The nausea left, which was a relief. When her eyesight returned, she discovered she was standing in the middle of a strange city. Underneath her feet, the hard ground felt very hot, and she was glad she had on her gardening boots. Sandals would not have been enough to protect her feet.

Two suns shone down from the pale yellow sky. The air smelled dry and dusty and scalded her lungs when she took a deep breath. It became hard to breathe. The inside of her nose went dry, and she wished for water.

Looking around, the old woman saw rows of stone-like buildings forming long lines in all directions. No plants or animals graced the areas between the buildings. A hard substance covered the ground between buildings. All around her, metal men scurried here and there.

She felt heavier than normal, making her feel sluggish when she moved. Looking around for someone to speak to about this, Esther found she was alone and unguarded. The portal through which she had been pushed stood to her left. A metal man was fiddling with some buttons and levers on a wall to one side of it. Presently, he stopped what he was doing. The next thing she knew, a metal man grabbed her by the arm, led her to the portal, and shoved her through it again. This time, when she exited the portal, she was pleased to see blue sky and only one sun.

Unfortunately, this place was also hot and dry. It was too hot for a cloak, so she took it off and carried it over her arm. Shade was the goal. At first glance, it seemed to be in short supply. There were no trees. A few plants with long spines on their leaves grew nearby and offered little shade. The portal disappeared.

Turning around, she discovered the metal men had built two buildings made of what looked like stone and a third was under construction. There were no rocks or signs of quarries anywhere nearby that she could see. Instead, the metal men were taking sand and mixing it with a liquid to make their own rocklike walls. The smell of the liquid was alkaline and harsh on her nose. She remembered Someisa's descriptions of the walls of the metal men's buildings that appeared in the girl's dreams. This must be how they were made. Room for the new building had been cleared in the sand for a hard surface creating the floor, and preparations for the last wall were under way.

The buildings provided shade, plus she was curious to see what they contained. None of the metal men paid any attention to her. Esther walked over to one of the buildings. The windows were small and very high up, just as Someisa described. She didn't see a door. After walking all around the first building, she was surprised to discover there were no obvious doors of any kind in this one either.

Someisa had mentioned a door in her dreams. Frustrated, Esther sat down in the shade of one of the buildings. No one came near. No one looked at her. It seemed odd that they had gone to the trouble of bringing her here by portal and then have no one to greet her or tell her why she was here.

Looking west of the encampment, Esther saw a vast wasteland where nothing grew that she could see from where she was standing. Rocky crags rose up out of the sand. Hills and far-off mountains were to the south and east of the barren lands. 'These must be the dead lands," she thought. A shiver of fear went through her body. "What if I get the wasting sickness? I don't feel sick. Perhaps this encampment isn't that far into the lands of sickness to cause me any harm."

She wandered back to the other side of the encampment and sat down in the shade of a building. The sun's heat beat down on her; she was tired, and soon dozed off.

Esther woke with a start. A smaller version of the metal men, close to four feet tall, stood in front of her.

"Does this unit require assistance?" it asked. The thing spoke in a monotone, which quickly became irritating.

"I would appreciate a drink of water," Esther answered. She thought it odd to be addressed as a unit, but let it go for the moment. She was very thirsty.

"Units do not require water."

"This unit does."

"We do not have water here. There is no need. Units do not require water."

"I am telling you, this unit requires water. It's built differently from your units."

"Units do not require water," it said again.

Esther sighed and decided to ignore it.

"Does this unit require oil to protect its joints from the heat?" The little metal man was persistent. She had to give him that.

"This unit does not use oil. It needs water," she stated as firmly as she could, using the voice she projected on her students when they got out of line.

"No oil," said the metal man as though he were committing something to memory.

"No oil," repeated Esther, "Just water."

"We do not have water. Units do not require water."

"Go away then. You have nothing of use for me unless maybe you have apple juice or cold milk. How about a nice glass of iced tea or even a cup of hot tea?"

"We do not have those things. We do not recognize those things. They are not useful for keeping parts moving freely." The metal man wasn't going to give up easily.

"Oh yes, they are. They are very important to keep this unit's parts moving freely."

"Units do not require these things. This unit will bring you oil."

With that comment, the metal man disappeared around a corner of the building. Esther felt a little dizzy from being in the sun too long without water. She got up and moved to another side of the building, looking for some shade. She knew she could not survive long without water. Aware she was not thinking too clearly, she sat back down again. She hadn't even noticed she rose to a standing position while she argued with the metal man.

Esther sat still, letting her thoughts wander where they would. Knowing this was getting her nowhere, she grounded and centered herself yet again, and reached out with her mind for contact with Everonius. At first, she found no energy signature for the dragon. Forcing herself to concentrate even more thoroughly in her mind about the dragon, she felt a faint whiff of the dragon's energy. It disappeared within a second or two. Frustrated, she tried again. This time, there was nothing.

"Perhaps Everonius is out of range or something," she thought. She put her consciousness on the energy signature belonging to Kanshisha. A barrier formed around her mind. She could feel it as she pushed out in her calls for help. Giving it one last try, she thought of her love for Someisa as she reached out for the girl. She could see the girl talking with Reisander and Kanshisha, but Someisa took no notice of Grandma Tea's presence.

Esther stopped and thought. It was obvious the metal men had figured out a way to stop her from communicating with her people. There was that slight link with Someisa. She would pursue that again once she drank some water. The need for water overcame all other thought. Her tongue was so dry she was unable to lick her cracked lips

A spiny plant called to her. Its energy field seemed friendly. Without another thought, she got up and walked over to the plant. She had heard about nopales cactus plants from Gobha and knew that they were edible. It had flat oval leaves covered with sharp looking spines extending from its rounded leaves. Reaching in carefully, Esther broke off one leaf. Liquid dripped from the break onto the hot sand. The inside of the leaf was filled with liquid. Not caring whether it was poisonous or not. She put the torn edge to her mouth and drank the liquid that dribbled out.

It was delicious. She thought she had never tasted anything so good. She reached in with a finger and scraped out the pulp and ate it. Not wanting to deplete the plant, she walked over to another one and broke off a round leaf. In the process of picking it, a spine caught her. It broke her skin. Blood trickled to the ground. Esther was prepared for this, only she didn't know that when she got up that morning. Because she had been planning on pulling up some of the pesky brambles that morning, she had put gloves and bandages in her pocket. She grabbed a bandage and pressed it against the wound. It wasn't very deep, and the bleeding stopped almost immediately.

This time, after drinking what liquid seeped out from the leaf she had just broken off, she pulled on her gloves for protection from the spines and broke them off one by one. Once she had the branch free of spines, she ate it. The leaf appeared older, and she found it was tough to chew. She went back to the first one she had discarded and ate it, too.

For the first time since arriving, Esther felt physically good. The sun was setting, and the air felt cooler. She knew she would survive. Now, if she could find a metal man that would talk with her about why she was here, all would be well. There wasn't a metal man in sight. The ones working on the building under construction disappeared. The little one insisting on giving her oil had not returned.

Chapter Eighteen

Worry neither heals nor does it speed up time. It does exhaust the worrier, which solves nothing.

M orning couldn't come soon enough for Someisa as she prepared for bed, even though it meant getting up in what would seem like the middle of the night. Going over the events of the day didn't help her get to sleep either, but she allowed herself the privilege of going over them once, and then she grounded and centered herself. It was a trick she had learned from Grandma Tea. By grounding and centering, she could clear her mind of worries and set an intention to sleep. Most of the time, it worked. She was concerned it might not work this time, but her body was tired and complied with her intention. Just before she drifted off, she remembered to set the intention to get up in time to meet Reisander at the trail's head.

***

Someisa was glad for the warm clothing she brought with her. It was cold at that time of night. Reisander led the way up the path. This time, she took a moment to ground and center again. Then she put her attention on her feet and followed Reisander to the spot on the trail where they turned off for the meadow without any mishaps. Going through the thick under-brush was another story. She kept to her feet, but the brambles seemed to like her and kept grabbing at her clothing, or worse, her bare skin. Luckily, she had on gloves or her hands would have been raw and bleeding by the time they got there.

They arrived first. Someisa took some jerky out of one of her pockets and offered some to Reisander. The two munched on it while they waited for the dragon. Time passed. The dragon was late and Someisa began to worry. "What do you think is delaying Kanshisha?"

"Don't know," said Reisander. "Not the usual thing for a dragon to be late."

It started to rain. Someisa pulled her hood up over her head and looked down at the ground. She felt miserable in the damp and cold of early morning. Reisander's posture told her he didn't feel any better than she did.

Thistle was off working at the wood sprite village. Someisa didn't even have the comfort of her company. Reisander didn't seem inclined to talk, so she stayed quiet for a long time. Unusual for her.

They waited. The sun came up and still no dragon. "Are we at the right place?" Someisa asked after thinking that thought for a while.

"We're where we're supposed to be. Call up Soonak and see if she knows what happened to Kanshisha."

Good idea." Someisa grounded and centered herself again and then sent her consciousness to look in the window of her mind. She pictured the black panther. For a long time, nothing happened. No bouncy black cat popped into her mind. Someisa increased her concentration, shutting out everything else.

Faintly, very faintly, she picked up a picture of the cat. It was hard to see the black panther very clearly as it was dark wherever the cat was. She could see it crawling on her stomach toward a goal that Someisa couldn't see. For a brief second, Soonak turned and looked at Someisa and hissed a warning. Someisa knew the cat well enough to back off. Normally, she would have come out of her meditative trance. This time her need to know had her pulling back to watch the cat from a greater distance. It also enabled her to see a broader picture.

Three metal men surrounded The Eldest Grandmother. Her hair was disheveled, and she looked red in the face. She was sitting in a chair with metal strings attached at various places on her body. Looking behind Grandma Tea, Someisa saw the familiar grey stone walls that she knew from her dreams.

To Someisa's surprise, one of the metal men seemed to see her and motioned to one of the other metal men. The picture of Grandma Tea disappeared. No matter what Someisa did, she couldn't get it back again. Focusing on Soonak, the cat hissed at her again. Fearing the metal men might learn of the connection with the cat, she let go of the image of Soonak.

"Now what do I do?" she wailed to herself.

Knowing Reisander wanted to know what Soonak had to say, the girl quickly related to him all that she saw and heard. It wasn't much to go on.

"We shall wait," said Reisander. The two of them sat together until mid morning. Neither one felt much like talking.

"If Kanshisha doesn't show up by noon, I'll put out a call for her. There must be a good reason for why she's late," announced Reisander.

Someisa didn't want to wait that long, but she didn't argue.

About an hour before noon, Gobha found them. He looked very distressed as he approached from the edge of the clearing. Reisander stood up to meet him. Someisa did the same.

"Kanshisha has been killed," sobbed Gobha, barely able to get the words out.

"What?" cried Reisander.

Chapter Nineteen

Our worst foes are not belligerent circumstances, but wavering spirits.

The Eldest Grandmother woke to find herself inside a building. She didn't remember falling asleep, but either she had done so in the cool of the evening, or the metal men had somehow put her to sleep. It may have been the plant she ate. It really didn't matter.

That she found herself inside abuilding changed everything. Not only was she inside a building, but she was sitting in a chair. Her attempt to stand up failed. Someisa's description of her dreams came back to the old woman. They brought a better understanding of what the young girl had gone through and an idea of what was to come.

Once fully awake, she looked around the room. It was very much like what Someisa had described: grey stone like walls to her left, windows high up and small, and a door off to her right. The door surprised her because there had been no sign of a door on any of the buildings she explored.

A table full of strange boxes stood to her right. She looked at the various items. None of them revealed what they were for or what they might do. She felt uneasy about them.

Presently, a metal man materialized in front of her. It observed her for some time without speaking. She waited for it to speak. It didn't. It wrapped a device of some kind around her wrist.

Another metal man came from behind her. It, too, looked her over closely. It took a small box from off the table and went round to her back. The metal man pushed her upper back forward, away from the chair's support. She needn't have worried about falling because whatever held her in place continued to do so, even with her in this position.

The metal man touched each one of her vertebras, starting at the top of her neck and working its way down to her tailbone.

When it finished, she sat upright again. It began touching her with the small box wherever there was a bone joint. It looked at a display on a larger box on the table that attached to the smaller box it held by a metal string. Not having facial expressions, it was hard for Esther to discern whether the metal man liked what it saw or not.

The last thing it did was place the small box over each of her seven primary energy centers. Again, it studied what was on the display. If the thing could frown, Esther was sure that is what it would do, for it was apparent by its actions, it was not happy with what it saw. It kept checking and rechecking the display shown on the box on the table.

"Where is the attachment for your energy system?" it asked in the same monotone the irritating little metal man had used when asking about her need for oil.

Esther said nothing.

A third metal man came around to where she could see it. It, too, studied what was on the display and then moved around her as though looking for something. None of the metal men gave off any form of facial expression. They were no different from the boxes they were using.

Esther thought about how body language, the use of hands, and facial expressions were such an important part of communication. Without them, there wasn't much to say in reply to their questions.

The third metal man, not that she was sure it was the third, as they all looked alike and had moved around some, adjusted a knob. "Where is the attachment for your energy system?" it asked in the same annoying monotone.

Again, Esther said nothing. In the quiet that followed its question, Esther felt a faint whiff of Someisa's energy. It gave her hope and the courage to defy these strange men made of metal.

One of the three touched her in places where the energy centers entered her body. It was as if by touch, the thing would get the answers it sought. It stopped after a while and repeated the question, "Where is the attachment for your energy system?"

Now The Eldest Grandmother knew the answer to that question and that it would not help them. She wasn't even sure she could put it into words, for the energy system is a multi-dimensional thing. So she sat there, staring back at them.

The staring match lasted a long time. Esther grew weary and eventually nodded off, or so she thought afterwards. When she came to, she found herself outside the building again. Dawn was hinting at the horizon over the mountains. That must be east, she thought. Why that was important, she didn't know, but it brought her some comfort.

She noticed the metal device was still on her wrist. She tried to get it off, but it was too small to fit over her hand. Being made of metal, she couldn't break it. Before it got too hot, she thought she would simply walk east away from the camp. She had an idea that if she walked east for a mile or two and then headed north, she would avoid the dead lands and begin the long walk home. '

Getting up off the ground, she headed toward the rising sun. Her thought was to keep walking until it got too hot and find some shade where she could rest until it cooled down enough to continue her journey. At worst, she could rest under her cloak. She hoped there would be plenty of spiny plants around for food, and especially water.

She made it about four hundred feet from the building furthest east, when the device on her wrist vibrated. Very shortly thereafter, a group of metal men appeared and forced her to turn around and walk back to the shade of the building.

"Do you need oil?" asked one of the metal men.

"No," she replied. She sat down with her back resting against the building. The thing on her wrist keeping track of her whereabouts was a big disappointment.

The following day was much like the first one. In the cool of the morning, she explored the camp. She decided not to eat any of the plants on the west side. They might give her the wasting disease.

Offering gratitude to the spiny plant people that fed and watered her gave her something to do. It felt good to thank them. She saw the tracks of little animals around the edges of the camp. A snake had come near and left again. The wind picked up, and soon sand filled in the indications of other life.

The temperature rose and The Eldest Grandmother followed shade as the sun moved across the sky. At night, she found herself in a building again. The metal men followed the same pattern as the night before. Just before dawn, they placed her outside. Either the metal men had great patience or they had no feeling for the passing of time. Esther waited.

Chapter Twenty

Yesterday's gone. There's nothing you can do to bring it back.

S omeisa began to cry, unable to talk.

Reisander wanted details. "Talk to me, Gobha. What happened?"

"Kanshisha heard Esther cry for help. The contact lasted only a second or two, but t'was enough for her ta get a bearin' on the location. She sent out a call ta the other dragons and took off o'er the dead lands. All we knows, is she went down somewheres in the dead lands and all communication with her stopped cold." Ere's no way she could survive where she went down."

Someisa pictured the lovely dragon in the window of her mind. Hoping for an answer, she sent out a call. Only silence came back to her. Memories of her contacts with the dragon came to mind. The first time they met was when the dragon awarded her with a red crystal.

The dragon had been so kind and so loving. Her contacts since that time were very brief, but she relished each of them and wished there had been time for more. Toshu had mentioned just in the past week that Someisa would get training from Kanshisha early in the season of a thousand greens. Now that wasn't going to happen. Every thought about Kanshisha, no longer living, brought pain.

Why it was different with the dragon and not like her fellow Cheschena-ki, she didn't know. Grief was not common among her people. A death was a time to rejoice with the one who had passed on and a knowing that you would meet again on the other side. Somehow, the loss of her dragon friend seemed more than just a death. It was as if Kanshisha had been wrenched away from her in a way that was acutely painful and left a void in her universe.

She wanted to ask Reisander about it, but knew it was not the time. She marked it in her mind for a later discussion and calmed down enough to continue to listen to the two men talking.

"Kanshisha went down about a hundred miles west o' them metal mens' buildin's. In a mountainy area, not explored by us in recent years. She was in contact with Everonius when she went down. All I know is, she cried out as if in pain. Everonius heard her say she was fallin' and that's the last anyone heard of her." Gobha looked drained of all energy. He walked over to a nearby log and sat down as his legs gave out from beneath him. His bottom almost missed the log. It sagged a bit from the big man's weight and released the heady smell of rotting wood, mushrooms, and wet ferns.

"The loss of a dragon is a terrible thing," said Reisander. "They are few and far between. Their territory stretches over the entire planet. To lose one means that much more work for the others and the chances of other invaders breaking through a bigger possibility. We've already had two breaches of their defenses. I fear there could be more."

"Now, don't go borrowin' trouble when we've enough of our own. Not goin' ta help."

"Yeah. You're right. So what do we do now?"

"Well, somethin's goin' ta happen that hasn't happened in recent years. "Ere's goin' to be a gatherin' of the dragons. They may even call in some dragons from off planet. While they're doin' their meetin', we rangers are ta keep guard. Not just Cheschenaki rangers, but rangers from all over the whole planet have been notified of what is happening here. Rocs from down south and way west on the other side of the planet are on their way here for ya ta ride while ya do your watchin' over us. They's more rangers than dragons. I be thinkin' this may be a permanent thing in future."

Someisa couldn't help herself when she had to ask, "What's a roc?"

"It's a very large bird. They live in a hot part of the world, far across the ocean. Most're big enough to carry a man. They look a bit like an eagle, only much bigger."

"Our cold, wet climate may be a bother ta 'em. I'll talk ta Zoenka about how we can keep 'em healthy in the wind and rain."

"How soon do you think they will get here?"

"It's a long ways, they's a flyin'. Especially o'er the ocean. They may come up ta the north and cross where the ocean's not so big. Tisn't certain they can fly high enough over the dead lands ta be safe from the wasting sickness that comes from 'ere. Tonguetied's called a meetin' of the rangers and Someisa, too, ta decide what ta do once them rocs gits here. He wants ta set up territories and such. Ya knows Tonguetied."

"Yup. When's the meeting?"

"Tomorrow morning." Gobha stood up, getting ready to leave.

"Okay. You're going to talk to Zoenka. Would you mind escorting Someisa home so she can pack, and be ready for whatever she's asked to do. I gotta talk to some folks and see what I can learn, both about Kanshisha and the dead lands."

"No problem. I'd be delighted ta walk the little lady home."

Sadly, Someisa gathered up her things and followed Gobha out of the clearing.

Chapter Twenty-One

When all hope seems lost, step forward anyway.

It began to rain again as Someisa and Gobha trudged down the path leading to Chehalem. Silent tears fell onto Someisa's cheeks. She wiped them away before Gobha could see them. A world without The Eldest Grandmother was unthinkable to her. The woman had always been there for her. Well, for everybody, for that matter. What would the people do without her?

That she might still be alive gave Someisa some hope. How to rescue her was another matter. It occurred to her a talk with Kahn, the Kewoyuspan leader, was in order. The two had become friends and Someisa had frequently visited the camp that had been set up for the Kewoyuspans until a way to send them home could be found. The one built in the high mountain desert was too cold for them. Of all the people Someisa knew, Kahn had had the most experience dealing with the metal men.

Even though they spoke different languages, somehow the two of them figured out how to communicate early on in their relationship. Kahn had gone to considerable effort to learn the Cheschenaki language before she met him face to face. Since then, Someisa worked with him to help the Kewoyuspan leader build his vocabulary.

"I would like to stop and visit with Kahn," she said to Gobha as they neared the path to the Kewoyuspan camp. "I haven't seen him in a while. It has occurred tome, he has the most experience in dealing with the metal men. Perhaps he can tell us more about them and what they might be doing with Grandma Tea."

"Good idea. Mind if I goes along?"

"You're welcome to join me. It would give Kahn an opportunity to work on his language skills using his voice. We' usually talk mentally. He wants to communicate with other people, not just Toolan and me.'

They arrived at the Kewoyuspan camp in the late afternoon. Someisa mentally called ahead to Kahn to let him know they were coming. Some of the Kewoyuspans were jittery about having Cheschenaki show up unannounced, so it was best to call ahead.

This camp followed the same layout as the older Kewoyuspan camps. Three buildings made of wood, arranged in a half circle, housed the Kewoyuspans. They much preferred wood for their buildings, whereas the Cheschenaki built theirs of stone with thatched roofs. Opposite the buildings was a large fenced paddock for their krebsrots which they used as pack animals and for riding. Between the two was empty ground for meetings, training, and other events.

Kahn motioned for them to enter the smallest of the buildings, which consisted of two rooms. He led them to a private office to one side of a general meeting room and greeted them with a pot of tea at the ready, and three cups waiting to be filled. "Learning to like your favorite drink," he said to Someisa ."Acquired taste, to be sure."

The Kewoyuspan found it awkward to hold the teapot. His hands were designed for different purposes. His fingers were long, delicate looking, and covered with a light grey fur. Someisa knew those fingers were anything but delicate from past experience.

"Finding management a teapot now, by using both hands. One hand tends to put too much pressure on teapot and smashes it. Takes practice."

Proudly, he poured tea into the three waiting cups. "Sit," he commanded. "Drink tea."

Someisa took a cup from Kahn and sat down. She nearly choked on her first sip. "A little on the strong side," she said, noting the abundance of tea leaves floating in the brew.

"This good?" asked Kahn. "If you like it that way, is good. Can drink it in small sips and enjoy it that way."

Gobha paid attention to Someisa's reaction to her first swallow of tea and took a tiny sip himself. Politely, he said to Kahn, "Yar skill at tea makin' has improved."

Kahn smiled. "What is pleasure of this visit, if okay to be bold and ask?"

Gobha sat himself down next to Someisa on a log shaped for sitting and took another sip of tea. The log sagged under his weight, nearly throwing Someisa to the ground. She caught herself and smiled, pleased to find most of her tea was still in the cup when she righted herself.

When Someisa didn't say anything right away, the ranger took it upon himself to bring up the subject. "The Eldest Grandmother's disappeared. They's no trace o'her. I be thinkin' the metal men have taken her off planet. Do ya have any idea what they might've done wit the wonderful lady?"

Kahn thought for a minute before speaking. "Off planet, they may have taken her; as a means of transporting her to another region on planet that not populated."

"Could be anywhere," said Gobha.

"No. A specific place. Long time they there, unknowing by peoples of your planet."

"Really. Do you know for how long?"

"Many trips around sun gone by since coming here. Many trips around sun before using us as spies and capturers. Not knowing how many."

"Do ya knows what they want?"

"Not knowing that. Communication with them not good. They not telling us what they want or why they here. Only tell us what they want us to do. Capture Cheschenaki. Send them some place via portal. Not tell us not eat. Big mistake." It was the closest Kahn could some to making an apology for having captured and eaten a few Cheschenaki people. Apologies were not a part of his people's way of life.

Gobha reached through his beard to scratch his chin. He disturbed a little titmouse who looked around, saw the Kewoyuspan, twittered a comment, moved further down the man's beard, and disappeared.

Someisa thought the best way for them to find The Eldest Grandmother was by a map. "Can you show me where this special place is, that the metal men live?"

Kahn nodded and took Someisa's hand. Together, they communicated by pictures in their minds. Kahn showed Someisa a picture of a dry, desolate land. Very few plant people lived there, none of them familiar to her. She could feel some heat coming through from Kahn's picture, but not much else.

Lots of metal machinery dotted the landscape where the metal men were working. Someisa could make out brown and barren mountains in the background. She saw no signs of water. She had no idea of what the metal men were doing, and from what she could pick up from Kahn's mind, he didn't either. The metal men were as strange to the Kewoyuspans as they were to her. Because they were working from Kahn's memory, there was no sign of Grandma Tea.

A haze formed in Kahn's mind, blocking the landscape. It became more difficult to make out a clear image of anything on the ground. Someisa had a sense the metal men knew they were looking at them, even though she thought she was being silly.

Committing to memory the picture of what she saw before the haze took over completely, she let go of Kahn's hand. "Thank you."

Quickly, she related everything she had seen to Gobha. "The only clue I can give you is that the weather was hot and dry. Other than that, neither Kahn nor I have any idea as to the location from here."

Kahn looked shocked. "Remembering gone,"

"What do ya mean, remembering gone?" asked Gobha.

"Gone," Kahn repeated. "All gone. Not in mind."

Someisa looked at Kahn while realizing what had happened. "A haze overshadowed Kahn's memory of the metal men's camp. I felt like they were blocking the picture Kahn had formed for me. I broke off contact with him before the same thing could happen to me and so I still have the memory."

"Draw it for Langor while ya still have it in ya mind. Put down everything ya kin remember, mountains, location of metal men, buildings, whatever." Someisa did as Gobha asked, having retrieved paper and a marker from her backpack. It took her a while. She had to start over a couple of times, as she was sure she had it wrong and there was too much to rub out. The last effort looked the best, which was a good thing because she was running out of paper.

They left Kahn with a warm farewell and continued onto Chehalem. Someisa's mind was going a mile a minute. She explored the memory of the metal men's camp over and over in her mind. Of course, that took her mind off her feet and she tripped over a root that just happened to be in her way. She landed flat on her face, unhurt, and disgusted with herself. Gobha laughed as he helped her up.

Chapter Twenty-Two

Stepping onto a brand-new path is difficult, but not as difficult as remaining in an unhealthy situation.

Kanshisha hurt all over. She knew she had several broken bones, which made movement almost impossible without making things worse. Keeping her eyes closed helped with the vertigo that plagued her. Pain was one thing, but vertigo was awful. Her spinning world made her sick to her stomach. There was no relief for that. She slept, as she knew that would help her body to heal.

When Kanshisha woke, she took careful stock of what was going on in her body. The vertigo had passed, for which she was most grateful. Some wounds were healing. She wished she had help in resetting some of the broken bones. Stretching out a wing brought tears to her eyes, and she cried out with the pain. Thankfully, it was enough to set one of the broken bones in the wing straight. Carefully, she relaxed the wing and waited for the pain to subside before working on another part of her body.

Movement out of the corner of her eye caught her attention, and the dragon learned she was not alone. Dozens of lizards the size of one of her feet surrounded her head. They watched her anxiously, not sure whether she was friend or foe.

"I won't hurt you," she said.

Her voice was so loud in the quiet of the dead lands, she scared the little lizards. They scattered in all directions. One by one, they slowly came back as she lay on the ground, overcome by exhaustion.

One lizard seemed braver than the rest and more receptive to the dragon's efforts at communication. Kanshisha formed a calming and loving thought in her mind and directed it to the lizard. It cocked its head as it studied her. Her projected thoughts must have worked because the little one stopped emanating fear. She waited for it to approach her face.

It climbed up on her nose and began licking one of her wounds. At first it hurt and then she felt a calm healing spread over her nose. The little lizard's saliva had some healing properties. Because she made no move to stop them, the rest of the lizards climbed up on her body and began licking her many wounds. A sense of peace that she had not known in many years came over her. She fell asleep.

When she awoke, all but one lizard had disappeared. The one that remained behind was the one who first approached earlier. The two looked at each other. Kanshisha started to rise. Alarm flared in the little lizard's eyes and it shook its head no. Kanshisha realized the lizards had healed all the cuts and scratches, but were unable to heal the broken bones. Pain brought the messages to her brain loud and clear.

She took inventory of the broken bones. From what the dragon could tell, she had three broken bones in one wing, a broken back right leg, and several broken ribs. She wasn't sure whether the breaks were due to the fall or whatever caused the fall in the first place. Probably both were the only conclusion she could draw.

Kanshisha had no idea of where she was or how she survived the fall. That she was smack in the middle of the dead lands, she was sure of. What surprised her more than anything was the good health of the little lizards. Whatever caused the wasting sickness in two-leggeds did not bother these little guys. She wondered how long would it be before the wasting sickness caught up to her. Surely she had been there long enough for her body to show symptoms. So far, she felt fine in that regard. Still, it would be a long time before she could walk or fly. And she didn't relish the thought of having the bones be re-broken and set straight if she ever did get home again.

Her stomach growled. It had been a long time since she had anything to eat or drink. Now that she thought of water, a terrible thirst hit her. It was hot where she lay and that didn't help. If it got much hotter, she would cook, and she didn't like that idea either.

All the while Kanshisha was thinking about herself and her body, the little lizard sat beside her as though for comfort. Before long, the other lizards came back and brought friends with them. It looked like an entire army of lizards arrived, each carrying something.

The first to arrive carried leaves full of water. They bravely climbed up to where they could pour the liquid held by the leaves into her mouth. Most of the time, compared to her size, the water content was little more than a drop or two. But they kept coming and coming until her thirst was satisfied. As if they knew this, the lizards took the empty leaves and laid them in layers all over her body. The leaves made shade from the scorching sun. It took a lot of leaves to completely cover her back, several layers thick. The lizards didn't seem to mind. They kept coming with more and more leaves..

The leaves did more than protect her body from the sun. They had a cooling affect that dragon found quite pleasing. She dozed off again. When she awoke, it was dark. The air she was breathing felt cold, but the leaves covering her body kept her nice and warm. The one lizard had stayed to keep her company.

"Thank you," said Kanshisha.

To her utter surprise, the little lizard answered her in her own language. "We thank you for guarding our skies," it said.

"You know about us?" asked Kanshisha.

"We know about the big ones who guard our skies and all the peoples on this planet. Yes."

"Have you always known?"

"Yes."

"How is it you have survived so well in these dead lands?"

"We have always been here. It is not in our consciousness to know that answer."

The dragon didn't know what to say. Could these gentle creatures have a natural immunity? Was it a part of the healing properties of their saliva? Had they passed it on to her when their saliva entered her bloodstream? Lots of questions. Few answers.

The little lizard interrupted her revelry with a question. "What do you like to eat? Stomach is grumbling."

Kanshisha started to laugh, only to find it hurt too much and stopped. "I like fruits best. Certain vegetables are favorable to me. I love fish, but I doubt they exist in this neighborhood."

"What is this fish?"

"They are animals we call the fish people who live in water."

"Here, water comes from underground."

"I thought as much. What about the leaves covering me? Where do they come from?"

"Places where water bubbles out of the ground have plant people growing around them. Some are good to eat. Some help with healing. Now that you are awake and hungry, my fellow lizards will arrive soon to feed you. Ah, here they come now."

The army of lizards arrived carrying leaves, some roots and some berries. Kanshisha wanted to sit up to eat, but the little lizard stopped her. "You are not to move if you can help it. The break in your leg is in three places.

When you were sleeping, we moved the bones back together as much as we could from the outside of your body. It is the best we know how to do."

"It is enough," assured Kanshisha. "Thank you."

"Open your mouth. We will put food in it. We think food that is good for us is probably good for you. I hope you also like insects."

Kanshisha obligingly opened her mouth. One by one, the little lizards dropped food into it. When her mouth was half full, they stopped to let her chew and swallow. It took some time for them to provide a few mouthfuls. Fortunately, it was enough, as she tired easily and didn't want very much by her standards. The lizards seem to understand this, and quit bringing food.

"Sleep now," said the lizard who stayed with her. "Time to rest and heal."

Kanshisha thought she saw Someisa's face in her mind just as she drifted off to sleep.

Chapter Twenty-Three

A single sunbeam is enough to drive away many shadows.

S omeisa trudged down the path with a heavy heart. There wasn't much conversation between Gobha and herself. Once home, she went straight to her room, lay down on her bed without even removing her boots, and stared at the ceiling. The pain of Kanshisha's death came in waves. She didn't even know why she felt such grief. It wasn't as though they had been close friends. She really didn't know the dragon very well. However, there seemed to be a connection between the two of them at a heart level that Someisa could not explain. It was as though the two of them had known each other for thousands of years. She passed the idea off as a possibility that the two of them had known each other in other lifetimes and let it go at that.

Still, she couldn't let go of her grief. There was pain deep inside of her she didn't understand. The more she looked at it, the more she realized it wasn't pain, but a deep longing to connect with the dragon. Somehow, that made her feel a little better.

It wasn't long before her mother called her in to dinner. Someisa was so upset she didn't even notice evening was approaching. It had been a very long day. She didn't think she was hungry, but once she sat down at the table, she found she was ravenous. The wonderful smell of a roast surrounded by vegetables and potatoes filled the room. Gobha joined them for dinner. He filled her parents in on what was happening. Someisa was grateful. She didn't feel like talking much.

She woke very early the next morning with Kanshisha still prominent in her thinking. She felt a pressure, a yearning, some sort of need to do something. An urgency filled Someisa's mind. The girl would have liked to consult with someone about this. It was too early to wake the Elder Grandmother or Fatidica. Thistle was still at the wood sprite village. Soon-ak wasn't waiting for her in the place she liked to be in Someisa's mind.

It seemed like the dragon was trying to reach out to her. That something was wrong, but different from death. She had heard Fatidica talking about contacting people who had passed on. She wondered if she could reach through the veil and talk with the kindly dragon. She knew it could be done, but wasn't sure how.

Determined, she grounded and centered herself and pictured Kanshisha in her mind. She remembered their times together and the understanding that had formed between them. She remembered looking into Kanshisha's eyes and seeing the kindness that always made her feel good. That the dragon had been dead almost a day now, as far as she knew, somehow made it worse. Why hadn't she felt the dragon die? Was it that the understanding between them so insignificant to the dragon that the connection Someisa thought was there wasn't on the dragon's side of things?

Using the window of her mind, she searched for the dragon, hoping to find where Kanshisha's body lay. Perhaps that would bring her closure with the dragon. Kanshisha's big, beautiful eyes took shape in her mind. The dragon blinked. Surprised, Someisa sat up in bed and the connection broke. But Someisa was left with the firm conviction the dragon was not dead, but lying somewhere in the dead lands, hurt and alone.

Someisa grounded and centered herself and again studied the dragon's face using the window of her mind. The picture wasn't clear. She pulled back a bit to where she could see the dragon's whole body. Leaves covered her body, many of which obscured the dragon's face. Her sides were moving to match her breathing pattern. This time, the dragon seemed to be asleep.

Someisa leaped out of bed and went to find Gobha. Fortunately, he was in the kitchen talking with Zoenka about possible herbal remedies for the wasting sickness.

Someisa burst into the kitchen shouting, "Kanshisha is still alive!"

"What?" said Gobha. "How do ya know this?"

"I saw her in the window of my mind. She is somewhere in the dead lands and she's hurt. I know this sounds strange, but her body is covered with leaves."

"Ya sure it wasn't just a dream, child?"

"Yes. It wasn't a dream. I saw her just as clear as I can see the two of you. Go get the Elder Grandmother. Get Fatidica. They will tell you I am not lying or dreaming."

"Sit down, Someisa," said Zoenka. "I'll make some tea. Take a deep breath and tell us how you came to this conclusion."

Someisa sat and explained about her sorrow over the loss of her friend. She talked about how she had used the window of her mind to see her friend one last time to create closure. Only the dragon she saw was breathing. It even blinked. She wasn't dead, but very much alive. She described the leaves covering the dragon's body.

"I know about 'em leaves," said Gobha. "The wee folk told me about 'em. Supposed ta have some healin' properties and can protect a body from the sun. I thought it was just poppycock. Ya know, just "em braggin' about somethin' tryin' ta impress me. Guess not. Shouldn't come to them conclusions so fast.

"I gotta tell the rangers an' talk ta the wee folk. Need ta know about 'em leaves. This changes everythin'."

Gobha took off for the Elder Grandmother's house.

Zoenka poured tea for Someisa and herself. "I know a little about the leaves you saw. Thistle's people know something about them. I'd ask her or one of her people, but I know they have their hands full with all that is going on in their village.

"You haven't asked about how they are doing. I can assume you have more on your mind than you can handle at the moment. Hara has made great progress in restoring their little homes and public buildings. He built them a hospital, much better than the old one, I am told."

Someisa took a sip of tea and discovered her mother had made her favorite tea. Even though it was hot, she took another sip and felt it go down to soothe her insides. "He said something about the two of you being in the way, but I admit I wasn't paying much attention. What is it that the leaves do that is helpful?"

"They weave them together to shield against the sun in hot climates. I don't know about any healing properties. I may have some in the root cellar. I'll have to check.

"Not all the dead lands are in hot climates. About half way across the continent due east of here is the largest of the dead lands that I know about. I don't think Kanshisha is there. It can get hot there, but also it can be very cold. Since it is early in the season of rest, I doubt very much she is there. From what you describe, I think she is in the dead lands east and far south of here. Do you know where The Eldest Grandmother is being held?"

"I don't. I caught a brief glimpse of her yesterday. She was inside a building."

"Do you think Kanshisha was on her way to rescue Esther?"

"No. The decision was for her to fly over the eastern edge of the southern dead lands to scout out a possible camp or village built by the metal men. She was to report back to us and the dragon guardians."

"Where is Reisander?" asked Zoenka.

"I don't know that either. He said he had to talk to some folks, and that I was to wait for him here. I don't know what he meant by folks. Sometimes he can be so secretive. He is supposed to be my mentor, but he doesn't tell me much. For all his storytelling abilities, he doesn't talk much when we're traveling."

"I'll bet that's frustrating for you," the healer smiled.

"You don't know the half of it. Most of the time I'm loaded with questions and all I get for an answer is 'now is not the time'. I could scream."

The two of them had a good laugh together. For Someisa, it was one of the best talks she had ever had with her mother. She felt like it was the beginning of a lifelong friendship and she liked it.

Chapter Twenty-Four

You can't 'should've' done something. You can only 'do' something.

R eisander got the message that a meeting of the rangers was to be held at The Eldest Grandmother's house. Leilanya would be there. She had volunteered to take care of the house and all of Esther's animals while Esther was gone. Leilanya lived next door to Toshu. She made wonderful crab cakes and clam fritters. He hoped she was making some now. He was hungry and the thought of her crab cakes made his mouth water.

The traveling ranger had covered much ground since he left Someisa with Gobha. First, he sought out the wood sprite village. Very few people even knew there was one. He wanted to talk to Chester Oak. He sent a message to meet with the king at the edge of the delicate village to prevent his large body from doing any further damage. The blast had done enough as it was.

Reisander didn't want to disturb the king any more than he had to, but the need was urgent and couldn't wait. Chester would know more about the dead lands than most wood sprites having been born near the edge of one. Possibly the very one that separated The Eldest Grandmother from where Chester was born.

Chester's parents didn't like the heat and the dryness of the south-ern territories and moved their family north to the rain forests along the coast. They found other wood sprites, made friends, and eventually settled down to build the wood sprite village. A few hundred years later, Chester's leadership skills got him elected as the current wood sprite king. Through the years, the king talked to wood sprites from all over the west side of the continent. He made it his business to know about everything that was going on in the wood sprite world. Hopefully, he knew something helpful about the dead lands.

The wood sprite village was located halfway between the haunted ruins and the ocean and many miles south of Chehalem. Distance wasn't a problem for Reisander, but the thought of having to make his way through the brambles again didn't thrill him. Sentries stationed in the brambles passed warnings to the wood sprites should an intruder appear. Scouts watched the approach of a visitor long before that individual reached the village. If the person or four-legged was undesirable for any reason, the brambles thickened and made it impossible to penetrate.

Reisander stopped at the edge of a particularly thick clump of brambles and chirped a greeting in the wood sprite language. A few minutes later a wood sprite fluttered in front of his face. The ranger's knowledge of the wood sprite language was limited, but he managed to convey to the wood sprite the urgency of his meeting with the king. The wood sprite let him pass and led the way through the brambles. Reisander arrived with nary a scratch.

King Chester Oak rarely left his home. He depended upon his people to bring him information and messages. In the few times Reisander had visited Chester, a long line of wood sprites would be fluttering, waiting patiently for their turn to speak with him.

With the destruction of the village and the number of wounded still undergoing treatment, the lines were even longer. Disputes arose over the placement of new homes and the problems of whose houses needed to be built first. The king had his hands full.

Until today, Reisander had always followed wood sprite protocol and waited in line. This time, he approached the king's home.

"Urgency," he announced.

The wood sprites in line held back and let him go forward. He let out a sigh of relief. Much of the journey here, he had pondered on which word would get the attention of the wood sprite king and if his people would respond as well. Wood sprites prided themselves on their brevity of language. They made up for it in body language and facial expressions.

"Speaking," said Chester as he came forward to greet his friend.

"I need your help and it's urgent," said Reisander as he politely knelt in front of the king.

Chester nodded to him and Reisander rose back to a standing position, which put him eye to eye with the little king sitting on a tree branch. "I need to know all you know about the dead lands."

"Forbidden," said Chester.

"I know it is forbidden to go there. Still, there is knowledge about the deadlands that I do not know. I also know you know far more than I do."

"Knowing,"

"Good. I have heard there are leaves, big leaves that grow there and can protect against the heat of the sun. Is that true?"

"True."

"Where do they grow?"

"Hot land."

Do they grow only in the dead lands, or can they be found elsewhere?

"Dead lands."

"Do you know where I can find some?"

"Knowing."

"Who gave you this information?"

"Lizards."

"Lizards? Do you mean big lizards like the dragons or another size?"

"Small."

"How small? Like the size of a wood sprite?"

"Bigger."

"How much bigger?"

Chester held up three fingers.

"Do you mean by three fingers the lizards are the size of three wood sprites standing together?"

"Knowing," said the king.

"Where would I find one?"

"Dead lands."

"Which dead lands?"

Chester pointed to the south and a little east. "Much long."

"Do they talk?"

"Knowing."

"That can mean many things. Do they talk with you by words?"

"Knowing."

Reisander was losing his patience. Trying another tact, he told the king about The Eldest Grandmother's kidnapping, to which Chester commented, "Knowing."

It was all Reisander could do to keep from laughing. The seriousness of the situation gave him the strength to gather himself, do a quick grounding and centering, and launch into the story of Kanshisha's sudden fall somewhere in the southern dead lands. He talked about how there was no communication with her since that time, and that it was feared she died. It was obvious from the sudden silence all around him that the wood sprites did not know about this.

"Thistle," called Chester Oak.

Thistle heard him even though she was much higher up in the tree and had been sleeping. It was the first opportunity she had had for a good nap and arose somewhat grumpy at being awakened too soon. She shook herself as a way of primping, before flying down to see what the trouble was and why her father had called her name.

Surprised to see Reisander standing in front of the king, she landed on a branch slightly below Chester and gave a small bow. Chester acknowledged her with a brief nod of his head. The two of them began to chirp and trill in their own language. Several times, Thistle turned to look at Reisander. He knew when she was told of Kanshisha's plight by the little he understood of her language and by the increased fluttering of her wings.

When the two finished their discussion, Chester pointed to Thistle and said, "Leading."

"Thistle fluffed herself up a little and announced, "Someisa."

"Does that mean you want Someisa to go with us to meet with the lizard people?" asked Reisander.

"Meeting,"

"You go tell Someisa I am coming to get the two of you. Possibly Gobha, too." He didn't mention the ranger meeting. "You can fly faster than I can walk."

Reisander left the wood sprite village and ran to The Eldest Grandmother's house.

Chapter Twenty-Five

We are all one and not one.

R eisander jumped up on the front porch of Esther's house. It wasn't the best choice for a landing, but he was in a hurry, and taking time to scope the area to see if anyone else was in the way wasn't on his agenda. Fortunately, the porch was empty. Reisander opened the door and walked in.

Apparently Gobha had also made good time arriving at the gathering. To his approval, all the rangers found ways of rapid transit to the house. Reisander walked over to an empty chair and sat down. His eyes lit up when he saw a plate full of crab cakes being placed in front of him. It didn't take him any time to think about being hungry. He grabbed three crab cakes off the plate and began eating. He was the last to arrive.

Before Tonguetied could officially call the meeting to order, Gobha stood up and announced with great joy on his face, "Kanshisha's still alive. She's somewhere in the southern dead lands where it's hot."

Tears came to Gobha's eyes as he related all that Someisa had told him. The rest of the rangers were quiet as they took in his words. No one doubted the authenticity of Someisa's vision.

"Sounds like a trip to the dead lands is in order,' said Langor. "But how can we do that safely? Even the dragons would have difficulty flying over it, if Kanshisha's fall has any importance, and I think it does."

"I would like ter know what caused her to fall before we roam around in country we know very little about other than it makes us sick and too much exposure can kill us," said Hara.

"Ya gotta point," said Gobha around a mouthful of crab cakes. Some crumbs flew out of his mouth and landed on his beard. The little titmouse was quick to remove them. "But Kanshisha's alive. Someisa picked up nothin' 'bout the wasting sickness. Only that she's badly hurt. And covered with leaves."

That brought Reisander's mind back to the leaves he wanted to know about when he visited King Chester. From somewhere in the back of his mind, he had heard about the leaves, but he couldn't remember where he got the information. It had been a comment in passing, most likely, possibly with either Gobha or Hara. He hoped one of them would enlighten the rest of the rangers about the leaves' properties. He wasn't disappointed.

"They's a low growin' plant that lives in valleys and shaded areas where water can be found. It has very broad leaves. I've seen lizards on the edges of the dead lands sleepin' under 'em. Never gave it much thought," said Gobha.

"Do you mean lizards live in the dead lands?" Langor was skeptical.

"Sure do," answered Gobha. "Least I've seen 'em running 'round in areas I didn't want ta go."

"Any idea of what protects them from the wasting sickness? It'd enable us to go into the dead lands without fear of it," said Reisander. "I intend to go there one way or another. King Chester told me about lizards who may be of help to us. He sent Thistle to bring Someisa to an area where Thistle knows of some lizard folk. It wasn't clear whether the lizard folk can communicate with us, but apparently they talk with the wood sprites."

"Seefar, what c-c -can you t-tell us?" said Tonguetied. "Can you m-make contact with the dragon?"

Perplexed, Seefar stood up and started pacing around the room. Because of his size, there wasn't enough room, and he finally gave up and sat back down on the only chair big enough to hold him. "I tried as soon as I heard Gobha talk about the possibility of Kanshisha still being alive. I got nothing. Well, not nothing. I ran into a wall. There is a barrier out there somewhere that won't let me reach the dragon. I would like to be present at the dragon meet before we go off half cocked, and see what they have to say. Surely they know more than we do."

"T-to bring in all the d-dragons would not be wise. With these m-m-metal men running about the planet, we still n-need eyes watching over what they d-do," said Tonguetied.

"That's up to the dragons. They're the ones who called for the meet. I would like to confer with them at least," said Reisander.

"How many dragons do we have guarding our planet? I never thought to ask," said Hara.

"Only four," answered Langor. "Kanshisha, Dragonis, Everonius, and Doragon. I haven't met Doragon. He's always on the other side of the planet."

"Only four and one out sick? Not good," observed Gobha. "I'd like ta meet this Doragon and see what he has ta say."

"Seefar, would you p-please contact the d-dragons and ask when and where the dragons plan to m-meet? I don't think we n-need to tell them how important it is that we be at the m-meet. I'm sure they already know. I'd also like to know m-more about the rocs. Can they fly high enough and far enough to m-meet our needs over the dead lands?" Tonguetied scratched himself on the side of his neck where a bug bit him.

"Give me a minute," said Seefar. He closed his eyes and was silent for several minutes.

"Rocs should be arriving any minute now. The dragons want all of us rangers present. A roc is on its way to pick up Someisa. Thistle is coming with her.

"The meet will take place in the high mountain desert on a plateau east of where the Kewoyuspan camp used to be. Better dress for snow. It's going to be cold there." Seefar heaved his bulk up out of the sofa, grabbed the last of the crab cakes before Gobha could get them, and prepared to leave. He so loved the slightly sweet and salty taste of crab.

A loud trumpeting sound came from The Eldest Grandmother's front yard. A roc landed. Large birds filled the sky.

"Guess our rides er here," drawled Gobha.

Chapter Twenty-Six

Destiny is not a matter of chance; it is a matter of choice.

S omeisa was relaxing with Pokela in the women's bath located in the center of Chehalem. Hot springs fed the baths. The men had one of their own, separated from the women by a wall. The long soak pulled out many of her aches and pains from recent travels. It helped to ease the stress fed to her body by her mind, which never seemed to stop worrying.

Someisa brought Pokela up to date on all of her recent adventures. The two girls had been talking for an hour while soaking in the pool. It was the first time they had had time to be together in several weeks. It was also nice that they had the pool all to themselves, a very rare event. They arrived early in the morning, hoping no one would be there.

"Nothing like girl talk to brighten the day," thought Someisa. She glanced down at her hands and realized her fingers were looking like prunes.

"I think it's time we got out of the water," she commented to Pokela.

Pokela laughed and climbed out of the pool. "Yup," she said. "I hate to go, but I have some chores to do for Makacega. I don't think he'll mind our time together, but I did promise him I would get them done before breakfast and it's almost that time now."

"Come to think of it, I expected to see Gobha before now. I didn't know it was so late," said Someisa.

The two girls had just finished dressing when they heard a loud cry from out on the lawn. Toshu came running in. "At last I have found you, Someisa. A roc is on its way to take you to a dragon meet. Run home and get your things. The meet is going to take place where it is snowing, so grab your cold weather gear. Take an extra water bottle, too. I have a feeling you're going to need it."

Someisa left the bathhouse and headed toward home. Out of the corner of her eye, she saw an extremely large bird. It scared her, but she hurried past it. After gathering up all her things, she bid a hasty goodbye to both her parents. Hoisting the heavier than usual backpack over her shoulders, she ran back to the central park. To her relief, Reisander was waiting for her beside a second roc. She had serious questions for him.

Unfortunately, there was little time for talking. Reisander took her backpack and stowed it in a bag attached to the back of a saddle on a roc's back.

Someisa didn't get to ask how she was to get up on the thing's back. It was much taller than she was.

Reisander sized up the situation, picked her up and literally threw her over the roc's back. The pommel on the saddle caught her in the stomach and knocked the breath out of her. She struggled to straighten up before Reisander placed her feet in the stirrups. They were a little too long for her legs. He finagled with them for a minute or two until he got them the right length on both sides. After handing her the reins, he leaped astride his own roc.

"By the way, your rocs' name is Skyhaven. No time now for proper introductions. We're heading for the high mountain desert. Dragon meet."

Both rocs took to the skies at the same time. Their wing spans covered the large grassy area of the central park completely. Someisa felt giddy as they rose high in the sky. She had never been so far off the ground. It was both scary and exhilarating. She loved it.

The wind blew strong in her face as they headed east up over the mountains. She wished Reisander had told her to wear warm headgear. The higher they flew, the colder it got. Holding on the reins with one hand, she reached into a pocket for some thick gloves with the other. In order to put them on, she would have to let go of the reins. But if she didn't cover her hands, she knew they would soon become numb with the cold. She wrapped the reins around a wrist to free up her hands. It wasn't all that easy to put on the thick gloves, but she did it.

The rocs knew where to go. She wasn't sure why she needed to hang on to the reins. Her roc didn't seem to need any direction. She wouldn't have known what to do, anyway. She settled down for a long ride.

However, it wasn't long before Reisander turned his bird downward. Someisa's bird followed. They landed in a barren spot on top of a high hill. He pulled out snow gear from his pack and put it on. Reaching into Someisa's pack, he pulled out a hat and a warmer cloak. Shivering, Someisa gladly put them on. She tied her hat firmly under her chin and then pulled the hood of the cloak up over the hat. Already she felt much better. Reisander stuffed her lighter cloak in the bag behind her saddle and they took off again.

Clouds obstructed her view of the ground and the sun. She knew they were flying east because that was where the high mountain desert was. She assumed they were going to the dragon meet. If anyone could solve the problems at hand, the dragons surely could. She had total faith in the ones she had met.

That there were only four dragons guarding the planet was unexpected. She had always assumed there were dozens. She had rationalized that their home was on a small, out of the way planet of little interest to anyone. How wrong that assumption turned out to be.

The metal men came to mind. Could they be sentient? In basic school, the term sentient meant being able to see and feel things, knowing about one's own mortality, and being able to make decisions accordingly. From her recent dealings with them via the dreamland, she knew the metal men could see, hear, and observe. But could they feel, not touch, but feel emotionally? When they asked for her soul, had they really meant the ability to feel emotions?

It got colder as they rose high enough to clear the mountains. Someisa stopped thinking about the metal men and concentrated on hanging on. Despite the warmer clothing, she still felt the cold. The wind at this height seemed strong enough to go right through her wool cloak. It was also harder to breathe. She needed to breathe more deeply at high altitudes to bring oxygen to her lungs. It was so cold she shrank from doing that, which left her a bit lightheaded.

Just when she thought she might pass out, she noticed the bird was no longer climbing. What a relief. The high mountain desert would be cold and windy, but she could breathe more easily once they landed. She relaxed a little, knowing her wild ride through the skies was about to end. If it hadn't been for the fact that they were flying through dense clouds and icy air, she would have liked to fly on forever. It was exhilarating riding high in the sky, so free of distractions.

The roc banked into a turn, and the clouds ended. They were still pretty high up. The view was breathtaking. Several snow-covered volcanoes rose into the sky on both sides of her. The high desert plateau stretched out as far as she could see. Lava fields meandered over the terrain. Cinder cones dotted the landscape here and there. Not much grew here, at least compared to the rain forest in which she lived. The lodge pole pines grew where they could find root space in the lava fields. Sage brush and junipers also grew abundantly. The rest of the ground was covered by brown grass. She wondered what it was like in the season of a thousand greens.

Three dragons and six rocs with riders watched them land. Someisa's roc landed gently. Her legs didn't seem to want to work after flying so many hours without moving. Embarrassed, but knowing the need for haste, she called to Reisander to help her down.

He laughed and came over to her roc. He whistled to it and it immediately folded its legs into a sitting position. Reisander lifted Someisa off the roc and sat her down on the ground next to Gobha, who grinned at her and handed her a cup of hot tea.

Once Someisa and Reisander settled themselves on the ground, introductions began. Each rider formally introduced his roc to the others and the dragons. Someisa remembered her roc's name just in time to do her introduction. She was glad she didn't have to go first, as she didn't know the protocol.

Proper roc introductions always began by reciting the name of the roc followed by its family lineage. Someisa didn't have a clue about her ride's heritage, much less its name, and didn't really care. Reisander stepped in to complete the introduction for her. The last thing said was the name of each roc's rider.

The dragons didn't bother with introductions other than to state their names.

Chapter Twenty-Seven

Don't believe everything you think.

E sther was frightened, although she didn't want the metal men to know it. They never displayed any signs of impatience, anger, frustration, or humility. They never laughed, joked amongst themselves, or spoke out loud to each other. Kindness was not in their lifestyle, either.

Inside the building, she had no access to the plant people who provided her with water and food. At some point she had wet herself, which dismayed her. She didn't remember doing it. Outside, Esther had no problems, but in this building, not only was there no place to relieve herself, but she was unable to move out of the chair. Bathrooms were not a part of the metal men's culture, she was willing to bet.

She didn't know how long she had been sitting there or that she dozed off. When Esther came to, she noticed metal ropes connected to various places on her body. This time, instead of connecting to the energy centers, they connected to the major and some of the minor acupressure points along the meridian lines through which energy flows within and throughout the body.

Her body ached from sitting so long in one position and not being able to move. Esther longed to shift her weight. The angle of the back of the chair did nothing to relieve the pain in her back. Something in her mind wanted her attention. Thinking it might be the metal men entering her thoughts, she pushed it away and set up barriers. Whatever it was, it pushed against the barriers. Anger in the form of a battering ram lunged at her barriers.

"Anger?"thought Esther. "The metal men do not have anger. Who is it trying to get my attention, then?"

With great caution, she lowered her barriers. Soonak immediately filled the window in her mind. "It's about time you let me in," said the big cat. "Has it been that bad that you had to block everything, including me?"

"I am so glad to see you, but what are you doing here?" exclaimed The Eldest Grandmother.

"Someisa is okay. A dragon meet is beginning. She flew in to the meet on a roc. All the rangers are there. Kanshisha is missing and presumed to be down in the dead lands somewhere west of here. She's hurt, and that's all we know."

"Whoa! What's this about a dragon meet? How did Kanshisha get hurt? What's going on?"

Suddenly the cat left the window of her mind and she was all alone with the metal men again.

"No talking," said one of the metal men.

Esther stared at him. "I'll do as I please."

"Not allowed," it said.

"Just try to stop me," said Esther.

"Just did."

That was what scared her most. Somehow, the metal men had cut off her communication with Soonak. Her fright turned to anger. "How dare you enter my mind! You have no right to interfere with what I am thinking."

"What is thinking?" Its monotone droned. "Stopped communication." Esther said nothing.

"What is thinking? Will thinking tell me where your soul is attached?"

She couldn't help herself. In spite of her condition and where she was, Esther laughed. She laughed so hard, tears rolled down her cheeks.

One of the metal men immediately began looking at the machinery on the table. It turned knobs and pushed buttons. Esther stopped laughing. All those lessons with Someisa about the power of the mind came to her. Why wasn't she using them? Nothing like a little panic to cloud one's thinking. She decided to play with it and see what it did to the metal men's reactions.

Starting with a red knob she could see clearly in front of a machine sitting on the table next to her, she focused her mind on it. She thought of the knob becoming very hot. Esther put all of her anger, her pain, her frustration, and her intent into melting that knob. Perhaps she hit it too hard, because instead of melting, it flared and then disappeared in a puff of smoke.

The metal men stepped back and watched the smoke fade away. One of them stepped up to another piece of equipment and adjusted a knob. Immediately Esther felt cut off from the world. It was a though she had no connections to anything substantial, or even insubstantial, to her surroundings and the rest of the world. It was so complete and so sudden, the force of it caused her to pass out.

When she came to, she found herself outside the building. Breathing in a deep breath of dry air helped her to clear her mind to a certain extent. A curtain of dullness covered part of her mind. She felt like she had been cut off from a part of the world she had taken for granted.

Thirsty, Esther crawled over to one of the spiny plants. The effort took most of her strength. Either she had put too much of her own energy into melting the knob, or whatever the metal men had done to her mind left her too weak to walk. Or both.

In her pressing need for water, she wasn't as careful to avoid the spines, and found she was holding a branch with a bloody hand. She didn't care.

She broke off the spines on the branch and bit into it. Her whole body sighed with relief as the blessed, slightly sour liquid ran down her throat. It took a while after eating the round branch before she could move again. She crawled over to a nearby rock and pulled herself into a sitting position. There she rested until she was ready to try standing. It took some effort.

Esther looked around for another spiny, fat bush. Her desire to take only what each plant could comfortably give prevented her from depleting this one. Wanting to thank this one, she made to connect with it. Only it didn't happen. She found she couldn't connect mind to mind. Thanking it out loud was the best she could do.

Despair swept over her. This was what it was like to be head blind. It meant the only way she could see or communicate was with the abilities of her body. There had to be a way around this.

In her despair, Esther cried out to her guides on the other side of the veil. The veil, in this case, is the place of separation between the spirit world and the physical world. She hadn't felt a need for contact with them for many years. Her self confidence had gotten in the way. Perhaps, in her vanity, she had depended upon herself too much. Also, she chided herself for becoming lazy about contacting spirit guides, because life had become easy with few problems she couldn't work out herself. That and the fact that she knew they were always there to help her. A little more gratitude for that quiet life she had been enjoying was definitely in order.

Wisdom said this was not a time for self recrimination. Instead of beating herself up for allowing herself to be in this situation, it was time to take action. The metal men had messed with her brain, shutting down the normal tools she used for communication.

But there were other ways of communicating that she suspected the metal men knew nothing about. The first thing Esther needed to do was to take care of her body. She selected another spiny plant. After eating its offering of food and water, she thanked it verbally and went in search of some shade. The sun was at midpoint in the sky, but the buildings still offered a narrow space of shade in the sand. Gratefully, she lay down in the shade and closed her eyes.

The heart was her best choice for communicating with her spirit guides. She didn't need the wonderful abilities of her brain to put her consciousness in her heart. Nothing blocked her. She sent out love to her guides, thanking them for all they had taught her through the years. Love and a joyous reunion with them greeted her. Tears of joy fell down her face. She lay in the arms of her compassionate guides and slept.

While Esther slept, one of her guides joined with her in her body and understood what had happened to her. The barriers in the woman's brain prevented the guide from communicating with other guides. Undeterred by this, the guide entered the cells of Esther's brain and made some changes. It found the pineal gland and noted that it was damaged.

The guide withdrew from her body and conversed with the others. They called in a guide who specialized in repairing damaged pineal glands. That guide entered Esther's sleeping body and repaired the damage. Once done, the guides left Esther to awaken on her own.

When Esther came to from her long sleep, she found it was night. The stars in this part of the world were slightly different from those in the night sky at home. Some constellations she recognized that were a little lower on the horizon than she was used to seeing them and some slightly higher. Once she realized this, the old woman was able to determine it was near the middle of the night.

It was also cold. Looking around for the cloak she had left somewhere on the ground near a building, she saw it was nowhere in sight. Esther got up and walked around the buildings until she found it. Putting it on made her feel better. Tentatively, she reached out with her mind to the world around her. The guides had healed her mind. The barriers were gone.

Knowing the metal men would detect her use of her brain, she went into her heart and thanked them. It was the purest communication channel she had. Love poured from her heart to theirs and back again. She sat in joy and love until morning.

The first rays of the sun meant she needed to get busy to help herself out of this situation. Meeting with her guides, she pictured in her heart what she planned to do.

Chapter Twenty-Eight

Do not wait until the conditions are perfect to begin. Beginning makes the conditions perfect.

D ragons don't usually mess around with protocols unless the situation called for it. Everonius, as the lead dragon and quite stoic, took his duties very seriously. He opened the meeting by getting to the point. "Our first consideration is to find and rescue Kanshisha. Once we have rescued her, we'll do what we can to find and rescue Esther. I'll hear from Dragonis first."

Dragonis normally patrolled the southern part of the planet, which is mostly water, thus enabling him to be free to help the other dragons when needed. The dragon stretched and pulled himself up to his full height, which scared the rocs. The rangers took a few minutes to calm them down.

"I wish you wouldn't do that," irritated, Doragon frowned at the offending dragon. "Nobody here is interested in how tall you are. Tell us what you know."

Neither dragon spoke in the soft gentle tones Kanshisha used. If anything, their voices were harsh and guttural. Uncomfortable in their presence, Someisa was glad she was seated between Reisander and Gobha. The rangers ignored the dragons for a couple of minutes and took the time to send the rocs hunting, as it had been along flight and they were hungry. It also prevented any further disturbances from the rocs.

"Thank you for taking care of the rocs," said Everonius. "I sensed their discomfort with us. We'll be gone before they get back."

Catching Everonius's stern eye, Dragonis knelt down to a level that made it easier for the Cheschenaki to see his face. "I haven't as much to report as I would like. There is a wide area of land at the east end of the southern dead lands on this continent that is surrounded by an invisible wall. It extends for many miles into the dead lands. I suspect Kanshisha flew directly into it, not knowing it was there, and that caused her fall. Because of her experience, I explored as much as I could. The lands within the barrier appear blurred, and it is hard to see more than a few hundred feet beyond the barrier. The barrier covers several hundred square miles. I tried to fly over it, but never found the ceiling. That's all I have to say."

Doragon was next to speak. "Coming from the other side of the planet, I have much to report. I have located three other areas that have barriers, like the one Dragonis described. Near those locations there have been sightings of metal men. All of these areas are on the fringes of dead zones. I don't know of any sightings away from these lands. The barriers are new. Until recently, there were reports of strange metal men sighted, but no activity.

"So far, I have no knowledge of any kidnappings. Esther is the most powerful and knowledgeable of all the Eldest Grandmothers, which is probably why they grabbed her. I haven't been able to fly over any of the lands that have barriers, either. I don't know why unless the barriers continue on into space."

Reisander nodded to Everonius. "Someisa has information that may be of value. I suggest you let her speak."

Someisa wished Thistle had come with her. Thistle brought comfort when Someisa was in a tight situation. Soonak wasn't available for support either. It was hard enough to address a group of Cheschenaki, but she did not know the proper way to talk to a group of dragons, especially when they looked at her with disapproving eyes. Not that the little wood sprite talked to dragons. Or maybe she could. Someisa didn't know if any of the dragons understood the wood sprite shrills and tweets that made up their language.

She swallowed and began. "I have had a brief communication with both Kanshisha and The Eldest Grandmother. Kanshisha is badly hurt. The vision I had of her showed her lying down, covered in leaves. Not much else. The vision I had of The Eldest Grandmother showed her in a grey stone room with three metal men looking at her. She looked hot and exhausted. Her hair was mussed. For a second, I thought I saw metal strings attached to her body. The vision came to an abrupt halt before I could be sure of the strings.

"Soonak sent me a vision of buildings and a background of some mountains. I gave Gobha a drawing of what I saw through her eyes. I don't think the metal men know Soonak is in their vicinity. The one contact was very short. I tried to re-establish it and she hissed at me and shut off the connection."

Reisander touched her shoulder. "Tell them about the dreams, gal."

Someisa told about the dreams beginning with the first one. When it came to the last one where they wanted to take her soul, the dragons grew agitated.

"Do ya know somethin' 'bout this soul business?" asked Gobha.

Everonius answered, "I have had messages about weird ones trying to capture souls from guardians of other planets. Nothing came of it and they soon disappeared. Nothing was said about the weird ones being composed of metal."

"How d-do we communicate with these m-metal men?" asked Tonguetied. "If they p-put up barriers to t-telepathy and around their stolen territory, how d-do we go about talking t-to them? I don't know how they b-block our visions and attempts at communication."

Gobha interrupted, "Have any of ya tried ta talk ta 'em?"

Everonius sighed. "We didn't even know they could communicate with us. We knew they had arrived several months ago, and so we have kept watch. Like Doragon said, we saw no harm coming from them. Just a few reported sightings. The barriers are new, though. We were unaware of the barriers until Kanshisha flew into one. It sounds like the barriers all went up at the same time."

Takin' down dem barriers is a primary concern. Trouble is, we don't got the machinery ta do it. Seems ta me one of us needs ta sneak in and turn off dem machines. Esther's there, but she's not in the best position for doin' it, unless ere's away Soonak can help her. What da ya see, Seefar? Ya haven't said much."

Seefar had been busy watching Hara build a small fire and putting a kettle of water onto boil for some tea. This is something Seefar was not likely to do. He enjoyed observing how other people did things. It took him a minute to notice Gobha was asking him a question. Realizing Seefar hadn't heard him, Gobha rephrased his question.

"Pay attention," said Gobha. 'Does ya know of a way ta see beyond dis here barrier thing."

Seefar shook his head, no.

Toolan spoke up. "There's one method of communication we haven't tried yet. So far, we have been using our brains. Which isn't a bad thing, it's just not working. If Kanshisha is conscious, we should be able to communicate telepathically with her because she landed outside the barrier. However, that would alert the metal men to her location and ours. How about we try communicating with Kanshisha through heart speech?'

Everonius smiled. It was a frightening thing. Dragons have big mouths and lots of teeth .Reisander was secretly glad the rocs weren't present. They might have lost them. The rows of teeth would have sent them home in a panic.

"The problem with heart speech is that it is done with pictures and feelings, not words, unless you're talking to a spirit guide," said the lead dragon. Why not use spirit guides? Better Soonak, but she is busy watching over Esther, which is not what she came here for. She is Someisa's power animal. Work around that," the dragon leader said.

"It's better than nothing," said Doragon. "Is there one among us who is good at pictures and has a love bond with Kanshisha? We dragons don't often form those kinds of relationships with each other. Ours is lonely work constantly scanning the heavens and the ground to make sure all is well."

All the rangers turned to look at Someisa. She sighed. "What is it you want me to do?"

"First, you need to feel for Kanshisha with your heart. Let your love for her flow into her heart. See it surrounding her, comforting her, and letting her know you love her. Following that flow of love, send a picture of all of us. That will let her know we are working on rescuing her. Then tell us what she sends back," said Everonius.

Someisa began to meditate. Once she felt centered and focused, she put her consciousness in her heart. Her heart radiated as she thought of the love she felt for Kanshisha. A ray of light took form. Someisa put everything she had into extending that ray of light to Kanshisha. She thought of how kind and loving the dragon had been to her. Building on that, she thought of the connection created between the two of them. The light flowed outward from Someisa's heart and into Kanshisha's heart. A connection took form.

Chapter Twenty-Nine

Love will find a way.

K anshisha had been sleeping when the connection occurred. In the dreamtime, she got the message from a spirit guide to look into her heart. It was an easy thing to do. So she put her consciousness into her heart and to her great joy found Someisa there. Not wanting to break the connection, she stayed in the dreamtime while entering her heart and sharing her love with the girl.

She could not see Someisa clearly, but the dragon recognized the girl's energy signature. Kanshisha allowed Someisa's energy field to merge with hers in her heart. It took a couple of minutes for them to be comfortable with each other. Both of them needed to trust the other, as that kind of bond left them vulnerable to each other. Kanshisha sighed with pleasure once the bond was complete.

Someisa's picture of the dragon meet came through clearly. Kanshisha sent a feeling of gratitude back to Someisa. Someisa sent back a feeling of curiosity. Kanshisha allowed Someisa to explore her body so the girl would know how seriously she was hurt.

Someisa came out of her meditation long enough to share with the rangers and dragons the extent of her injuries. "At least none of her internals is injured," observed Gobha. "That broken wing's gunna take some fixin'".

Gobha moved around to where he could sit behind Someisa. Then he put his hands on her shoulders. "Go back in ta your meditation. I'll be followin' along with ya," he said.

Someisa didn't think that would work. "I have an idea. You and I need to connect heart to heart before we can reach out to Kanshisha."

"Little Lady's right," Gobha said to the others. "We don't have the love connection she has with Kanshisha. But 'ere's way around that. Would some a ya fellers build a fire ta keep us warm while we work? "

A couple of rangers set about building the fire.

Gobha moved around until he sat facing Someisa. He held his left hand palm up and his right hand palm down. "The left hand receives and the right hand gives. Ya remember that when ya were learnin' healin' from your ma?"

Someisa nodded.

"Put yar hands in mine."

Someisa put her left hand under Gobha's right hand and her right hand on top of his left one.

"Now," he said. "Place your consciousness in yar heart again and let energy flow from yar heart into yar right arm."

Someisa did as he directed.

"Good. Now let da energy flow into my left hand. I'll do the same. Let my love energy flow in ta yar heart through your left hand and arm."

It only took a few seconds. Someisa could feel Gobha's love energy flowing into her heart. She felt warm and wonderful.

"Now, little lady, make your connection again with Kanshisha."

A bit of doubt flowed into Someisa's mind. She wasn't sure she could focus on Gobha and Kanshisha at the same time.

Gobha picked up on the doubt. "Leh go of reason and logic," he said. "Allow love energy ta flow freely. Takes no effort at all. That's the girl. Let it flow. Now put yar consciousness in ta yar heart and feel the love ya have for Kanshisha."

Kanshisha's worry and fright flowed into Someisa. At first, she thought the metal men had somehow broken the bond between the two of them. Once she felt Someisa's presence in her heart, she breathed a sigh of relief. Gobha gently made his presence known to her. Kanshisha was so surprised she nearly broke the connection. Gobha went into healer mode and worked on healing the dragon's broken wing. He let his love flow into her body until he connected with her body itself.

The dragon felt the love flowing throughout her body. She relaxed and let it happen. Gobha centered his love around the broken wing. The wing had three breaks in it. He figured she must have landed on it when she fell. Wing bones are fragile. Two were easy to heal, being simple stress fractures. He let his love energy flow into one of the broken bones. It had begun healing on its own. Her body had cleaned away the debris from the break and some cartilage grew from both sides of the break. Using his love as energy, he speeded up the healing process. The cartilage connected and bone began to replace the cartilage. He held it until the bone was strong enough for her to use with caution. He did the same with a second bone.

The third break was more serious. The bones didn't match up. They needed to be manipulated to where the two ends faced each other. He knew of only one way to do that. He went into his heart again and called for his favorite healing spirit guide.

The healing guide brought in other spirit guides. Gobha sat back and let them do their work. The spirit guides gently massaged the bones back into place. He knew this would be painful for Kanshisha. He felt the dragon shudder with the first massage maneuver. Kanshisha was made of stern stuff. She held her ground and let the spirit guides do their thing. To avoid shock to her body, it needed to be done slowly. Each stroke to a bone had to be ever so gently maneuvered to prevent further damage to surrounding tissues. Finally, it was done.

Kanshisha let out a sigh of relief. Gobha set about growing the bones together. They wouldn't need to go through the cartilage stage because the ends were touching each other. An hour later, the repair to the complicated bone fracture was completed.

Both Gobha and Someisa let their love energy flow into the break in her right leg. They found a compound fracture that required the same level of energy work as did the nasty break in the wing. The leg bone was also in three pieces. The spirit guides came in again and spent another hour massaging the parts of the bone so that they lined up with each other to begin the process of growing of the bones together.

Normally, Gobha would have stopped the healing work to let Kanshisha's body adjust to the changes. Even healing work needs time for rest to allow the healing to integrate with all the systems of the body and make it whole. They didn't have the luxury of a few weeks or even days of time. So, Gobha set about working on the ribs. Another hour passed. Someisa began to get restless from the drain of having to sit still for so long. Gobha didn't let up until the ribs were at least in alignment. More work needed to be done, but he felt Kanshisha was too tired to continue to do much more.

Kanshisha gingerly stood up and put her weight on the healed leg. She still experienced some pain, enough to remind her not to abuse the leg and wing with too much activity until they had completely healed. Kanshisha expressed love and gratitude to both Someisa and Gobha through a warmth of feeling in her heart.

Slowly, she extended her damaged wing. There was some residual stiffness in the wing and a little pain. Other than that, it seemed functional. She knew enough not to use it right away. Taking a deep breath remained painful. She understood Gobha had done what he could without putting her body into shock. The complete healing of the ribs would have to wait.

Again, she sent gratitude to her two friends, followed by much love. A bond had formed between the three of them that would last for the rest of their lives. Healing with so much love is a marvelous thing, and she felt grateful that they cared that much about her.

Before the connection broke, she sent pictures of the lizards who had helped her. She hoped Someisa and Gobha would pick up on the unspoken message that the lizards were useful allies.

Kanshisha lovingly sent farewell and closed the connection. She had work to do. She needed to know where she was, what had caused her to fall from the sky, and what she could learn about the metal men from here. But for now, she needed to complete her healing by herself. Her body needed rest. She closed her eyes and went to sleep, safe knowing that she had help from many quarters.

Chapter Thirty

It's easy to forget that life is the greatest gift of all.

S omeisa came out of her trance completely exhausted. She had never been in a trance that long, not even close. To hold her focus and concentration took everything she had to keep it together. She stood up too fast and fainted. Gobha caught her before she hit the ground. Even though she had been sitting the entire time, her body gave out and could no longer support her, even in a sitting position.

"That's a brave girl, ya got 'ere for a foghlamach. Seems ta me yer trainin' her well. And I think ya could learn a thin' or two from her, too." Gobha grinned as he held the girl. Reisander pulled a blanket from his pack and laid it on the ground. Gobha gently laid the girl on the blanket.

Tonguetied covered her with a second blanket. "I wouldn't have believed she c-could hold the connection that long. Let her sleep. She'll c-come to soon enough. What did you learn from Kanshisha, Gobha?"

"Looks like 'em little lizard critters are of some importance. I kind a got the message we should talk with 'em. Langor, ya got any idea about communicatin' with a lizard?"

Langor shook his head no, but Reisander had an answer. "Thistle can talk with them."

Everonius nodded his head. "The wee folk have connections with the lizards, and so do we. They are distant cousins of ours. I suggest we meet with them and see what they can tell us.

"Gobha, did you notice any sign of the wasting sickness in Kanshisha?"

"None. In fact, other than the broken bones, her body seems ta be in good shape. I saw several places where broken skin had been recently healed. Much faster 'an normal, even for a dragon, if ya don't mind my sayin' so. I noticed some sort of healin' medicine at work there."

"Interestin'," said Reisander. To the dragons, he asked, "Where do you think we should go from here?"

Everonius glanced at the other two dragons. A private line of communication flashed between them. Facing the rangers, he said, "We are in agreement with each other. The dragon pack will continue to monitor the metal men's activity as much as we can. Dragonis and I will continue to monitor the area where Kanshisha fell to find out whether she landed inside or outside the barrier. I am hoping she is outside the barrier so we can talk directly to her. This barrier business is beginning to annoy me in no uncertain terms.

"Doragon will go back to his territory on the other side of the planet. He patrols most of the northern continents. Dragonis patrols much of the southern half of the planet. The land in that part of the world is scarce, as it is mostly water and doesn't need as much surveillance. It does require a lot more flying. As far as we can ascertain, there has been no activity in the southern hemisphere, so I do not mind assigning him to find Kanshisha.

"We think Esther's location is a couple hundred miles north of the equator. I'll start patrolling that area. I may not be able to get close because of the blasted barrier, but I'll do what I can. I'll meet up with Dragonis and Kanshisha once we find her and she can fly again. Also, I'll explore how far up the barrier goes. Perhaps it is not so high that we can't fly over it. We dragons can handle being in space for short periods of time, but I know you Cheschenakis cannot.

"Before I start my patrol duties, I would like to meet with these lizards. Call your rocs back. We need to do some flying to the edge of the nearest dead lands a bit south of here. Hopefully, we can talk with some lizards there.

"Seefar, I sense you would like to go home and work from there. That is all right with me. I'll keep in touch with you telepathically when I have something worthwhile to share with you, and you do the same with me. I want you to explore the edges of these barriers and see if you can mark them on a map. That way we can avoid any more mishaps like Kanshisha's."

Tonguetied nodded his approval. "Wh-what about the girl?"

"Have Reisander stay with her until she wakes. She'll need to eat. Her body used a lot of energy to maintain that meditation for so long. I also sensed she channeled healing energy to Kanshisha along with Gobha. She'll be ravenous which will cause her to wake up shortly."

To Reisander, he said, "Fly back to the wood sprite village and pick up Thistle, if they can spare her. That space on top of the cave is big enough for a roc to land. Then go find some lizards and have a talk with them yourselves. If Someisa doesn't come to within an hour, wake her. She needs more rest, but we have not the time for that. Food will have to do."

The rocs arrived just after the dragons took flight. Seefar found his roc and headed home. Reisander stayed with Someisa while the other rangers jumped on their rocs and followed the dragons into the air.

Reisander took the time to go into a deep meditation. When he came out of it a short time later, he felt like he had had a few hours sleep. He had no idea when his next opportunity to sleep would be, and took advantage of the brief respite.

Someisa woke shortly after Reisander completed his meditation. She stretched as she slowly came into awareness of her surroundings. It was cold, and she had no desire to leave the comfort of the warm blankets. The fire was almost out and not giving much heat. Reisander made no move to build it up again.

"Have I been out long?"

"Probably not long enough," said Reisander.

"I'm hungry."

"Figured you would be." He handed her a large meat filled sandwich.

Looking around her while eating, Someisa saw that the two of them were alone. "Where is everybody?"

"The dragons and rangers took off. We've all been given assignments. There is so much territory to cover, even for dragons. "

"Dragons don't say much, do they? I noticed they let us do most of the talking."

"Yeah. They like to keep to themselves pretty much. It said a lot when they all showed up here. I don't think they liked it when you communicated so easily with Kanshisha and they couldn't.

"We're to go get Thistle and then fly to the edge of the dead lands to find some lizards. With Thistle's help, we may communicate with them. I, for one, would like to know how they have survived all these centuries in the dead lands. I want to know if there are other critters that have survived and what's their secret for survival."

Thistle fluttered in to view. "Talking," she said.

"Talking to who, Thistle?" The little wood sprite took Reisander completely by surprise. There was no communication between the two of them. He hadn't sent any messages to the wood sprite village requesting Thistle to meet them. Yet here she was, saving them a lot of time and effort to go get her.

Thistle looked smug, as though she were reading his thoughts. Reisander realized they knew very little about wood sprites. Until Someisa's rescue of Thistle and subsequent friendship with her, the Cheschenaki people had little contact with the creatures.

"Lizards," announced Thistle.

"Great. Where do you want to go to make contact with them?"

Thistle flew over to Someisa and landed on her shoulder. "Waiting."

"Oh ,bother." Sometimes Someisa lost patience with her little friend's language issues. "Here we go again. How many questions will it take to get a complete answer out of you?"

The wood sprite crossed her arms over her chest and glared at Someisa. The girl grinned and said, "Waiting."

Reisander laughed. "Come on, you two. This is no time for quarreling."

"Not quarreling," said Thistle.

"You could have fooled me,."

"Hmph."

Now it was Someisa's turn to laugh. She saw behind where Reisander was sitting the head of a lizard poking out from behind a rock. "I don't think we have to wait any longer. The lizards have come to us." She pointed to where the lizard was standing.

Reisander turned to look. Three lizards crept cautiously from behind the rock. They were fairly good sized as lizards go. The largest one was about three feet long, counting its tail, which extended out quite a ways behind it. It stood about twelve inches high. The other two lizards were slightly smaller.

The larger lizard took charge. It trilled something and Thistle answered with chirps and trills of her own. Someisa and Reisander held still so as to not frighten the creatures. One of the other lizards trilled, followed by the third. Someisa got the impression they were introducing themselves to each other as Thistle respectfully answered each lizard with a soft trill and a chirp.

Reisander understood a little of what Thistle was saying. The lizard's trill was of a dialect he couldn't make heads or tails of.

The fire had died down to nothing but a few small coals. The lizards gathered around it appreciating its warmth. Reisander wanted to add more wood to the fire to keep the heat going, but was afraid he would scare the lizards away.

To Thistle he asked, "Would the lizards mind if Someisa puts some wood on the fire? It will go out soon if she doesn't."

Inwardly, Someisa groaned. She felt like she was back in the familiar place of a foghlamach left to do menial chores.

Reisander grinned at her, knowing what she was thinking. "I thought I would spook the lizards if I got up to get the wood. I am a lot bigger than you are."

Someisa smiled. "Where is there wood? I don't see any near us?"

Reisander looked around at the sparse landscape. "I guess Gobha found all there was. We'll have to do without the fire. Well, I doubt we'll be here long, anyway."

"Hmph!" said Thistle, clearly upset by their conversation, which didn't include her or the lizards.

"I'm sorry, Thistle. I didn't mean to ignore you." He said.

"Normal," replied the wood sprite.

Reisander sighed. For some reason, Thistle was out of sorts and he didn't know how to bring her back to her normal cheery self. So he got down to business.

"What were you saying to the lizards?"

"Knowing."

"Do you mean introducing yourself to each other?"

Because she was so little and rarely held still, it was hard for Reisander to tell if she was nodding her head. He went on that assumption, but carefully, in case he had missed something again.

"Are the lizards ready to answer our questions?"

As if to say yes, a lizard crawled into Someisa's lap. She stroked its head while it curled up into a ball and settled itself comfortably there. "I like it," cried Someisa in delight." It feels much softer than I expected."

Another lizard climbed into her lap, nudging the other one to make room. There was a bit of a scuffle before the two settled down and beamed at Reisander, quite content where they were. The ranger smiled back at them.

The larger lizard stood its ground in front of the ranger. Its firm stance caught Reisander's attention, and he turned to face it. It trilled something.

Looking at Thistle for translation, he waited for her to say something.

The wood sprite looked troubled for a moment. Then she brightened and said, "Hello."

Reisander looked back at the lizard standing in front of him. "Hello."

The lizard trilled again.

"Does the lizard understand what we are saying?" asked Someisa.

"Not understanding words."

Someisa nearly fell over backwards. It was very rare she heard Thistle say more than two words in a row. Most often, Thistle only said one.

Reisander thought for a moment. "Pictures?"

Thistle jumped up and down on Someisa's shoulder with glee. "Pictures."

There was plenty of sandy soil around them. Reisander cleared a space of rocks and debris so he could draw a picture. But then he didn't know what to draw.

"Where do I begin?" he asked Thistle.

"Dragon."

Reisander drew a picture of a dragon beside a very tiny lizard. Even though greatly different in size, in a simple drawing, they looked alike. His ability at art wasn't so good either, but he got the idea across.

The lizard trilled.

Thistle responded. The lizard responded again.

"Dragons knowing," she said.

Reisander erased part of the dragon he had drawn and replaced it with a broken wing.

The lizard trilled excitedly.

"Knowing," translated Thistle.

"Can it tell us where?"

Thistle trilled. The lizard answered.

"South,"

Reisander sighed. He already knew that. Trying a different tact, he said to Thistle, "We saw leaves covering Kanshisha. What are they for?"

Thistle trilled. The lizard responded.

"Shade."

"Okay. What did the lizards do to prevent her from getting the wasting sickness?"

Thistle trilled again. This time the lizard didn't trill back. Instead, he spat upon Reisander's leg, where some skin was exposed between his pant leg and his boot. He shifted his foot away in surprise. The lizard jumped back several feet and trilled.

"Healing," announced Thistle.

Someisa was the first to catch what the lizard was trying to show them. "I think it is trying to tell you its saliva has healing properties."

Reisander looked first to Someisa. He glanced at the two lizards snuggled happily in her lap and then back to the larger lizard. "Tell the lizard I am sorry if I scared it. I wasn't expecting its demonstration."

After trilling to the lizard, it cocked its head. Tentatively, it walked over to where Reisander sat and crawled into his lap. Reisander was afraid to move. The lizard raised itself up to where it could look Reisander straight in the eyes. They stared at each other for several minutes until Reisander felt a warming sensation in his heart. Focusing on the lizard from his heart center, a picture formed in his mind.

He saw Kanshisha sleeping all covered with leaves. Some lizards were replacing dried out leaves with fresh ones. Another lizard licked a small wound that had opened when Kanshisha tried to stand. Reisander watched the wound close and heard Kanshisha give a small sigh in pleasure. The lizard broke contact.

Reisander smiled down at the lizard in his lap and said, "Thank you. That answers a lot of questions." To Thistle, he asked, "Kanshisha does not have the wasting sickness. Does the lizard's saliva pass on a way to prevent that?"

"Telling."

"Is that a yes or a no?"

The wood sprite shifted from side to side on Someisa's shoulder in agitation.

"Telling!"

Reisander looked down at the lizard resting comfortably now on his lap. The lizard nodded its head up and down.

"Do you understand me?"

The lizard stared back at Reisander with unblinking eyes.

"Does the lizard understand me when I talk to it, Thistle?"

"Trying."

"Does it understand our language?"

"Not knowing."

Does that mean you don't know the answer or that it doesn't understand the Cheschenaki language?"

Thistle flew off Someisa's shoulder in fury, disturbing the two now sleeping lizards in the girl's lap. Fluttering in front of Reisander's face, she put her hands on her hips and hollered, "Language!"

Someisa couldn't help laughing. She had experienced all too often the difficulty of conversations with the wood sprite. The little lizards in her lap took fright and scampered away behind a rock. "Skittish little things, aren't they?" She laughed again.

Reisander glared at her in exasperation, which brought on another spasm of giggles.

"This isn't funny, Someisa."

"I know. It's just that I have had so many exasperating efforts trying to get information out of Thistle, just like you're experiencing now."

"My trilling isn't much better. Probably worse, as I can't make many of the sounds in Thistle's language. Toolan can, but I don't know how he does it." Reisander suddenly jumped.

The large lizard was acting strangely. It had scratched his arm and started licking the wound. Reisander jerked his arm away. Thistle flew into his face in fury.

"Preventing," she cried.

"Preventing what." Exasperated, Reisander kept his arm away from the lizard and covered it with his sleeve.

Thistle shook her fist at him and said, "Wasting disease."

Someisa got it first. Tentatively, she offered a bare arm to the lizards who had returned to her lap. Immediately, one of them scratched her arm and then began licking the wound. It hurt initially. She didn't like the scratching part at all. After a few licks, she noticed the wound started to heal. At the same time, she felt a calming peace flow through her entire body. It was wonderful. It didn't last very long as the scratch healed quickly and the lizards settled back into her lap and went to sleep.

Reisander watched all of this with a skeptical eye. Thistle continued to flutter around him, encouraging him to raise his sleeve and let the lizard finish its work.

"It's all right," said Someisa. "Look. The scratch disappeared, leaving no scar. I feel fine. While the lizard licked the wound, I felt a sense of peace surge through my body, which stopped when the lizard stopped. I think what Thistle is trying to tell you is the saliva of the lizards prevents the wasting disease."

Chapter Thirty-One

Fear: False Evidence Appearing Real

Reisander fought with himself. For some reason, he didn't trust the lizard standing patiently in front of him. Someisa seemed unharmed by her experience. Thistle was all for it. Yet some part of him held back. It took him a while to realize it was just plain fear. Fear of what, he wasn't sure. He could take time to analyze it, but now wasn't the time or place. An opportunity to enter the dead lands was in front of him. It was time to get going. Reisander pulled up his sleeve and held out his arm to the lizard.

It nodded its head in approval. There were no marks left by the first scratch. The lizard made another one and began licking. The two lizards in Someisa's lap came over to help. They moved the sleeve of his other arm out of the way and made another scratch a little longer than the first one. Both of them began licking.

"I think one lizard is enough," said Reisander, brushing the last two away from his arm and addressing them. "I've had enough trouble with just one. I think the two of you're two too many."

Their saliva had the same effect on Reisander as it had on Someisa. She smiled at him as she saw his face relax. She couldn't help herself. It was the first time she talked Reisander into doing something he didn't want to do, and she liked the sense of pride it gave her.

Despite her pride in persuading Reisander to let the lizards do their thing, deep down inside, she had her own misgivings. When she was very young, a man with the wasting disease came to her mother for help. Her mother couldn't save him. His death had haunted Someisa for months afterward. It wasn't that he died that upset her. It was what he had to go through to get there that bothered her. It was an agonizing time for him. She still had occasional bad dreams about it.

That was the beginning of the rift with her mother. Someisa had lost trust in Zoenka, although she soon forgot the reason why. The power of the disease was more than her mother could do to help him. A small trickle of fear wafted through Someisa's mind. Could a small amount of lizard saliva actually prevent the disease? She wasn't as sure as she pretended to be. Thistle flew in front of the girl's face. Noticing the little wood sprite, Someisa put the fear aside to be explored at a better time.

"Drink," said Thistle.

Someisa got out her water bottle. Until Thistle brought it up, the girl hadn't noticed she was thirsty. The lizards finished with Reisander. The scratches on his arm disappeared. Thistle told him to drink, which he did, emptying his water bottle.

"We're going to have to find a supply of good fresh water," he said to Someisa.

"Knowing," said Thistle.

"Okay, Thistle. Where will we find a source of good, clean water?"

Thistle flew off to the west. Someisa shooed the sleeping lizards off her lap and got up. The lizards got to their feet and followed as she took off after Thistle. Reisander pushed dirt over the last reaming coals before leaving. The other lizard and the two rocs were not far behind.

Thistle led them downhill to a ravine. Snow dotted the surrounding landscape. At the bottom of the ravine, the underbrush thickened. Pulling aside some bushes, Someisa beheld a little trickle of water. It was barely enough to fill a water bottle. She filled hers, drank it dry, and then filled it again. She moved aside to make room for Reisander. Downstream, the rocs and the lizards had their heads over the water, lapping up what they could from the tiny stream. At last, all finished drinking their fill.

"What now?" asked Someisa.

Reisander looked around at the ravine. "I suggest we go back up to the top of the ravine. It'll be hard for the rocs to take off from here. We fly south."

"Is there a more dignified way of getting on a roc's back than you picking me up and throwing me on its back?" Someisa asked as they climbed back up the hill.

Reisander didn't answer until they got to the top of the hill. He went to his roc and touched the back of its knee. The bird bent its legs and sat down. Reisander had no trouble climbing on.

"I think it would be best if Thistle rode with you. I am not sure where we are going other than to find the dead lands south of here. The wind would blow Thistle right off your shoulder. Have you got a pocket where you can keep her safe/"

Someisa was having some trouble with her roc. She touched the back of its knee and nothing happened. She tried pushing on the back of the knee and still nothing happened.

Reisander shook with laughter. "You have to let it know who's boss."

Someisa walked to the front of the roc and glared at it. Its head was many feet above hers. She couldn't make eye contact with it. Noting that glaring at its chest got her nowhere, Someisa tried pushing on the knees again, this time using both hands. The roc lowered its head and just looked at her as if saying. "What do you think you are doing?"

Someisa got mad. She wanted to kick its knee, but knew that meant she was out of control. It also meant she would use violence, which, of course, was forbidden.

"Turning to Reisander she said, "Okay. What do I do now?"

Still laughing, he got down off his roc. He grabbed Someisa's roc by its long neck and pulled its head down to where he could look into its eyes. Then he let go.

"Now you do it. It takes only once for you to look into its eyes, tell it you're the boss, and instruct it is to do as you tell it to. You'll have no trouble after that."

More than a little dubious, Someisa grabbed her roc by the neck using both hands. It was strong and resisted her. Planting her feet firmly on the ground, she grabbed its neck and pulled. The roc ducked its head so quickly she fell back on her butt. Looking up, she could have sworn the roc was laughing at her.

Not to be outdone by a bird, Someisa got back up, planted her feet, and pulled on the neck of the roc. This time, she was prepared for it to drop its head. As the head came down, she stepped a little to its side. Reaching up, she grabbed the roc by the feathers on each side of its face and pulled until it had to look at her. "You will obey me," she said firmly. "Now bend your knees and sit down so I can climb into the saddle on your back."

To her delight, the roc did as it she commanded. A few minutes later, she was sitting in the saddle with Thistle gently tucked into a pocket of her tunic.

Reisander nodded to her. It was the only recognition she got. His roc lifted up into the air and Someisa's roc followed.

Chapter Thirty-Two

Things turn out best for the people who make the best of the way things turn out.

When Kanshisha woke, it was dark. At first, she thought she had forgotten to open her eyes. She blinked, and it made no difference. The overcast sky prevented moonlight and starlight from braking through, keeping the night very dark.

She felt a sense of urgency she couldn't explain. Gingerly, she stood up. The back leg was sore, but it held her weight without too much complaint. A deep breath told her that her ribs still needed work, but were an improvement over the day before. Stretching out her wing, she was delighted to find it moved freely without pain. Breathing in a sigh of relief, her ribs reminded her to go easy on heavy breathing.

Not knowing the terrain, she didn't want to move yet. Where should she go? Knowing it was futile to try traveling in the dark, she decided to stay where she was until morning. In the meantime, she thought she would try communicating with Everonius. The sense of urgency seemed to tie in with her desire to talk with him.

She grounded and centered herself. It had been a long time since she had done that and was glad she did. It helped clarify her thinking. She made herself comfortable as best she could and formed a picture of Everonius in her mind. Nothing happened. Sighing, she remembered she had to work through her heart. She could understand communication being blocked inside the barrier. It worried her that communication outside the barrier didn't happen either. She hoped it had something to do with her proximity to the barrier, which, she guessed, was about twenty feet from where she had fallen.

Kanshisha rarely communicated much with any of the other dragons. Unless something came up, none of them were very talkative with each other. However, there was a bond between all of them through the heart connecting them over vast distances while patrolling the planet. It wasn't that they were solitary creatures by design. It was a big planet and there was a lot of ground to cover.

They spent more time over the populated areas, even though the people below didn't know they were there. Almost nothing occurred in the dead lands. Those areas were only given a brief overview a few times a year. Obviously, that was a mistake pointed out by the arrival of the metal men who seemed impervious to its dangers.

Kanshisha went into her heart and found the bonds with the other dragons. She wanted to talk with Everonius without including the other two. Everonius, as lead dragon, would want her report. She separated out her bonds with the other two dragons and settled specifically on Everonius. Then she activated the bond with him. Everonius responded immediately, letting her know he was ready to receive her report.

She began with a picture from her memory of the terrain beneath her as she headed toward the metal men's camp where she thought they were holding The Eldest Grandmother. She held the moving pictures until she hit the invisible barrier. At that point, the pictures she sent Everonius went dark. There was a brief pause, and she began again, showing him her memories of the kindness of the desert lizards and how they had helped her to heal. She showed him the leaves that covered her body and kept out the heat of the sun and the night's cold, the way they fed her, and brought her water.

Everonius sent back feelings of approval and appreciation. He then sent pictures of Reisander and Someisa on their way. The wounded dragon smiled.

An idea had occurred to Kanshisha during her recovery time. She pictured what she planned to do and Everonius sent back a feeling of approval. With that, she severed the connection and went back to sleep.

Chapter Thirty-Three

Fear can rule the mind if not controlled.

It had been a long ride to the northern edge of the dead lands, much farther than Someisa expected. It grew dark by the time they reached their destination. Someisa was stiff and sore from sitting in an unaccustomed pose for so long and she badly needed to pee. The saddle was wide, covering the broad backs of Skyhaven. Her legs straddled the roc in a position that took its toll on her comfort level.

Her exit off the roc was not what could be called graceful. Her legs buckled when she landed after falling out of the saddle. She found herself flat on her back. It was a struggle to get back on her feet. The roc left her there to go hunting for its dinner. She sighed. It would have been nice if it had waited. She could have used it as a brace to help herself up.

Someisa looked over at Reisander and saw that he was walking a little awkwardly away from his roc. It, too, took off in search of food. Neither roc seemed to mind the saddle on its back. She marveled at that, thinking they would feel more freedom flying without them. She didn't know that as long as the roc wore a saddle, its duty was to stay with its rider until released. Hunting for food was the one freedom it had while wearing the saddle. That was the agreement between the rocs and the rangers. But, of course, Someisa didn't know that.

The countryside was warm, even with the coming of night. The vegetation grew sparsely. Reisander had picked a location on a hillside with a nearby small spring bubbling out of the earth and downhill to fade away into the sand at the bottom.

Thistle worked her way out of Someisa's pocket and fluffed out her wings. The wood sprite was thirsty and immediately headed for the spring.

Someisa took off her cloak and set her backpack on the ground beside her. Fortunately, she had the presence of mind to take it off the saddle and drop it on the ground before she got off the roc's back.

It had been a long day. There was nothing with which to build a fire nearby, so they made do with trail bread, dried fruits, and jerky washed down with water from the spring. The water tasted a little bitter to Someisa, but she drank it anyway. There was nothing else "It will get cold as the night progresses," said Reisander as they settled down to sleep. "I suggest you keep your cloak nearby. Your blanket may not be enough to keep you warm a couple of hours from now."

Someisa had just finished folding it up and put it in the pack. Grumpy, she got her cloak back out of the backpack, wishing he had said something earlier. She set the cloak beside her and lay down on the warm sand. Sleep came immediately.

She dreamed. Pictures of people with the wasting disease formed in her mind. The girl could see them with sores on their faces, the bleeding from their noses, and what looked like burns on their arms and legs. Many of them were throwing up. She heard them moaning and sometimes crying out in pain.

This dream was not fun, and she struggled to come out of it. But the pictures kept coming. She felt hot and uncomfortable. Her stomach complained. Overcome with nausea, she finally woke herself out of the dream.

Looking up, she could see thousands of stars. Watching them helped her to come back to reality. A trickle of worry entered her mind. What if the lizard's saliva didn't work, and she got the wasting sickness? She didn't like the thought, but the worry stayed with her as she went back to sleep.

The dream was still with her the next morning. Without saying much, she went about doing the few chores assigned to her before they took off again. She didn't tell Reisander about the dream. She was afraid he would call her silly to worry when precautions had been made. The lizard's saliva had worked on a dragon. But what if it didn't work on people? The pictures from her dream continued to haunt her throughout the day.

"You're quiet today," observed Reisander.

She smiled at him, although the smile didn't reach her eyes, and he noticed. "I'm okay. Just a little more tired than usual. Yesterday took a lot of energy." She hoped he would leave it at that.

Reisander was still concerned, but accepted her answer. They needed to get going. "We'll ride east along the northern border of the waste lands until we reach a point north of where we think Kanshisha went down. I don't want to risk flying into the barrier. The rocs haven't been immunized and can't go into the dead lands. We'll walk from that point on.

"Make sure both your water bottles are full. I don't know where our next source of water is going to be. I am hoping the rocs will land us near water. They often do that without being asked."

Someisa wasn't too happy with this news. She checked her water bottles, and yes, they were both full. Thistle flew from the spring and landed on her shoulder. Someisa held open her pocket for Thistle when the little sprite announced, "Leaving."

Someisa felt a tinge of dismay as she watched the little wood sprite fly out of sight. She couldn't make out the direction as Thistle flew straight up and into the sun. By the time she set her direction, Someisa could no longer see her.

"Thistle's gone," she announced to Reisander.

"Something must have come up for her to leave us so quickly and without an explanation. We'll just have to do without her and her knowledge."

This time, when Someisa touched the roc's knees, it sat and waited for her to mount. Reisander nodded to her in approval, and they took off.

Someisa watched the scenery as they flew over it. The ground below was barren in most places. They flew low enough for her to make out some ruins here and there. She saw no villages or other signs of habitation by her people. It gave her a sense of loneliness, looking at all the emptiness on the ground.

Plants, unfamiliar to her, grew here and there. They were flying too high for her to see them clearly. At the beginning of the flight, she could make out scraggly trees scattered here and there over the landscape. The trees thinned out as they flew eastward and disappeared completely by noon.

Mid morning, Reisander spoke to his roc, and it led the way to a landing spot near a little oasis in the rocks and sand. Some vegetation grew there, and he was hoping for a water source, enabling them to have a long drink before taking off again. He emptied one of his water bottles during the flight and noticed Someisa drinking from hers. The climate here was very dry.

Letting his roc lead the way to water, he watched it dig in the sand that had settled in a little hollow in the middle of the oasis. About a foot down, water trickled into the hole. The roc waited a minute until enough water filled the hole and then bent its head to drink. A short while later, they took off again.

Chapter Thirty-Four

What you fear will come upon you.

L ate in the afternoon, Reisander instructed his roc to land on hot dry land. Someisa's followed.

"Time to let the rocs go free," he said to Someisa. "We no longer need their services. We go on foot from now on."

He untied their packs from the saddles to prepare for sending the birds home. Someone there would remove the saddles and give the rocs their freedom. As he worked, he thanked each bird for their service and gave them a treat. Each one nodded its head to Reisander, and then the two took off. He watched them soar into the sky for a minute or two and then turned to Someisa.

Someisa felt a wave of fear go through her. It was hot. She was tired. And she wanted no part of entering the dead lands. She regretted her enthusiasm over the lizard saliva as a preventative. Her fear leftover from the dream engulfed her.

Reisander was still talking. "We'll rest until dark. It's too hot to walk in the desert during the day. There is almost no shade in the dead lands. So we will travel by night."

Someisa sighed with relief. They ate a quick meal and settled down in the shade of a couple of weird plants covered with spines. It wasn't much, but it was all there was. Reisander fell asleep almost immediately. Someisa lay on the hot sand and worried.

It wasn't like her to worry so much. Perhaps if she had never seen the man with the wasting sickness, she might not feel so strongly about it. The dream had brought up all her fears from when she was so young. She wished her mother hadn't included her in nursing the man. It took him several days to die. But her mother believed her daughter should not be spared the realities of life, so Someisa had to help with the caring for the poor man.

A few hours passed before Reisander touched the girl's shoulder to awaken her. It was dark, but the moon had just risen, making the way a little easier to see.

"The ground will be easy for walking," he said. "It's fairly firm. According to Chester Oak, sand, like where we are standing, will become less and less. There will be little vegetation as we go along. It's hilly between where we are and where we think Kanshisha may be. Fortunately, we don't have to go very far. You up for a twenty-mile hike tonight?"

Inwardly, Someisa groaned. Twenty miles to her was a long way to walk in a single night. How many nights would it take for them to get to Kanshisha?

And then another thought hit her. How long would it be before she got the wasting disease? She was sure she was going to get it no matter what she had originally thought about the lizard cure. Masking her fear as best she could and pretending it was the long hard walk ahead of them that bothered her, she nodded her head.

"Piece of cake," she said.

The sun set, but the light from so many stars lit the way. An hour after they began their journey, the moon came up. Someisa enjoyed the coolness of the night. She had to work hard to keep up with Reisander.

"Heh, could you slow down a little? I'm running out of energy trying to keep up with you," she said.

Reisander laughed and shortened his stride. "I forget sometimes that my long legs make it difficult for you to keep up."

"Thank you," she said, smiling back at him. There was no more conversation for a long time after that. Someisa had all she could do to keep up. All the while, she worried about the wasting sickness and what it might do to her body. An unusual tiredness bothered her. She felt slightly sick to her stomach. At first she thought it came from the effort of keeping up with Reisander, but deep down she just knew she had the wasting sickness. Grimly, she kept going.

"It was when she stumbled and fell that Reisander saw something was wrong. A small trickle of blood was forming under Someisa's nose. At first, he thought she had bumped it when she fell. But she had caught her fall with her hands and her face had not hit the ground.

"You feeling okay, gal?" he asked.

"I'm fine," she said, wiping away the blood with her handkerchief. "It's this dry climate. My lips are chapped and I think it's making my nose bleed. I'll be okay."

Reisander watched her anxiously as she got up to stand and continue their journey. They resumed walking. An hour later, she threw up.

"You lied to me," said Reisander sternly. "You are not well. What is the matter?"

"I think I have the wasting sickness," she said. "I have been afraid of this."

"Lay down," instructed Reisander. H checked her pulse and noted that it was more rapid than usual for a girl her age. He could feel the heat of a fever from her skin and he noticed a small sore forming at the base of her neck.

"We're not very far from Kanshisha. Can you walk?"

"Yes."

"Let's get going. It's only an hour until dawn and I am hoping we reach Kanshisha by then."

Reisander watched Someisa struggled to her feet and took her backpack to make walking a little easier for her and they continued on their way. The going got slower as time went on. It was obvious to Reisander that Someisa was having a rough time of it. Her walking gait slowed to a shuffle.

He was deciding whether or not he should put the packs down and carry her when several lizards showed up. The lizards were anxious and kept pointing in a different direction. Putting down Someisa's pack and removing the one on his back, he picked up Someisa and followed the lizards. Somewhere they had gone off course a little bit. The lizards stayed with them until the sun came up. It was at that point he saw Kanshisha. If he had stayed in the direction he had been originally heading, he would have missed her entirely.

Kanshisha was waiting for them. One lizard had run ahead to let her know they were coming. She was surprised to see that Reisander was carrying Someisa. He set the girl gently down on the ground in front of Kanshisha. Several lizards gathered around, looking concerned.

"What happened to Someisa?" asked Kanshisha.

"She has the wasting sickness."

"How is it she has it and you don't?"

"We met with some lizards before we began our journey here. They scratched our arms and then licked the wounds closed. It was supposed to keep us from getting the wasting disease, but for some reason, it didn't take on Someisa."

Someisa groaned and threw up again. There wasn't much left in her stomach. The retching exhausted her, and she fell back onto the ground. One of her arms hit a sharp rock which cut her skin. Immediately, a lizard sprang forward and began licking the wound.

Someisa shrank back in fear of the lizard.

"It's all right, child," said Kanshisha. "The lizard won't hurt you. It's only trying to help."

"Nothing can help me," said Someisa.

"And why is that?"

"No one can escape the wasting disease. I have seen it before when someone came to Mother for help. She couldn't save him and he died." The effort of talking caused Someisa to close her eyes and she drifted out of consciousness.

"I need to go back and get our packs. I left them not far from here when I picked up Someisa. I'll be right back." Reisander took off running.

***

Kanshisha watched the unconscious girl. Talking to the lizards, she said, "It is obvious to me Someisa had brought the wasting disease upon herself. I don't know why or how. Your saliva worked on me and it worked on Reisander. It should have worked on Someisa unless she had somehow blocked it. I am determined to find that out."

The lizards nodded their heads as if in agreement. The dragon settled down to patiently to wait until the girl woke up.

Chapter Thirty-Five

Your mind will give back to you exactly what you put into it.

R eisander returned to find Kanshisha hovering over Someisa with her hands held a little above the girl's body. He put the packs down and walked over to them.

"You can join in and help with this healing. It won't last, but will enable Someisa to wake, and then we can deal with her mind," said the dragon.

"Where do you want me to put my hands?"

"At her feet, if you don't mind. She needs to be grounded. Her fear has led her far afield from where she needs to be in order for us to complete the healing. We can bring her field back into balance, but that is only part of the process. It is her belief in the power of the wasting sickness that is causing her to manifest its symptoms."

"Oh bother. She is stubborn. Do you think we can talk her out of it?

Kanshisha was quiet for a minute and then said, "She gave me a hint before she passed out. She mentioned a man coming to her mother for healing from the wasting disease. Apparently, the man died despite her mother's efforts. I suspect, knowing Zoenka, the woman gave her daughter a long dissertation on the wasting disease and warned her against ever stepping foot in the dead lands. When she comes to, we must heal the damage done to her consciousness."

"You can do that?" asked Reisander.

"Of course. So can you. We all help each other in ways that bring peace to our fears. Remember, thoughts are things. When we take on a fear, it is usually formed by the influence of someone we hold in authority. In this case, it is false evidence appearing real. Once a person sees that what they believe isn't true, and accepts that with all of their being, the person heals. Zoenka unknowingly, and with the best of intentions, planted the fear in Someisa's mind. When she wakes up, we'll have a little talk.

"In the meantime, I see our lizard friends have brought us lunch. And, by the way, they are sentient and can talk."

"The ones I met conversed with Thistle by trilling in her language, which I assumed was close to hers. It was a dialect I couldn't follow and had to rely on Thistle to translate. They didn't chirp like Thistle does when talking to other wood sprites."

'I don't know if they can speak in your language, but they know mine."

"Interesting," said Reisander.

Three lizards approached him, carrying leaves full of water. He gratefully accepted the leaves, one by one, and drank. More lizards arrived with leaves. Reisander drank until he was no longer thirsty. As if the lizards knew this, they began offering him fruit. The grubs they offered him did not thrill him. They looked better than some of the things he had found to eat during his travels and so he tried one. As long as he didn't look too long at what they were, he found them edible. No, they did not taste like chicken.

The lizards had brought food for Kanshisha as well. It took many trips, but they kept coming. Even though she could have eaten more, she stopped them when she felt she had had enough to sustain her.

The lizards took the leftover leaves and covered Someisa with them. The sun was well above the horizon by now and it was getting hot. Lizards began replacing dried out leaves on the dragon's back in preparation for the rest of the day. One of them tentatively held out one to Reisander.

"I suggest you sleep now," said Kanshisha. "It will be too hot soon to do much. The leaves will protect you from the sun and allow you to sleep. I will watch over the two of you and wake you if Someisa wakens before you do."

Reisander obligingly lay down on the ground and placed his backpack under his head for a pillow. The lizards scampered over his body, completely covering him with their leaves. He was surprised at how pleasant and cool it was under the leaves. Tired, he immediately fell asleep.

It was late afternoon when he woke. Kanshisha was doing more energy healing on Someisa. He saw the concern in her eyes. "How is she?"

"Her field is in balance for now. I have just finished working on her again. It doesn't stay balanced for very long. Something in her mind keeps changing it. She has not waked on her own. I was about to wake you. I think we need to bring her back to consciousness. She needs water.

"I have also talked with the lizards. They are making juice from some plants that they think will help. Their bodies are much like dragon bodies. They know what can heal us. They are not familiar with two-leggeds. There is some concern whether their medicine can help her. I am thinking nothing will help her until we can talk to her."

That makes sense," agreed Reisander. He crawled out from under the pile of leaves covering his body and approached the unconscious girl. He put his hand on her shoulder and called her name. There was no response. He shook her a little and still there was no response.

"Do you think she thinks she is dying?" he asked Kanshisha.

"That is a good possibility. We may have to go through our hearts to reach her. I suggest we work together this time."

"Sounds good to me." Reisander sat down next to Someisa with his back to Kanshisha. The dragon placed a hand on each of his shoulders. He could feel her energy fill his heart with comfort and warmth. It felt wonderful. The ranger felt a part of his gruff exterior melt. It frightened him a little. It had taken many years of rough living to achieve the tough personality he presented to the world. It kept him strong.

Kanshisha nudged him and he quickly got back to the business at hand and sent back love to Kanshisha. A bond formed between the two of them. Reisander could feel the energy building and allowed it to flow down his arms into the unconscious girl. He put one hand under her back, at about where her heart would be and the other on top of her body over her heart. He could feel the fever produced by her body to ward off infection.

Kanshisha then explained what needed to be done to begin the healing. "We will enter the dreamtime in order to journey through the underworld to where this all began. We may encounter another lifetime. I have called for Soonak to come as a guide. She knows Someisa's other lives history."

"I'll follow your lead," said Reisander. "I have never done a healing journey before."

Kanshisha led the way. The two of them entered a dark grey tunnel. Soonak greeted them a little way down the tunnel and took over the lead. Someisa's guardian angels and spirit guides flanked them on both sides and behind them. Slowly, they all ventured down the tunnel. It spiraled down and down.

A picture formed at the bottom of the tunnel. It showed another lifetime Someisa experienced. In this incarnation, a nuclear war raged, and the planet was doomed to total destruction. Someisa stood on a hillside, watching others frantically trying to help others or to help themselves. A place of healing stood to her left. The building was overflowing with dying people. People lay on the ground as there was nowhere else to put them. The people caring for them were not much better off.

Someisa's own body was covered with sores. Blood dripped from her nose and mouth. She had stopped eating because nothing stayed down and throwing up exhausted what little strength she had left. Tears fell down her cheeks. There was nothing she could do.

Soonak appeared to Someisa and spoke to her, "Let's look at this scene from another point of view."

The girl nodded, and the scene changed. The sick and dying still lay in the healing area and on the ground, but a feeling of love covered the entire scene. Soonak, Kanshisha, and Reisander added their love. A golden white light shone over the people on the ground. The light revealed a slightly different scene. Angels and spirit guides surrounded each person. They gently eased the souls out of the suffering bodies and carried them home.

The love and the comfort filled all hearts, including Reisander's and Kanshisha's whose attention stayed with Someisa. A look of radiant joy spread over her face. A guardian angel surrounded her, filling her mind with its love. She heard it say, "It was a matter of choice. It is not your fault. Each of these people chose to experience this event and this way of dying. Their reasons are their own. They will go on to other lives and make other choices. It is the way of things."

The scene faded. Reisander felt himself being pulled back up the tunnel. Scene after scene of radiation poisoning passed in front of his eyes as he moved back up the tunnel. Each one closed with an aura of love and golden white light. Then they stopped.

The scene in front of Reisander was of Someisa as a child. It looked like she had completed six trips around the sun, a very impressionable age for their people. A sick man lay on a bed in the guestroom of her house. He was dying of the wasting sickness. It wasn't a pretty sight.

A golden white light came down and filled the room. Someisa didn't see the white light. She was too wrapped up in the horror in front of her. She had squeezed her eyes shut to avoid looking at the man.

"Open your eyes, little one," said Kanshisha. "See the miracle that is happening in front of you."

The child heard the dragon, although she did not know the source of the voice. It was loving and kind. She clung to its sound.

"Watch what love can do,"

A guardian angel stood at the head of the sick man. She reached down and touched the area over his heart. The man looked up at her and smiled. "It's time," he said. The guardian angel nodded in agreement. Slowly and gently, the guardian angel helped ease the soul out of the body. The body gave a slight sigh and ceased to function. The expression on the body's face was one of great joy.

"It's all right," said the soothing voice of Kanshisha. "The man is happy now. He chose this sickness as his method of going home because he wanted to experience what it was like. In his next life, he will study ways to heal the wasting sickness."

"It's awful," sobbed Someisa.

"It may seem unpleasant to you, and it is not an easy way to go home, I will admit. But it was his choice before he came into this world."

The scene faded, and Reisander felt himself moving back up the tunnel again. They left the tunnel and moved out of the dreamtime into present time. Someisa lay on her back with her eyes closed. Her breathing was labored, her body still feverish. Reisander saw he still had his hands above and below Someisa's heart. He didn't move them, as he knew that the healing was incomplete.

"Open your eyes, child," said Kanshisha once again. The girl struggled against the soft voice. "We have healed your other lives and worked with you as a child so that you might realize it was a matter of choice in each life. There is no horror here, only that which you perceive in your mind. Let it go. The wasting disease you have is nothing more than an illusion. It isn't real. It is based on memories best forgotten, as they no longer serve you, especially in this lifetime."

Someisa took a deep, shuddering breath. Her eyes remained closed. There was no change in her condition.

It dawned on Reisander that he was contributing to Someisa's illness. Instead of seeing her as healthy and whole, he had been focusing on her disease and its causes. He closed his eyes to stop seeing her as she was, caught in the illusion of illness brought on by fear. It was real to her. He replaced the sight of her lying in front of him dreadfully sick with a picture of her laughing with friends, running after him as they trudged up a trail, how she faced Kahn and offered him forgiveness.

Slowly, ever so slowly, the illusion Someisa had formed began to crumble. Kanshisha added her memories of Someisa, such as when she received her red stone. She included her joy and her pride in all that Someisa had accomplished.

Soonak joined in with other memories, some of them funny where they laughed together, and impressed upon the girl that she needed to accept the disease she felt in her body for the illusion it was.

Soonak, Reisander, and Kanshisha waited patiently, pouring their love into Someisa's heart. They had no judgment about what she chose to do at this point. It was not their place to make choices for the girl. They had asked her to let go of the illusion of sickness and showed her what it really was. It was now all up to her.

Reisander felt the fever leave Someisa's body. Her face went from very pale to its normal color. Her breathing softened and resumed a healthy rhythm. She opened her eyes.

The three healers cheered with joy. "Well done, Someisa. Well done!" exclaimed Kanshisha. "It will take a while for the sores to heal and your hair to come back, but the important thing is that you decided to live."

Chagrinned, Someisa sat up and looked at her healers and mentors. "I really made a mess of things, didn't I?"

"Not really," said Soonak. "You felt a need to learn more about how the mind can bring on disease. So, you created a situation in which you could study how that works. You did a good job of it. Scared us all. But now it's over and we can move on to other things. There is another important lesson here for you to understand. In order to be fully compassionate, you must let go of empathy."

"What does that mean?"

"When you empathize with someone, and most healers are empathic, it means you're sharing the feelings and emotions of another. In so doing, it's easy to become embroiled in their pain and sorrow. While in that state, it's difficult to think clearly. If you're so locked into another's suffering that you lose your sense of self, there is no room for a desire to help. By letting go of the empathy, you are then free to think of ways to help alleviate the suffering. When you're in a compassionate state, you can let go of your attachment to another, step back, observe the problem, but not get involved with it. Then you can make wise decisions and be of service to the person who needs your assistance. Do you understand, little one?"

"I think so. While being empathic, I took on the suffering of the man with the wasting disease and allowed it to become a part of me. When we arrived here, I still held those empathic feelings. I was ashamed of my belief that I would get the wasting disease and refused to ask for help."

Reisander stood up and said, "Shame is a useless emotion and serves no one. I suggest you let go of that thought as well. Let's get going. We've a long day ahead of us."

Chapter Thirty-Six

When the going gets tough, the tough get going.

S oonak was waiting for Esther to wake up. Except for assisting in Someisa's healing from the wasting sickness, Soonak had been busy patrolling the area around the metal men's building site and keeping an eye on The Eldest Grandmother. Esther seemed to hold her own. Soonak was waiting for the best opportunity to speak with her. Night was her first choice, but the metal men, up till now, kept her inside one of the buildings at night.

Soonak had explored every inch of the ground around the camp. She found nothing of interest to her. Much of the camp comprised of three buildings, wires, equipment and machinery. The roof had been placed on the unfinished building and it looked complete from the outside. Other than the buildings, none of it meant much to the cat. She wondered if Esther had any idea what it was all about.

Esther stirred and shivered. Soonak watched her look around for her cloak. Once the woman found it, Soonak made her presence known. Esther was overjoyed to see the cat, even though the two of them did not always get along. Soonak was well known for ignoring the rules and doing as she pleased, which annoyed Esther. Still, the two of them were civil with each other.

"I see you finally asked for help from your spirit guides," said Soonak.

"I feel a little silly for not thinking about doing that sooner. I need to get out of here. Where exactly am I?"

"You are on the south-eastern corner of the southern dead lands."

"That explains why it is so hot and dry."

"Help is on its way."

"That's good. I need to go home. I don't think I can teleport yet. I haven't used teleportation for many years. It sets me aside from the others. Besides, I don't want the metal men to know when I leave, and I think they would notice if I used teleportation. I fear they would simply come get me again. I tried to teleport earlier and nothing happened. Do you know why that is?"

"They have some way of blocking many mental abilities, even telepathy," said Soonak. "But I have better plans. First, we have to find some lizards."

"Lizards? Are there lizards out here? I have not seen any," said Esther.

"They live in the dead lands."

"The dead lands? I did not think anything could live there."

"You would be surprised at how much life there is in the dead lands. But right now we need lizards." Soonak led Esther around the back side of the buildings.

Somewhere west of the camp lay the beginning of the dead lands. There was no distinct line where they began. Esther felt uneasy on that side of the camp and had avoided it most of the time she spent there. She felt they were closer than what met her comfort zone. However, so far she had no symptoms of the wasting sickness.

"Wait here," said Soonak, while indicating a spot in the shade of some spiny plants. It was getting hot. "I'll go find you some lizards."

The cat disappeared.

"Oh, to be an angel in black panther form," she thought. "They have such freedom."

While waiting, Esther helped herself to a couple of round branches from the spiny plants. As she ate, she watched a few metal men moving about. Their movements were stiff and awkward, reminding her of Someisa's comments about puppets made by a toy maker in Chenault. None of them paid any attention to her, much to her relief. They seemed to be busy fussing around some of the equipment and machinery dotting the landscape.

For some reason, she felt the need to be on the south side of the spiny plants. It would be brutally hot out of the shade. The spiny plants provided little shade, but it was better than being in the full sun. Even so, she obeyed the urging, telling herself she would only stay a few minutes and then return to the shade.

Two lizards sat on the ground as though waiting for her. Their size surprised her. She thought that if anything survived in this heat and in the dead lands, it would be very small. She had seen very few signs of life on this side of the camp and what she had noticed, with the exception of a snake, were about the size of mice.

Soonak appeared just then. "Good. They're here. I know this is going to sound weird. The lizards are going to scratch you deep enough to make you bleed. It is important you let them do this.'

Esther frowned. "Why?"

"They will lick the wound. Their saliva has healing properties and will prevent the wasting sickness."

"Are you serious?"

"Yes," the panther switched her tail in agitation at the need to explain. She thought The Eldest Grandmother would do as she asked without a lot of questions. They needed to hurry.

"It worked just fine for Kanshisha and Reisander. Someisa had a little trouble with it, but she is doing just fine now. They were about fifty miles due west of here early this morning. I imagine they have shortened that distance quite a bit by now."

With some hesitancy, Esther extended her arm to one of the lizards. It scratched her from her elbow to her wrist. It hurt, and she jerked back in pain. With Soonak's nod of approval, she held out her arm again. Both lizards began licking it. The sensation was pleasant, and Esther relaxed.

As soon as the lizards finished, Soonak said, "Let's go. The lizards will lead the way."

The lizards held back, refusing to move. They trilled something at the black panther. One of them pointed to a pile of large, soft green leaves lying in the shade of a rock.

"Sorry. I forgot about your need for leaf covering to protect you from the sun. I'll keep an eye out for the metal men while the lizards help cover you with leaves. Before they do that, do you have anything on you that was put there by the metal men?"

Esther held out her wrist. "It lets the metal men know when I get a certain distance from their buildings. I have tested it out in several places."

Both the cat and the lizards studied the thing on her wrist. To one side, Soonak could see an odd shaped hole. "I wonder," she said. "If that hole allows the insert of a piece of metal to open the thing."

She trilled to the lizards. They looked the hole over very carefully. One of them stuck its tongue into the hole and moved it around. Soonak fidgeted while it did so. Presently they heard a click, and the thing fell off of Esther's wrist. One lizard took the device in its mouth and ran to the east side of the camp and on into the desert. Metal men immediately appeared and followed the device carried by the lizard.

The other lizard handed Esther a hat made of leaves and led the way down into a ravine and headed south along the bottom. They followed the ravine out of sight from the metal men's facility, running when it was feasible to do so. The terrain was quite rocky. At one point, they heard a strange noise. Looking up, the lizard trilled to Soonak and pointed a foot at a flying machine coming toward them.

Soonak pushed Esther and the lizard under a rock with a slight overhang. She arranged her black body over the two of them so that from above, she looked like a shadow of the rock. It was hot enough that the cat didn't think the heat from their bodies would be noticed. The thing flew on by and continued down the ravine. It stopped, hovered for a minute or two, and then banked right and returned to the metal men's compound. It followed a serpentine path as it swept over the ground to the west of where they were hiding. Soon it passed out of sight. They waited for a long while and then got up to resume their travels.

They came to the edge of a cliff that ran east to west. It provided shade, which made the going easier for Esther. They eased along the cliff bottom, heading west.

"This is where I must leave you," announced Soonak. "I am being summoned elsewhere."

The cat disappeared, leaving Esther to wearily follow the lizard.

Chapter Thirty-Seven

If you're making mistakes, it means you're out there doing something.

S omeisa came into consciousness slowly. It took some time to figure out where she was and why she was there. Seeing Kanshisha bending over her brought joy to her heart, and she reached up to hug one of the dragon's legs. "I am so glad to see you," she said. "I was so worried about you."

Someisa looked at her arms that were around the dragon's leg. "My sores are almost gone," she exclaimed. "You healed me."

"No, child. You healed yourself," said Kanshisha. "We simply let you know your fears were groundless. The wasting disease was of your own making coming from your fear of it. It wasn't real, but your mind believed it was. Your body followed your brain's pictures and created the disease. Once you understood that, the disease went away."

"I made a big mistake, didn't I?"

"No one expects you to be perfect, you know. You were quite young when you saw the man dying of the wasting disease. It frightened you so much you stored the vision in your subconscious until you faced the possibility you might catch the disease yourself. At that point, your subconscious mind took over and, out of fear, created it for you."

"Huh. How did you clear my mind of the fear?"

"We entered your heart and did a little shamanic journeying. It was the best way to get through to you. Originally, we did it so that there was no way the metal men could interfere. We knew they had the ability to approach you in the dreamtime, which is mental. We followed your heart, which guided us to the core of your fears, cleared up a few lifetimes of anguish, and ended up at your childhood experience. You are now free to either keep the fears or to let them go.

"If you decide to let them go, forgive yourself for having them. You can accept them as a mistake once made, but no longer having any hold over you. It is just something that happened long ago and no longer serves you. You'll have no need to do it again."

Someisa let go of Kanshisha's leg and sat up. She kissed the dragon on the nose, looked her in the eyes, and said, "Thank you. From the bottom of my heart, I thank you." Turning to Soonak and Reisander, she added, "Thank you. You all saved my life, not just my physical body, but also from a fear I didn't even know I had that could have killed me, eventually."

To her surprise, she began to cry. It embarrassed her, but she didn't stop herself. Reisander handed her a handkerchief and kindly walked away. Soonak wandered off to survey the surrounding terrain and then returned to Esther. Kanshisha cuddled the girl in her arms until she had cried all of her tears. Once finished, she said to the dragon, "I am done with that now. It is time to move on."

"Well said, child. Well said."

"What do we do now?"

Reisander came back at that point and heard her question. "We need to get through that barrier to rescue Esther. Soonak tells me she's escaped and is following a lizard. They're somewhere east of here. Esther's strength is waning and I'm concerned for her. We need to get to her. We could talk heart to heart, but I doubt she knows where she is or how far away she is from us. Soonak tells me to go due east until we can see a cliff to the south. She says Esther and her lizard leader are somewhere along that cliff depending upon how fast Esther can walk."

"We need to get past the barrier. Anyone have any ideas?"

Someisa looked stunned. Reisander, up to that point, always knew what to do. This was a side of him she hadn't seen before.

Kanshisha trilled to the lizards, asking for advice.

The lizards all made digging motions in the sand beneath their feet. "Of course!" exclaimed Reisander. We can dig underneath it. Your lizard friends are amazing. Very intelligent. I'd like to know why we haven't worked with them before. But now is not the time.

"Gather up your things, gal. We may have a long walk ahead of us."

"I could carry you," offered the dragon.

"Not with those broken ribs, you can't. They'll have to heal on their own. Gobha set them, but didn't grow them back together. Your body was already going into shock from the rapid healing done on your wing and hind leg. I suggest that once we're out of sight, you make your way west to a point where you think you can safely fly home."

Kanshisha hung her head for minute. She didn't have the heart to mention she wouldn't be able to fly until her ribs healed. There were always other ways. Dragons often needed to move around the planet faster than they could fly.

Someisa thought she was upset at not being able to go with them. Little did she realize the dragon was deep in thought, with plans of her own.

"You are right," said the dragon. "If you are to crawl under the barrier, I doubt you will be able to dig deep enough for me to crawl through. I would become a hindrance. I will seek out Everonius and have him meet you here."

"Good thinking," said Reisander. Before we go, do we have enough water?"

"I only have half a bottle," replied Someisa. "What are we going to do about the sun? It's only early morning and already I am sweating heavily."

Kanshisha trilled to the lizards. They had thought about their new friends' problems with the heat and the need for water. They produced cloaks made of fresh leaves. Someisa wondered what held the leaves together as she could see no sign of thread or other means of attachment. She got her answer by watching a lizard making a hat for Reisander. They made the crown from smaller leaves. The lizard layered leaves together by spitting on them and pressing them together. It formed a wide brim and attached it to the crown with spit.

She felt a small hand on her leg. Turning away from Reisander, she saw another lizard was trying to get her attention. It held a similar hat in its other hand. She sat down and the lizard spat on the middle of the top of her head. It then pressed the hat onto her head. Someisa shook her head, and the hat stayed firm. The thought crossed her mind that she might not be able to get it off, but decided not to concern herself about it right then.

Tied to the cloaks the lizards had made were water bottles made from some sort of round leaf. The leaf was thick and hollowed out so that it could carry water. The hole at the top had been stuffed with a rock to keep the water from leaking out.

"These guys think of everything," Someisa said to Reisander. They were ready to go, but there was no sign of Soonak. "Now, where did that cat go?"

"She's a cat, even if a big one. She's her own agenda. I assume she thinks, from the directions she gave us, that we can find Esther on our own." Reisander yawned and stretched, readying himself for the long walk ahead of them.

"I don't think we are on our own," said Someisa with a laugh. "It looks like we will have lots of company." A half dozen lizards surrounded the two of them as they headed east.

The barrier was much closer to where they found Kanshisha than they thought. They had only taken a few steps, when Someisa sensed the barrier was somewhere right in front of them. It wasn't anything she could explain. She just knew it was there.

The lizards trilled a warning.

She was about to say something to Reisander, who was a few steps ahead of her, when he bumped into the barrier. It caught him off guard, as he wasn't expecting it to be solid. That was a mistake on his part, as he had not thought through what had caused Kanshisha's fall. He didn't considered it as something so physical, especially since he couldn't see it.

A lizard fussed around him, making sure that he was okay. He patted it on the head and assured it he was all right. He didn't know if the lizard understood him, but it backed off and joined its buddies, who were already digging.

Reisander touched the barrier at a spot away from where the lizards were digging. Using his eyes, there was no sign of anything there. The wall had no reflection, no shadow, no deviation of light going through it. Yet he could touch it. It had no warmth or coolness. It was just there. He pushed on it. Nothing happened.

The lizards, however, were busy digging. They had made a hole wide enough for the Cheschenaki to go through one at a time. It didn't take the lizards long to come up on the other side. That meant the barrier wasn't very thick. It seemed to rest on the surface of the ground as the lizards' hole wasn't deep, either. It was a little tight for Reisander. He paused mid way from crawling underneath the barrier to reach up and touch it to see how thick it was. It was paper thin, yet had stopped a full grown dragon from flying through it. The two-leggeds and the lizard people emerged from the other side and continued on their way east, leaving behind a mystery.

Chapter Thirty-Eight

There can be no greater gift than the giving of one's time and energy to help others without expecting anything in return.

Esther was having a rough time of it. The going got more difficult as the lizard continued to lead her west. The ground was covered in small, sharp rocks that threatened to cut through her moccasins. She was careful of her footing, as it would be easy to turn an ankle on a rock. Because her attention was mostly on her feet, she missed much of the scenery she passed through.

It was when she called a halt to rest that she saw what she had been missing. A little to the north of where she sat, a large patch of lush plants with big, soft green leaves covered the ground. Small creatures played in and around the plants.

The heat was becoming oppressive. Shade from the cliff shielded her from the direct rays of the sun until now. It was nearly noon and the cliff no longer offered shade.

Her lizard friend scampered over to one of the plants and picked some leaves. He made quick work at designing a hat for Esther, which he brought back and offered to her. The one she had been wearing had dried out. She placed the hat on her head and immediately felt a little cooler. Not knowing its language, she nodded her head in thanks.

Thirst was becoming a serious issue. She had long since emptied the round branch she had used as a water bottle. Without thinking it might be of use now, she had eaten it to get the last of the moisture out of it. Communicating her discomfort to the lizard began with pantomiming drinking. At first, the lizard looked at her with a blank expression. Then it was as though a light dawned in its eyes. It pulled on the edge of her robe, leading her away from the cliff and into the patch of green plants.

She stepped on the leaves of plants, not knowing it was a taboo. The lizard trilled in anger and some thorny spines rose off its back. She jumped back in alarm, stepping on more leaves in the process. That didn't help the situation. The lizard pointed to bare ground between the leaves where she was to put her feet. From then on, she walked with care to avoid any further damage to the plants.

To her delight, in the middle of the patch of plants was a pool of water surrounded by the sacred leaves. The only thing she could think of to do was to step over the plants and into the pool. She removed her moccasins and stepped in to the water. It was only a few inches deep where she stood. Bending over, she drank her fill. Unable to resist, she moved further in to the pool and lay down in the water. She had not had a bath since her capture. The pool was a luxury she had no desire to leave.

After a few too short moments, the lizard trilled for her to get out of the water. Sighing, she reached for the hat which had floated off, and put the thing back on her head. She found her shoes and put them on, ready to walk again.

"It would be nice if you had a name," Esther said to the lizard. "I think I'll call you Thorin, because of the way you led me to water. You show strong leadership qualities."

Pointing at the lizard, she said, "You Thorin." Pointing back to herself, she said, "Me Esther."

The lizard cocked its head as though taking into consideration what she had just said. Then it turned its back on her and led the way back to the cliff. She was careful where she put her feet. It wasn't always easy, as the space between plants was often small. Once at the edge of the cliff, they made their way west over the rocky terrain.

Esther had time to think as they walked. The premise that nothing grew or lived in the dead lands was obviously wrong. All her life she had heard stories of what happened to animals and people when they strayed too far into the dead lands. What had changed?

How long had the lizards survived in this forbidden land? Why was it no one had noticed plants growing? She had seen insects moving about on the plants near the pool. Even Hara thought insects could not survive in the dead lands.

She knew of no sightings of plants along the western edge of the dead lands. The dragons had shared no knowledge of life east of there. But here it was all around her. Perhaps the lands were beginning to heal themselves. Perhaps the planet was healing these lands. The growth may have been too slow at first for anyone to take notice. Besides, the wasting sickness was a strong deterrent, preventing anyone from getting close enough to see the changes. Esther was eager to confront a dragon about it. They had to know.

By late afternoon, Esther was thirsty again. The cliff had turned a little south, allowing the sun's rays to hit them from time to time. The rocky terrain prevented walking in the shade at the very bottom of the cliff.

Scanning the horizon, she saw no plants of any kind. It would have been nice if some spiny plants with the strange round branches grew here. She had not seen any since they entered the dead lands. Exhaustion brought about a need for rest. She called to Thorin, who was a little ahead of her, and headed to a shady spot shielded by some rocks.

Thorin jumped up and down, trilling to her. Esther was too tired to even look down at the lizard. Weariness took over, and she rested her head on her arm draped over a rock. Esther had gone as far as she could go. She let her mind go and drifted into unconsciousness, unaware of the two people appearing on the horizon to the west of where she lay.

Chapter Thirty-Nine

Universal intelligence often laughs when plans are made.

They found Esther lying on the ground. Reisander brought her back to consciousness by wiping her face with a cloth made wet by water from the bottle he carried. He dribbled some water into her mouth.

"I am not sure whether you are an illusion or reality," she said, while trying to smile. Her lips were so dry and cracked they bled from the effort.

"Oh, we're for real, old woman," said Reisander. "You gave us quite a scare." He gently wiped the blood off her mouth. "Easy on the water now. Your system isn't used to a lot of water at the moment. You need to give it time to absorb it."

"I will be all right, thanks to you," said Esther. Noticing Someisa for the first time, the old woman sat up and beckoned the girl to her. "Come here, girl and give your Grandma Tea a hug. It is so good to see you."

Someisa, in her delight at seeing her beloved Grandma Tea, embraced her mentor. Reisander was all smiles as he watched the two cling to each other as if afraid to let go. Esther released an arm and brought Reisander down into a group hug, much to his chagrin.

The lizards watched this behavior with some curiosity. Not having had much contact with two-leggeds, their behavior was new to them. The six lizards who had traveled with Someisa and Reisander nodded to Thorin and he nodded back. All six lizards joined with the Cheschenakis to form a bigger group hug.

Reisander planned to return immediately the way they had come. He didn't like being inside the metal men's barrier. It made him feel exposed and wary, but Esther's condition changed his mind.

"Easy there," said Reisander as Esther struggled to stand up. "Give yourself some time to move. You've been dehydrated, and that can slow your body's recovery."

She stood looking at him fondly. "I would like to return home now, but you are right. I think I need to rest for a bit. It'll be more comfortable walking at night, anyway."

Reisander nodded his agreement. He glanced at Someisa. "I could do with something to eat. Do we have anything in that pack of yours that is soft enough for Grandma Tea to eat?"

"The best we have is some travel bread. I know it is hard, but I'll break it into small pieces for her to suck on. What we need is more water."

Turning to the lizards, she pointed to the water bag and raised her eyebrows. The lizards just looked at each other. Someisa tried again, this time pouring a precious drop into her hand and holding it out to the lizards.

Thorin approached her hand and licked away the water. He turned and chittered to the other lizards. Before they could respond, a droning sound came from across the desert.

"We're in trouble," Someisa said. "I know that sound all too well. They're coming to get us. I don't see any place to hide, not that it would do us much good, anyway."

The lizards ran around in a frenzy, looking for places to hide. It took only a few seconds for them to disappear completely.

Reisander picked up Esther and headed for some large rocks at the base of the cliff. Someisa followed close behind him. They ducked out of sight just as a flying machine floated over head.

Someisa held her breath for fear the slightest sound would give them away. The thing hovered over them for what seemed like an eternity. Then it left, heading back the way it came.

"We've been spotted," said Reisander. "I don't know how it knew we were here, but it did. We've got to get out of here, and fast."

He led the way, and the two women followed him. It was clear Esther could not run as tired and out of shape as she was. Reisander threw the old woman over his shoulder and ran with her to the west, with Someisa scrambling to keep up with him. They hugged the cliff as much as they could, both for what little protection it offered and to keep them going in the right direction.

The cliff grew shorter, letting them know it was about to end. Reisander kept an eye on the horizon and also watched the sky behind them. Too soon, he saw three of the flying machines approaching. The barrier wasn't far away, but he couldn't remember where the hole was that went under it. He knew they were south of where they had come in.

They were closer to the barrier than he thought as he ran headlong into it and he nearly dropped Esther. Stunned, he stepped back and then followed the barrier with his hand as he went north. Someisa stayed close behind him.

A small ravine hid them temporarily from the flying machines. But it also kept them from seeing how close the machines were. Reisander hoped the ravine would provide a hole under the barrier. To his disappointment, the barrier followed the natural shape of the ground. He didn't remember seeing a small ravine when they came in, but then he wasn't looking in this direction.

Over Esther's labored breathing, he heard the flying machines approaching and knew they were going to have to make a stand where they were. Even so, he kept going north, hoping to find the underground opening.

It didn't matter. The flying machines landed on three sides of them, with the barrier behind them. There was no place to go. Reisander gently placed Esther behind him and stood quietly, waiting to see what the machines would do.

At first, nothing happened. Then one machine spoke in the monotone of the metal men. "You come."

Nobody moved.

"You come," it said again.

Someisa wasn't sure which of the machines was speaking, but it sounded to her like it was the one in the middle. Unable to control her curiosity, she asked, "Why?"

Reisander gave her a warning glance, but she wasn't looking at him. She was staring at the machine in the middle. "Why?" she repeated.

"You come," said the machine again.

Someisa thought talking with these metal flying things was about as difficult as talking with Thistle. Obviously, this wasn't going to be a very involved conversation. She put her hands on her hips and continued staring at the one speaking.

"You come," it said again.

"Come where?" asked Someisa, trying a different tack.

The machines were quiet, as though pondering an answer to her question. It didn't come. Instead, long sinewy arms that made Someisa think of snakes shot out from all three machines. Each machine grabbed a Cheschenaki around the waist and flew into the air.

The machines headed back east.

Chapter Forty

Listen with your heart. You can hear everything.

K anshisha suddenly had a feeling something had gone terribly wrong. She had been sleeping, working on speeding up the healing of her body, when the feeling came. Fearing the worst, she wondered what to do. She couldn't fly over the barrier and the hole under it was much too small for a dragon to go through.

She needed help. Doing her best to ignore the fear that came over her, she thought of Everonius. To her delight, he immediately came into her mind as though he were waiting for her call. She wondered why all of a sudden she could communicate telepathically, but let the thought go because of the more important pressing matters.

"Something is very wrong," she said, speaking to the image in her mind. He caught what she was feeling.

"I have felt it too. I dislike this,' he said. "Let me think. I will be back." He shut off the communication between the two of them and called for the other two dragons. Instead of returning to their normal patrol routes, the dragons stayed close together. They were a team and one of their own was in trouble. But worse, the people they were sworn to protect were in trouble. The normal routines hadn't worked, and they were planning strategies to prevent further intrusions.

The metal men had to go. That much was clear. How to rid the planet of their presence without the use of violence was part of the puzzle. The dragons considered the matter of whether the metal men were intelligent but not sentient, and if that bound the dragons' actions to the Accords. Of all the laws written in the Accords, the one that said 'do no harm to sentient beings' outranked all the others.

To guard and protect was their sworn duty. But they had other obligations as well, such as to observe how the people lived together without rancor. It was a peaceful place to live. Sometimes they got bored with their work. Often, not much happened that caught their interest on the planet itself. Communications with dragons off planet brought them news of what was happening galaxy wide and sometimes beyond.

They knew the rangers did most of the work, keeping the peace with storytelling and ferreting out the truth when there were disagreements. The dragons' primary job was to prevent beings whose homes were off planet from interfering with the peaceful relationships and restful conditions this world provided. They also had their own agendas and their own opportunities for personal growth that would not be understood by the two-leggeds.

Because Kanshisha's broken ribs prevented her from flying, the three male dragons decided to meet with her in the dead lands where she lay healing herself. As soon as they landed, they found themselves surrounded by the little lizards. The dragons submitted to the lizards' scratches and their licking of the wounds.

Everonius suspected the dragons were immune to the wasting sickness, although they never discussed it between themselves. He had spent enough time in the dead lands himself, with no repercussions, that he was pretty sure he was immune. However, he allowed the lizards to do their thing as a measure of good faith.

Dragonis had brought food for everyone. For the first time since Kanshisha fell, she got to eat her fill, and she relished every morsel. There was plenty for the little lizards, who danced with glee at the sight. It became a merry picnic. The dragons couldn't help but smile as they watched their little distant relations gobble up their meals and play with each other.

Everonius felt a twinge of envy at their ability to enjoy the moment. With a soft sigh heard only by himself, he talked about the business at hand. "Help is coming. We do not have the knowledge to combat these metal men. How to communicate with them is a problem. We do not understand what they want. I have sent messages to the Galactic Union of Federated Planets. They know we do not have the resources to handle this situation."

"Who is coming?" asked Doragon.

"I am not sure." Everonius popped five apples into his mouth. "It will be technology specialists who understand robots, which is the correct name for the metal men."

"I have heard of robots," said Dragonis. "I do not know why I did not put the two together as the same thing."

"None of us did." Everonius ate another bunch of apples. They were one of his favorite foods. "They should arrive in a day or two."

"How are they traveling? Will it be by portal or ship?"

Everonius looked thoughtful. "I didn't think to ask them, Dragonis. Plum forgot. I'll be talking with them after this meeting and I will let you know. I suspect it will be by portal."

"The only working portal in this neck of the woods is at The Eldest Grandmother's island," said Doragon.

"I know." Everonius nodded his agreement. "Because they will bring a lot of equipment with them, I assume it would be by ship."

"Assume nothing." Doragon grinned at Everonius.

Everonius let that comment pass. "Where would be a good landing place that provides space to set up tents and equipment? I am thinking it's too hot here, and would the robots expect us so close to their barrier?"

"I think we need a place outside of the dead lands. We cannot depend on the lizards all the time."

"Good point, Dragonis."

Doragon spoke up. "What about the mountains east of the metal men's encampment? They would not expect us coming from that direction. It is many hundreds of miles to the east coast and there are no villages or habitations of two-leggeds until you get to the end of the continent. We need a map of the area around the robot's compound. On that map, we need to know the extent of the boundary the robots have set up and how high it goes? Has anything about the barrier changed since the two-leggeds dug underneath it?"

Kanshisha listened to what the other dragons were saying and decided it was time for her to add to the conversation. "Do not forget the captives. I am assuming all three have been captured. They can provide us with a map of the compound by sending us pictures of everything they see on the ground. Their perspective is much clearer concerning individual items than what we can see from the air. I would also like to see pictures of what is in the buildings to share with your technology specialists."

Immediately, Everonius was all business. "You contact Someisa, or whoever, and get that done. How soon do you think you can fly?"

"I do not know. Soon I hope."

"I would like our meeting place to be somewhere in those mountains east of the captives. Doragon, you scout out a good landing place for an incoming ship. Dragonis, find out the dimensions of that barrier. All of you contact your rangers to see if there is any activity we need to know about. I suspect our three two-leggeds are not the only ones they captured. We will have to set up rescue plans for all two-leggeds once we have a better idea of what we are dealing with. And I want it done before any harm comes to any of them."

Doragon and Dragonis flew away, leaving Everonius alone with Kanshisha. He asked her, "Do you think the robots will harm them?"

"I do not know. So far they have not. But I am thinking they do not know pain and would not know that they are causing harm to a two-legged. Why are they working only with two-leggeds? If it is souls they want, all living things have them."

"It depends upon what they want with souls. I do not think souls are their true objective. I guess we will just have to wait until the techs get here. We just don't have enough information."

Chapter Forty-One

Separation from friends and family is a very lonely thing.

The three Cheschenakis were dumped unceremoniously on the ground next to buildings, now familiar to Esther. The flying machines disappeared over the roof of the nearest building. Grandma Tea took Someisa and Reisander on a tour of the compound.

Reisander studied the wires, collections of metal shapes and sizes, and where things were in relation to each other. He had a feeling it was going to be important to know that information in the near future.

Someisa was curious about everything. The various metal structures fascinated her. The sun was setting, making it more difficult to see. She reached out to touch a piece of metal. The heat of the day had not yet cooled. The metal was hot, and she burned her fingers. It wasn't a severe burn, but enough to let her know she needed to be careful about touching things.

Esther slumped down on the east side of a building out of the way of the rays of the setting sun. She looked utterly discouraged. With her back to the wall, she brought her knees up to her chest and rested her head on her knees with her arms around her shins. She refused to even look at Someisa, who, seeing her dismal form, had put a hand on her shoulder. The girl left her, sensing the old woman wanted some alone time.

Night set in and the temperature dropped. Esther had dropped her cloak when she was taken. Reisander noticed it was missing and covered her with his. The old woman nodded thanks and lay down on the hard ground and went to sleep. Reisander watched her sleep. She didn't look well. He lay down beside her to help keep her warm. Someisa, noticing Reisander no longer had a cloak, lay down on the other side of him and shared her cloak with him.

Restless, Someisa had trouble going to sleep. Reisander had learned long ago to sleep when time was available and had drifted off within a few minutes. She didn't want to move for fear of waking the others. It made it difficult for her to get comfortable. She would have liked to get up and pace around the compound.

A metal man suddenly appeared. It stood at their feet and aimed a piece of machinery at them. The next thing she knew, they were inside a building. The formation of the three of them didn't change, and neither Reisander nor Grandma Tea woke to the change.

This puzzled Someisa. That Reisander didn't wake seemed odd to her. He usually woke to the very slightest change in sound or light around him. She passed it off as him being overly tired and didn't think about it.

Metal men were in the building with them. Someisa didn't move at first, not wanting them to know she was awake. She soon realized they weren't paying any attention to the three people, so she sat up and looked around.

The metal men were setting up three chairs, very much like the one she saw in her dreams. Next to each chair, they set up equipment and metal boxes. The boxes had lights that flashed at times as the metal men worked with them. In the center of each box was a display of pictures or drawings. She dreaded what was going to happen next.

One of the metal men noticed she was sitting up. It stared at her. If it had a face that showed an emotional response, she would have thought it was surprised. Instead, it pointed a machine at her and suddenly she found herself in a chair. She struggled to get free, but as in her dreams, she found she couldn't move.

They attached metal strings to various places on her body, even in places no Cheschenaki would touch without permission. She felt violated and gave the metal man who was doing the work an angry stare. She wanted to kick it and might have, if her legs weren't already bound. The metal man ignored her. It dawned on Someisa they had no knowledge of the touching rules of her society. Any one part of her body was the same as another. Just the same, she hated the thought of one of these metal creatures touching her anywhere.

While they were vaguely shaped like men, Someisa no longer thought of them as men. She wished she had a better word for them. The creatures worked as a unit. None of them seemed to have a mind of its own. When they started attaching the metal strings, they all worked together in unison. It was weird.

This time, instead of walking around her and merely looking at her, one metal man pressed a button on a machine. An uncomfortable sensation surged through her body. She cried out in shock and woke Reisander. He immediately ran to her side and began pulling off the wires. The unpleasant sensation stopped.

"Do you require assistance?" said one of the metal men.

The absurdity of the question caused Someisa to giggle. She couldn't help it. Here was Reisander, pulling off all the metal strings so carefully placed by the metal men, and one of them was offering him assistance.

Reisander finished removing the wires and turned to the metal man who spoke to him. "No,' he said.

"Assistance is needed," said the metal man.

"Assistance is not needed," said Reisander.

"Assistance is needed," insisted the metal man.

"No, it is not." Reisander bent to help Someisa out of her chair and found he could not move her. When he removed the wires, he took hold of them at a polite distance from Someisa's body and hadn't noticed the surrounding barrier. That he could remove the metal strings but not touch Someisa was another mystery. The metal men had no trouble touching her, Reisander could not.

He stood up and commanded, "Release her."

"Do you require assistance?"

"Yes. I want you to remove the barrier around this girl's body."

"That does not require assistance," said the metal man. Other metal men began reattaching wires to Someisa's body. They didn't seem to care about her clothing. They attached wires to clothes and skin alike.

Reisander followed along behind them, pulled out a knife from inside his tunic, and began cutting the wires. This seemed to get a reaction from the metal men, and some of them placed themselves between Reisander and Someisa.

"This is not assistance," said the metal man who had been talking to Reisander.

"It is to me," said Reisander.

All the metal men stopped what they were doing and faced Reisander. Undaunted, he put his hands on his hips and said, "I command you to release this girl."

At first, the metal men did nothing. They stood where they were and looked at him.

"You do not have permission to attach metal strings to this girl," he stated.

"What is permission? We do not have permission. We do not need permission. Do you need assistance?" said the metal man.

"Remove the barrier around this girl's body."

"That is not assistance."

"It's the assistance I need."

One of the metal men picked up a machine and aimed it at Reisander. He suddenly found himself back outside the building. Esther appeared moments later, followed by Someisa.

"Now that was weird," said Someisa.

"You got that right, gal. I don't know why they didn't simply put me in one of the other chairs."

"Perhaps they thought you were different because you stood up to them. Maybe they took you for a commander, or leader, or something."

"I don't know." Reisander sat down and stared at the mountains in front of him. They glowed softly in the moonlight. Startled, he looked more closely. For a brief second, he thought he saw a dragon flying between two mountain tops. It was so fleeting, he decided he had imagined it. However, he kept an eye on that area just in case he saw it again.

"Did you see anything moving over in those mountains?" he asked Someisa.

But the girl was looking elsewhere. "Sorry. I was looking at Grandma Tea. I am concerned about her."

"I am too. There isn't anything we can do for her right now. I think the best thing is to let her sleep as much as possible. I doubt she slept much when she was alone here."

"Did you see something over there?" Someisa pointed in the direction of the mountains.

"Wishful thinking is more like it, but I thought I saw a dragon flying between those two peaks over there."

"Nice wishful thinking," said Someisa. "But I'll help you keep an eye out for another sighting. For some reason, it brings me hope."

"It does for me too."

Chapter Forty-Two

When life gives you lemons, throw them back and ask for chocolate.

When Esther woke up at dawn, she showed them the round leaves of the spiny plants.

"Gobha calls these plants cactus," said Reisander. "I remember him talking about them while on a hike together, exploring these warmer climates. He showed a few to me. You happened to find edible ones."

"They are the only source of water and food that I have found. When I asked for water from the metal men, they kept offering me oil. It would have been funny if I weren't so terribly thirsty at the time."

"How far out did you explore, Esther?"

"I never found the perimeter. I would start to walk toward the east or north, but it either was too hot and I would come back to the shade, or the metal men came after me. The metal men always took me into one of their buildings at night. Why, I don't know."

"Perhaps their machines don't work as well in the heat," said Someisa while reaching over to pick a cactus branch and getting pricked by a spine. "Ouch. How did you manage to pick these cactus leaves without getting hurt by the spines?"

Esther grinned. "It took practice. If you bring your hand straight into the plant, you'll have fewer problems with spines. Coming in at an angle invites trouble."

"I see what you mean," said Someisa after successfully pulling off a branch and then snapping off the spines. "There aren't many of these cactus plants close by, but I see a whole patch of them off to the south of here."

"I think the plural of cactus is cacti," said Reisander. "I wouldn't be surprised if there are other edible plants around here. It is surprising what the desert can supply in the way of a meal. For example, this bush over here has edible seeds. They're dry but nourishing." He noticed signs in the sand of a snake that had passed through. "Do keep an eye out for snakes. Rattlesnakes and coral snakes live in these desert regions. Their bite is poisonous. Gobha gets around and shares stories about them with me. He says rattlesnakes make good eating, though. There may be other critters we don't know about. "

Someisa shuddered at the thought of snakes. There weren't any poisonous snakes in the rain forest that she called home. Even so, her mother kept a supply of anti-dotes on hand and was sometimes called away when someone in the southern region of their nation encountered one in an unpleasant way. Mother Nature has a way of providing anti-dotes for poisonous species, be they plants or animals. Zoenka was the leading Cheschenaki authority on such things.

Someisa noticed the number of nearby cacti with all their branches intact dwindled close to where Esther sat. Quietly, she set about using Hara's training and caused the cacti to grow new branches. From then on, there were always plenty available for the three of them to eat.

Reisander meandered toward the east. The terrain changed further away from the buildings. Where the buildings and machinery were located, the ground was somewhat smooth and flat. The further east he went, the more rocky the ground became. A small hill rose ahead of him and a couple miles beyond that, the mountains rose up out of the desert floor. They looked liked lumps left over by some sort of cataclysm.

He climbed to the top of the hill and saw traces of a dry stream bed. He called to the women to come join him. "Gobha taught me to dig holes in dry stream beds in the desert. The rocs do the same thing. With luck, we will find water within a few feet down."

The stream bed had a layer of sand on top, but a few inches down, the soil turned hard and difficult to dig with bare hands. Reisander sent Someisa searching for sharp rocks to use as hand shovels. She came back with one and handed it to Reisander and then went searching for more.

Looking around the hill, she found no more sharp rocks. However, she remembered seeing some sharp rocks when she was exploring around some of the metal stuff in the compound. Soon she came back with two.

Reisander studied them for a moment. "These have been cut," he said. "Look at how sharp the edges are. No signs of wear from the wind and blowing sand like the first one you brought me. Interesting." He took one of the sharper rocks and began digging. Part of the edge of the rock broke off, but it still served the purpose.

The ranger was about to give up when he noticed a slight darkening of the soil. Renewing his efforts, a small pool of water took form at the bottom of the hole. Tasting the water, he found it pleasantly salty.

"I think it is safe to drink this. The water tastes briny, but is palatable. A wee bit of salt in the water will help keep our bodies from losing too much salt by sweating. I suggest you try it, Esther. I think lack of salt may be one reason you are so weak."

"That and other minerals," said Esther after taking a taste of the water. Then she dipped both hands in the water and began drinking deeply. Once finished, she made room for Someisa. The girl didn't like the taste much, but she drank anyway. Reisander drank his fill once Someisa finished.

Someisa noticed the sun had risen, and the air was growing warm. Soon it would be too hot to go wandering around. "I am going to explore over in this direction," she said, pointing southeast. "It's getting hot. Perhaps we should spread out and find what we can."

"Good thinking. Gal," said Reisander. "I'll go north of here a bit. Esther, I suggest you check out that patch of cacti and then head for shade."

The Eldest Grandmother didn't like being the weak link of the three of them. She grumbled to herself as she walked over to the cacti plants. Because of Reisander's warning about snakes, she kept her eyes on the ground. She was glad she did when she spotted something that brought a sudden intake of breath. In front of her were the unmistakable footprints of a very large cat.

Calling to the others to come see, she pointed out the footprints. "Have you made any attempts to contact Soonak?" She asked of Someisa.

Shamefaced, the girl answered, "It didn't occur to me. We were using heart language and so I never gave her any thought. It's unusual for her to leave any footprints. Perhaps these are a message for us. "

"Well, contact her now," said Esther. "No, wait." Let's pick a few cacti branches and head for shade. Then you can contact Soonak.

Once fed and comfortably seated, Someisa closed her eyes, grounded and centered herself, and entered the part of her mind where she would find the window that gave her access to other places and beings. She expected that there would be a barrier. Instead, she found a large black cat with a twitching tail that meant it was unhappy.

"Why is it you have a tendency to forget about me?"

"I'm sorry. So much has happened, and I thought the barrier the metal men had created would stop all contact. And, in truth, I forgot."

"Thank you for being honest with me. I am more than a cat, as you well know."

"Well, I know that, but I don't know what you really are."

"For now, a cat will do," said Soonak, to Someisa's disappointment. "Explanations will take too long and I have much to share with you. The metal men, they're known as robots by the way, can't stop me from entering your mind. First, good news. The dragons are setting up a station over in the mountains yonder."

"Then Reisander really did see a flying dragon?"

"Don't interrupt, little one. Yes, he might have seen one. Doragon got a little careless and was in sight of the robot compound for a second or two. Hopefully, they didn't catch sight of him or they might send the flying machines to check things out.

"They would like the three of you to learn all you can about the equipment and machines the robots are using. Every chance you get, memorize what you see. That especially goes for the stuff around the compound. Help is coming in the form of some technical experts that know about this stuff. Send those pictures to Everonius and he can pass them on to the tech people. Use heart communications. It's easy to send pictures that way and avoid the notice of our 'friends' here."

Someisa got so excited she came out of her meditative trance to tell Grandma Tea and Reisander what the cat said.

"Will the tech people be able to talk with us while the barriers are still up?" asked the ranger.

"I didn't think to ask. I broke concentration and cut off communication. She did say to use heart communication with Everonius."

"Well, get back to it, gal. I'll bet that cat has a lot more to say."

Someisa re-grounded and centered herself. She entered the window in her mind and found a cat pacing, its tail twitching from side to side, almost like a dog's. She knew she was in trouble with Soonak and apologized.

"No need for that," said Soonak before the girl could say anything. "I understand your enthusiasm. But would you please wait until I am through with my messages before you go running off to tell others? "

I'm sorry," the girl stammered.

"That's not what I asked for. Didn't I say there was no need for an apology? Are you listening to me?"

Someisa had never seen the cat so angry. But she had to be honest. "I can't make a promise I won't break. When I get caught up in troubles, I get so involved I forget to ask you for help. I sometimes form a barrier of my own. I am sometimes ashamed of my little issues and think that they are not important enough to ask you about them. So I don't think to ask about the big stuff either and I don't know what is big stuff and what is little, anyway."

"Well, start thinking. Nothing is too small for me. In reality, it is all small stuff."

Why can't you show yourself to us instead of going through me?"

"And have the metal men notice another being out here?"

"Oh, yeah. I hadn't thought about that."

"Use your head, girl. Why do you think Reisander and Grandma Tea told you to use your mind?"

"Uh."

Soonak continued talking. "The more we know about the machines the robots are using, the better. The techs are more interested in what's outside, but that doesn't mean you can ignore the inside."

"In some ways, the inside machines are easier. I can picture them because I have seen them more than once. Grandma Tea probably can too."

"They weren't very kind to Esther. She may not have been in a place to notice anything. We're counting on you because you are nosey."

"I'll take that as a compliment."

Chapter Forty-Three

Magic is believing in yourself. If you can make that happen, you can make anything happen.

"I wonder what this is for," said Someisa. "It moves very slowly, like it's following the sun. Have you noticed? This morning it was facing east. Now it is facing toward the sky and a little to the west, just where the sun is."

Reisander came over to where Someisa was standing in front of a large, shiny disc. "Interestin'. I haven't been here long enough to pay much attention." He reached out to touch the disc and quickly drew his hand away.

"That thing's hot."

"There are three of them like that. This one and two more over there," she said, pointing in two different directions. "Could they be converting heat from the sun into some kind of energy and using it?"

"I don't know, gal. But I'll bet the techies do. Send this on to Everonius."

"I'm having trouble connecting with Everonius heart to heart. He isn't exactly a warm fuzzy, you know."

Reisander laughed. "I'll bet he isn't. Give it a try anyway."

Someisa sighed and sat down in the shade near Grandma Tea.

"He's really a big old teddy bear."

Someisa jumped. "I thought you were asleep."

"I was. I woke up a little bit ago and couldn't help overhearing your conversations with Reisander." She rose to a sitting position beside Someisa.

"I have trouble imagining Everonius as a teddy bear."

A big grin crossed the old woman's face. "That's because you haven't had the time to look below the surface of the dragon. Everonius really cares about this planet. He has enforced the Accords for over a thousand years. That takes dedication. The hours are long, often boring, and never ending."

"I never thought of that."

"You're young. Those kinds of thoughts have yet to enter your mind. Don't worry about it."

It took some patience on the part of Everonius, before Someisa could send him a clear picture of the moving discs.

"Good noticing," he said.

A warm feeling flooded through Someisa's heart, quickly followed by pictures of an offworlder sneaking down from the east with Soonak leading the way. Everonius broke contact.

"We have company coming," Someisa announced.

"Where from and who is it?" asked Reisander.

"It's an offworlder. One of the technology people. Soonak is guiding him here."

"Good. It's about time. I thought they would never get here. That means Soonak knows at least one of these people. That should make communications easier." Reisander walked over to look at another grouping of metal strings and unknown objects, leaving Someisa alone with Esther.

"I don't understand something," she said to Grandma Tea. "I've been under the impression Soonak is my power animal, and now I find she communicates with one of the off-world people."

"It's hard to explain. I always thought Soonak was something personal, kind of like a doll, and not something to be shared. Like when she told me not to tell other people her name. Yet both you and Reisander knew her name. I felt betrayed by that. I thought our way of talking was special just to the two of us and now I find she is talking with other people I have never met. This hurts, and I don't understand why."

"It's called jealousy, what you are feeling. You must understand, Soonak is not a cat and Soonak is not her real name."

"What is her real name, then?"

"You'll have to ask her. It is probably something neither of us can pronounce. We brought in Soonak as a power animal because we thought it would be an easy transition for you to make from the world you have always known to that of the spirit world."

The wind picked up and Esther brushed some hair out of her eyes as she gazed at her young foghlamach fondly.

"Is Soonak some kind of spirit guide? I know about them. Mother uses them all the time when she has healing work to do."

"Soonak is more than a spirit guide. She is very high up in the angelic hierarchy. I don't know much more than that. But it means she can be in more than one place at one time and that she serves more than one person. It doesn't mean she loves you any less."

Someisa continued to sit beside Grandma Tea and stare out at the landscape in front of them. The heat shimmered up from the valley floor and blurred her vision.

"Sharing my special friend is a difficult thing for me to accept. Not that I have any choice. What's this about being in more than one place at the same time? How can she be in more than one place at the same time?"

Someisa frowned and tossed a pebble across the sand, aiming at nothing in particular.

"For now, it is just something you'll have to accept. I admit, I don't understand it either." Grandma Tea sighed and adjusted herself on the hard ground. She had lost a lot of weight and lacked her normal padding for sitting on the ground.

"I suppose it really doesn't matter," she said to Grandma Tea. "I feel a little selfish."

"That's perfectly normal, child," said Grandma Tea and gave the girl a hug. "So how is it going with the techs? Are they making any progress?"

"Soonak says they have landed. She is leading one here. She says his name is Peter."

"Interesting," said The Eldest Grandmother. "I am sorry I am not much help."

"What did they do to you?"

"Who? Oh you mean the metal men?" Esther sighed a long drawn out breath. "I don't know for sure, but I think they did something that has damaged my insides. I don't feel my normal self. I am constantly tired. It is an effort to walk anywhere. Even for water."

"I have an idea," said Someisa. She jumped up and ran over to the patch of cacti. Picking an especially large branch, she hollowed out its center, putting the pieces in her pocket for later. Then she walked over to the water hole they had made.

It had filled in again. She set the cacti branch down and re-dug the hole. While waiting for the silt to settle, she looked back at the compound. The sun would set soon. She looked forward to the coolness of dusk, but not the chill of the middle of the night. The cold was at its worst just before dawn.

The water cleared, and she filled the cactus branch with water and took it back to Grandma Tea. The old woman took a long, grateful drink.

Someisa realized she hadn't seen Grandma Tea go for water since early morning. That worried her, and she intended to talk to Reisander about it. She pulled the bits from the center of the cacti branch out of her pocket and offered them to Grandma Tea. Esther nibbled on one for a minute and then put it down in her lap.

"I think I'll take a little nap," she said to Someisa. "That drink refreshed me and I can relax a little now."

Someisa left her beloved mentor and walked over to talk with Reisander. After telling him what Grandma Tea had said, he sighed. "I don't like the sound of this, gal. I think the robots hurt her and hurt her bad. I don't know what to do. Why don't you ask Soonak?"

"I don't know why I keep forgetting about her." Someisa sat down beside where Reisander was standing. He joined her on the ground and waited. Someisa grounded and centered. Soon she had the vision of the cat in her mind. She passed on to the cat what Grandma Tea had said and then pictured what the old woman looked like now.

Soonak bristled. "Why didn't you tell me about this sooner?"

"Grandma Tea has kept it to herself. Today is the first day I thought something might be seriously wrong. I'm worried."

"And so you should be. Not that worry does much good, but in this case, it caused you to speak up."

"Is there anything we can do for her?"

"I'll ask Zoenka and get back to you." With that, the cat disappeared.

"Soonak has gone to talk with my mother," said Someisa to Reisander.

"That is a surprise. Didn't know those two had connected. I hope she knows if one of these plants can help. What about doing some energy healing? You up to that?"

"Yes. I think it would be more effective if we worked together," said Someisa.

"Let's go then."

The two of them performed energy healing on Esther for some time. Someisa was concerned about how weak the woman's field was. It seemed to respond to their ministrations for a while and then leveled off. It did not return to the strong field that Someisa had always known her mentor to have. The lower energy centers were weaker than the upper ones. Someisa knew that to be common for people who were close to making their transition. She didn't say anything to Reisander as she didn't want to discuss her findings in front of Grandma Tea.

Esther opened her eyes when they finished. "Thank you. I feel better." She struggled to sit up. Reisander reached over and eased her into a sitting position.

We've got to get you out of here," he said. "I am going to see how far east I can go before I run into the barrier. There may be a way we can dig under it again or something. I've got to try."

The two women sat in the shade watching Reisander as he moved east. When he disappeared over the little hill they had explored earlier, Someisa decided she wanted to do some exploring of the compound. She was curious about all the metal stuff. It seemed to her that the metal strings were the weakest part of each installation. She found one of the sharp rocks Reisander had been playing with and carried it with her as she wandered around. Grandma Tea had gone back to sleep. Someisa thought that was probably the best thing for her and took care not to wake her.

Someisa studied the strings and metal pieces and even some glass things. Most of the glass was too high for her to reach. However, a small conglomeration of strings, metal, and glass on the west side of the compound caught her attention. This time, before she rushed madly into taking action, she stood in front of the thing and tried to contact Soonak.

Sweat ran down her face and some got into her eyes. She hadn't thought to bring water with her. Her thirst and the heat made it difficult to concentrate. She walked around to the shady side of the thing only to find it offered little in the way of shade. There were no walls or other solid items that could provide enough shade to shield her from the sun, especially when it was near noon.

A mass protrusion of wires held together by glass interested her. She wanted to sit down, but the sand was too hot. She made a mental note of the place and returned to where Grandma Tea lay sleeping.

There was no sign of Reisander. Someisa went to the water hole and dug it out again. After she finished drinking, she filled the cactus branch with water and brought it back to Grandma Tea. Normally, in this heat, the woman was red in the face. Now Grandma Tea's face had gone pale. Someisa knew enough about healing from her mother to know this was not a good sign.

Someisa gently touched the old woman's shoulder, hoping to wake her. Her mentor opened her eyes and gave the girl a weak smile.

"I brought you some water," she said, holding the cactus bottle to the older woman's lips. Esther drank a little of the water and let the rest dribble down her chin. Someisa took her handkerchief and wiped up the water. Adding more water to the piece of cloth, she gently washed the older woman's face.

"That feels good." Grandma Tea smiled and looked at Someisa. Her smile turned into a frown and she said, "Whatever happens, don't let the metal men attach metal strings to your skin. They had metal strings everywhere on me. But the ones attached to my neck, hands and feet were awful. When I didn't answer their questions with something they understood, they pushed a button and a nasty tingling sensation ran through my body from where the metal strings touched my skin."

In a hurry, Someisa thought of the cat. Soonak appeared and Someisa passed on what Grandma Tea had told her. "I felt something like what she describes the last time I was in the chair. I didn't share that with her because I thought it would cause her more worry."

"I'll talk with Peter and learn what I can. In the meantime, keep Esther cool. Don't leave her alone, if you can help it." The cat disappeared from Someisa's mind.

A few minutes later, Someisa felt a sudden pressure on her butt, like she had been kicked. It took a second kick before she realized the cat was trying hard to get her attention.

"Peter says there are two other installations like this one. Some of the captive people have experienced sensations just like you and Esther have. However, the people involved are much younger and don't seem to have the same serious reactions. All of them reported feeling more tired than usual. None of them liked the experience."

Someisa passed on the information to Grandma Tea. The woman nodded her head as she listened. The effort to talk to Someisa brought on another wave of tiredness to Esther.

"I need to lie down," she said. Sitting up seems to be too much for me."

The Eldest Grandmother sighed and would have toppled on her side if Someisa hadn't caught her. She laid the old woman gently down. Wanting something to cushion her head, Someisa looked around and found her cloak. She folded it and placed it under Grandma Tea's head and sat down beside her. Wondering where Reisander was, she tried to contact him through the heart connection. He didn't answer. Someisa felt a moment of panic and stood up to look around. There was no sight of him.

***

Reisander was surprised by how far he had to walk before he found the eastern barrier. He explored it both ways before coming back to where he started. Movement caught his eye. On the other side of the barrier, a lizard appeared. It looked familiar, even though he had to admit they all looked alike in his eyes. This one felt familiar might be a better way of describing his recognition of Thorin.

Reisander put his hand on the barrier, and Thorin put his hand opposite the ranger's. Reisander smiled. He wasn't sure how Thorin could be of help, but it was nice to see the lizard's friendly face.

Thorin scratched a picture in the sand. He drew an outline of the mountains to the east. He made a circle between the two peaks where Reisander had seen the dragon. Off to the side, the lizard drew a picture of a dragon and then added an arrow going from the dragon to the circle. Reisander took that to mean the dragons had stationed themselves at that place.

The lizard wasn't done yet. Once he got Reisander understood about the dragons, he erased the dragon picture and drew a picture of a man. He drew another arrow from the man to the dragons' meeting place. The ranger nodded his understanding.

The lizard erased the drawing again, and replaced it with a much bigger drawing of the man. This drawing showed a large pack on the man's back that extended above his head. The man held things in his hands.

Reisander assumed this was a drawing of one of the techs and again nodded in understanding. Thorin erased that picture and drew one more. This was of the local landscape, with the sun setting. He placed an arrow at the spot where the two faced each other.

The ranger raised his hand in farewell and returned to find Someisa resting against a wall, with Esther sleeping beside her.

"Rest while you can, gal. I found the eastern barrier. It's about a mile from here. We know the western barrier is a good ten to fifteen miles from here. I'd check north and south, but we've got company coming.

"I met Thorin on the other side of the barrier. He drew pictures for me. Somewhere close to where I saw the dragon flying is their meeting place. Thorin also drew a picture of one of these technology guys. We're to meet at the same spot at sundown.

"I know you'd like to go with me, gal, but I think one of us has to stay with Esther. I don't want her alone in this condition."

Disappointed, but knowing Reisander was right, Someisa nodded in agreement. She repeated everything Grandma Tea had said about the metal strings and the strange sensation that went through her body when the metal men were interviewing her. She also mentioned her experience and her brief contact with Soonak.

"I tried to contact you through the heart connection, but you didn't respond," said Someisa.

"Sorry about that. I was too busy with Thorin to pay attention. Get some rest. I have a feeling things are about to change." He lay down in the sand next to The Eldest Grandmother and promptly went to sleep.

Chapter Forty-Four

Love is heaven, and fear is hell. Where you place your attention is where you live.

Someisa woke a few hours later. Reisander was gone. Esther appeared to be sleeping. Something about her breathing bothered Someisa. It seemed more labored. The girl rose and went to gather some cactus branches. She wasn't sure if she should call them branches or leaves. Grandma Tea had named them branches and so she let it go at that.

She picked several, pulled off the spines, and brought them back. Grandma Tea was awake when Someisa sat down beside her. After handing her a piece of cactus, Someisa sat down and ate. The cactus tasted okay, but it was somewhat bland and Someisa was tiring of it as a steady diet.

Grandma Tea accepted her piece and set it in her lap. Someisa noticed. "Aren't you going to eat that?"

The old woman sighed. She broke off a small piece and held it. "My stomach isn't wanting food right now," she said. "I feel queasy."

"Maybe it's from hunger. You haven't eaten hardly anything since the metal men released you."

"I don't think it's from hunger, child."

Esther took a tiny bite, but Someisa suspected the old woman just wanted to ease her mind. Her mentor chewed it slowly, letting the plant's juices run down her throat. Someisa was pleased to see that it stayed down.

Evening came. There was still no sign of Reisander. Someisa took that as a good sign. Grandma Tea had swallowed a couple of small bites of cactus and keep it down. Things seemed so right and so lovely at dusk. The world slows down preparing for rest. Someisa dozed off and woke to find herself inside a building.

The robots had Grandma Tea in one of their horrible chairs. She slumped over in her chair, seemingly unable to hold up her head. The robots were busy checking their instruments. Metal strings hung from all over the woman's body.

"This unit is defective," said one of the metal men.

Someisa was free to move around. She had a feeling she was going to be next. Two of the chairs from their last visit were missing. Either that or they were in a different building. Someisa stomped her foot to get the robot's attention. "She is not defective!" She stormed over to where the metal men had formed in a group around Grandma Tea. "This woman is a living, breathing Cheschenaki. There is nothing wrong with her."

"This unit is defective," said the metal man. "There is no place to attach a soul. There are no ports, sockets, or conduits. It no longer responds to us. It is defective."

This scared Someisa. "You idiots! I don't know what those things are or what you are talking about. She is not made of metal. This woman is made of flesh and blood. She needs medicine to cure her of whatever damage you have done to her. She needs water and food. She's not made like you. And neither am I."

By the end of her tirade, the robots finished unfastening the wires from Grandma Tea's body. One of the metal men pressed a button on a machine, and Grandma Tea slumped down out of her chair. Someisa caught her before her head hit the floor. She sat down and laid Grandma Tea's head in her lap.

"It's all right, child." The woman's voice was so weak, Someisa could barely hear her. "It's my time. I have known it was coming for some time now. You must let me go."

Tears fell as Someisa realized what Grandma Tea was saying.

"You needn't cry, child. It is a good thing. Listen to me carefully. You are to be The Eldest Grandmother. Age has nothing to do with the title. But before you can take on the mantle of The Eldest Grandmother you must complete your training and achieve mastery of the rest of the stones. Do you hear me, child?"

"Yes," stammered Someisa.

"Then I can leave in peace. Reisander is a good man. Listen to what he says. He won't leave you until you have completed your tasks. After that, he will continue as one of the best friends you'll ever have."

The robots tried to pull Grandma Tea away from Someisa. She held on tight to her beloved mentor, but the robots were no match for her. Fearing they might injure Grandma Tea by their tugging, the girl finally let go and they placed the old woman in a corner. Someisa could see that her beloved friend was still breathing, but she wasn't sure for how long.

Someisa let her anger guide her. This event differed from when she stood up to the Kewoyuspans. She had faced down Kahn, their leader, but she could still communicate with him on more than one level. He had a flesh and blood body. These things in front of her had no life to them as she knew it.

"You idiots! How dare you treat that woman so badly! She is the matriarch of my people. She is our leader, wise and much loved."

"She is defective."

"If she is defective, then so am I. So are all the people on this planet. When are you going to figure that out? Will your machines and wires and equipment actually assist you? You have no love, no feeling, no hope. I've got news for you. There is a whole lot more to living than do and not do. We enjoy kindness, friendship, and family. There is beauty, appreciation of good things, help for those who need it, and the wonderment of who we are and what we are doing. We have so much more of life than you do. I pity you!"

The metal men stood and listened to her shouting at them. She thought they would put her in the chair when they gave up on Grandma Tea. Instead, they fiddled with knobs and peered at their equipment, leaving the angry girl standing there with her fists clenched.

The next thing she knew, she was outside the building with Grandma Tea on the ground beside her. Grandma Tea's breathing was soft and slow.

Someisa looked toward Grandma Tea's head and saw the crown energy center glowing an iridescent white. Rainbow colors sparkled throughout and it had expanded to several feet above her head. That was when Someisa knew her beloved grandma Tea was leaving her and going home. Not to her earthly home, but her actual home on the other side of the veil.

Someisa gave a cry of anguish as Esther took her last breath. The girl reached out with both her heart and her mind to anyone who could hear her calling for help. At the same time, she held The Eldest Grandmother in her arms and let her tears fall. All the Cheschenaki heard her. In that moment, every living thing knew that a great woman had made her passing. It was a time for rejoicing and a time of great sorrow. Rejoicing for the life the woman lived. Rejoicing for all the gifts she gave to all who knew her and even those who didn't. But their leader was gone. And for that, they felt sorrow. They would sorely miss her.

Someisa felt a hand on her shoulder and looked up to see Reisander standing beside her with tears in his eyes. He looked old and tired. "It's all right, gal. She'll be there for you when you need her. There is no need for sadness. She knew her time was coming long before we began this journey.

Give her time to adjust to going home. She will let you know when you can talk with her again."

"Does that mean she will become a guide?"

"It's possible. I don't know what she will decide to do now that she is on the other side of the veil. I doubt she will ever be very far away from you. It is important that you let her go in peace. She must make her own way. And you must make your own way. You have learned much, and she is proud of you, and so am I."

Someisa stopped crying. She gently laid her friend and mentor's head on the ground. The two of them straightened out her body. Stepping back, it looked like the old woman was only sleeping. She took a long deep breath and thought, "Goodbye. I love you."

Out loud, she said to Reisander," We need to get her body back home so we can celebrate her. I don't like her leaving us without a party."

"It will be the greatest celebration we have ever known in many hundreds of years,' said Reisander. 'For now, we must leave her be. We have work to do. Help has arrived. Come with me."

"Leaving me no time to grieve?"

"You can do that later."

Chapter Forty-Five

Seeing is believing.

"Do you feel it?" asked Someisa. Not wanting to be left alone, she followed Reisander to the eastern border of the metal men's compound. All around her, she felt the energy of ethereal beings singing with great joy.

"Yes."

"Do you hear singing?"

"Yes."

"Is it always this way?"

"Most times. There have been a few crossings that were done quietly. The person felt no need for celebration, only a desire to rest from a tough life."

"I thought we were all here for a rest between other difficult lifetimes."

Reisander changed course to avoid having to climb over a rocky area. Once around it, he continued talking. "Not all lives on this planet are simple. Look at yours. Do you consider your life to be without strife? Could you stand the boredom without it?"

This set Someisa back a bit and she stopped walking. Noticing Reisander's frown when he turned to see what had stopped her, she gathered herself together and continued to follow him. A life of boredom was her biggest fear before her Wasaru. She had not been able to put it in words before. She felt a sense of freedom, like she had let go of a heavy weight. But before she could ask more questions or even think about things, they reached the barrier.

To her delight, a large hole had been dug under the barrier. A man was crawling through the hole, shielding a small piece of equipment. He was trying to keep the equipment free of sand and other debris. Reisander leaped forward to give him a hand.

"Thanks," said the man. Once through, he stood up and dusted off his clothes. He wore pants, and a shirt made of a fabric new to Someisa. The fabric was green, gray, and brown in splotchy patterns. He wore a tool belt over his hips from which dangled strange things.

The man picked up the piece of equipment and then reached back through the hole to retrieve an odd-looking pair of scissors. The thing had long handles and slightly curved blades that were much shorter than the handles. He handed it to Reisander and picked up his piece of equipment.

"Someisa, I'd like you to meet Peter. He's the tech person I told you about." Turning to Peter, he continued, "Peter, this is Someisa. She is one of our top communicators, even though she is still in training."

"Pleased to meet you, miss," said Peter.

Formalities over, the three of them ran back to the compound. Someisa had trouble keeping up with the two men and let them go ahead of her. Top communicator. Reisander had called her a top communicator. Where did that come from? Although she was overjoyed at the compliment, she wished she understood it.

The two men reached the compound. She watched as they went over to a stand of metal and wires. Peter set down his whatever-it-was and took the large scissors from Reisander. He walked around the installation, studying it from all angles. One of the short metal men suddenly appeared next to him.

"Do you need assistance?" it asked.

"No, thank you," replied Peter. The man continued his study of the installation. Turning to Reisander, he said, "This isn't what I need. Let's move on to the next one."

The two men completely ignored the little metal man. They moved on to another mess of metal strings and ropes and enormous pieces of metal. Peter shook his head and moved on to the next one. The metal man followed them.

"Do you need assistance?" it repeated.

"No, we're all right by ourselves," said Peter as he took the strange scissors and began cutting metal strings. The metal ropes were hard to cut and Reisander lent his strength to the handles as they cut first one wire and then another. Sparks flew. The metal man disappeared.

"Stay away from the cut metal strings," Peter instructed. "They are dangerous and can kill you."

Someisa jumped back out of the way. Some of the metal strings moved like snakes and they scared her. Peter and Reisander took great care to avoid them. The tech grinned and said. "I think we have found the heart of this installation. Once we cut this metal rope, we'll shut the whole thing down"

Cutting the metal rope not only stopped the live metal strings from moving around and giving off sparks, but shut down everything. Someisa hadn't noticed the low grade humming that came from all the equipment and piles of metal and metal strings. Now everything went quiet.

Someisa felt a lightness in her head like a heavy weight had been lifted. She heard Kanshisha's voice in her mind. After doing a quick grounding and centering, she went to the place in her mind that held the window where she could see and talk with distant people and dragons.

"We'll be there in a few minutes, little one. Tell Reisander and Peter not to let any of the robots leave the compound," said Kanshisha.

Someisa relayed the message. Peter fiddled with the piece of equipment he had brought with him. She watched him, fascinated, as he moved his fingers over small buttons and soon saw an image of a man, on what looked like glass, pop up. Below the image, writing appeared. Then the tech began talking with the image of the man. Someisa couldn't hear what they were saying.

Turning to Reisander, he said, "Check all the buildings. We need to know where all the robots are located. Hopefully, we have disabled them, but that has yet to be confirmed."

"Come with me," said Reisander to Someisa.

Grandma Tea's body was where they left it. Someisa felt some relief when she saw it. She didn't like the idea of the metal men taking it away and doing who knows what. They found no signs of the robots outside the buildings.

Finding a door into the buildings proved to be difficult. Someisa remembered Grandma Tea mentioning something about that before they were cut off from communicating. She used another tactic. "If there were a door, where would it be?" she asked Reisander. "From what I remember seeing from the inside, the doors were visible. Could the lack of visible doors be an illusion?"

"I don't know, gal. It seems to me that if we've shut everything down, that illusion would go away."

"Perhaps we haven't shut everything down. There's lots of stuff inside made of metal with knobs and buttons sticking out all over them. Could they be working on their own? "

"Let's go ask Peter," said Reisander. They rounded a building and found the tech sitting on the ground, still talking with the image on the glass.

They waited until Peter looked up at them. "We aren't finding any robots outside the buildings and we can't find any doors into the buildings.

The gal here thinks the lack of doors might be an illusion. That would mean they've another source of power somewhere on the compound, most likely inside the buildings."

"Rats, I didn't think of that. I thought we'd be done when we shut down this installation." He spoke rapidly with the image of the man in the glass. Turning back to Reisander, he said, "We're to cut every wire, metal string, as you call them, we can find. There may be something I missed."

Someisa followed them around as they checked every mound of wires and metal. They cut every wire they found. Someisa helped them find wires. Her smaller hands could reach areas the men could not. When that happened, Peter handed the girl a small version of the strange scissors and she cut the wire.

Once done, they walked around the nearest building. They found no doors. "I know they teleported us in some way, because one minute we were outside and the next I was inside. I could only see a door from inside," said Reisander.

"Tell me more," said Peter.

"Well, the only time they took me inside, I had been asleep and woke to find myself inside along with the two women."

Someisa interrupted. "I was awake. A metal man appeared. He aimed a machine at us and suddenly we were inside." She smirked at Reisander.

"Did they use that machine to transport themselves? I didn't see anything like that when the robot spoke to us."

"Not that I noticed," said Reisander.

"Me either," replied Someisa. "Can you teleport into the building?"

"Not really, but even if I could, but it would be a fool-hardy thing to do. With no knowledge of what is in the room, I could find myself teleported into a table or piece of machinery and that would be very hazardous to my health." The twinkle in his eyes let Someisa know she had asked a dumb question, but he wasn't going to reprimand her for it.

"Interesting." Peter spoke again to the image. There was a rapid exchange of information.

"The boss would like the two of you to walk around that nearest building, there, and see if you can feel a door. The robots don't use the sense of touch as far as we can tell."

Before Someisa could make a move, Kanshisha arrived, followed by Everonius. The dragons filled most of the empty space between where the three people were standing and the desert.

"The other compounds have yet to be breached," announced Everonius as he landed. The barrier is down around this one. We must make haste and capture the robots if we possibly can."

"That is what my boss told me to do as well," said Peter. We seem to have a little problem of finding a door into those buildings."

Everonius took off and flew over the top of the buildings. He paused over one of them. "I can see a door up here. I'm going to open it."

The dragon landed on the rooftop and studied it. He cocked his head this way and that, looking at it from different angles. "I think I'll need a little help. I am not familiar with how this thing works" The dragon flew down and offered Peter a ride up.

Peter blanched at the idea, but bravely climbed up on the dragon's back. It occurred to Someisa the man may not have met a dragon before. "Are you secure back there?" asked Everonius.

"Yeah, I think so. Will I hurt you if I grab one of your scales? I need something to hang on to."

"There's a notch at the base of my wing that works best. Find it?"

"Yeah, I got it," called back Peter. Everonius wasted no time and rose to the top of the building. Someisa and Reisander watched from below. Peter found a latch and struggled to open the door. The latch refused to budge. Everonius reached down and with a claw pulled on the latch. It gave free suddenly. Three flying machines lifted out and took off over the dead lands.

"Rats, that wasn't supposed to happen," he yelled. "May as well bring the others up. And let me bring the computer up. The boss is not going to like losing those planes, but he'll be wanting to see pictures of the inside of this building, anyway. Rats. Why did I leave my computer on the ground?"

Everonius flew Peter back down. The tech picked up a thin rectangular thing, climbed back on Everonius's back, and they returned to the building's roof. Peter jumped off Everonius's back and waited for the dragon to fly both Reisander and Someisa up to the top of the building. There wasn't much room for the dragon on the edge of the roof as the open door prevented him from having a firm foothold. Everonius flew back down and joined Kanshisha on the ground. The two of them explored the rest of the compound.

Looking down, Someisa could see one whole wall covered with equipment. The rest of the building was empty. There was no easy way down. "I think I'll leave this building to the two of you. I'd like to see if I can find doors in the other two buildings."

"Keep Kanshisha with you," admonished Reisander. "I don't want you confronting the robots alone. Not after what happened to Esther." Having said that, he dropped down into the building.

**

Everonius flew up to where Someisa could jump on his back and then lowered the girl to the ground.

'Thanks, Everonius. I'm okay now. I have a feeling we'll have better luck finding the metal men in the building on the east side of the compound, away from the dead lands. Don't ask me why, I just feel it."

"Kanshisha, you stay with Someisa as best you can. No heroics now, with those ribs not quite healed."

Kanshisha sighed and nodded her head.

The young woman and her dragon friend headed over to the building she described. Someisa walked around the building, trailing her hand along the wall. Sure enough, on the east side of that building, close to where The Eldest Grandmother's body lay, she found an indentation in the wall. It was so subtle in the way it fit into the structure of the wall that her eyes completely missed it.

"I've found something," she said to Kanshisha. "There's a change in the wall that I can feel, but I can't see clearly. Now that I am very close to the wall, I can make out a very thin, almost invisible, crack."

Someisa continued to follow the crack with her hands. She missed the top of it. Searching around, she found it much lower down than she expected. It dawned on her that the little metal men were much shorter than she was. She would have to duck her head in order to go through it.

Frustrated, she couldn't find a doorknob or other means of opening the door. She carefully went over every inch all around the edges of the door. Turning her back on it, she leaned against it and gave a push. The door opened so suddenly that she fell back in to the room.

"I think you found the doorknob," observed Kanshisha dryly. "It looks to me like it must be in the middle of the door."

Someisa stuck out her tongue at the dragon and got up, brushing off her clothes as she did so. Turning around, she saw that the building was empty. Totally empty. No metal men, no machinery, no wires or metal bits. Nothing but a little dust.

"Huh," she said. "Let's try the next building."

Kanshisha pushed her head through the door. She could barely get it in far enough to look around.

"Don't be so hasty," said Kanshisha."This doesn't feel like it looks."

Someisa turned back into the room and reached out with her mind to explore it. "You're right. I think I'll explore by feel, like I did with the door."

Someisa began her search by walking around the perimeter of the room. She could feel the energy of things that she knew nothing about, but were no longer there. "It feels to me like they left, taking everything with them except an energetic residue."

"I was afraid of that," said the dragon. "Quick, let's check out the last building."

Someisa left the door open so that others could find it and ran over to the last unexplored building. Feeling along the walls, she came to a similar indentation in the wall. Over the middle of the door, she found a tiny button. Pushing on it, she opened the door.

Chapter Forty-Six

The obstacle is also the path.

S mall robots filled the room with activity. The taller metal men were
not present. Everywhere she looked, the short metal men were fiddling with knobs and buttons. Some seemed to move around in a random fashion. Their activity made Someisa think of an ant colony that had lost its queen.

"Kanshisha," she called. "Go get Reisander and Peter. They'll want to see this."

The dragon was in the process of putting her head through the door. She backed out and gave a loud roar. Everonius responded. "They'll be here in a moment," she said to Someisa.

The girl walked over to one of the short metal men and said, "Do you need assistance?"

"Assistance," it answered. Then all the metal men replied in unison, "Assistance."

"I can't give you assistance," she said.

"Assistance," insisted the short metal men together.

"I'm sorry. I can't help you."

"Assistance," they said. Someisa almost felt sorry for them.

"What have you found, gal?" called Reisander from outside the door. He bent down to get through the door, with Peter doing the same right behind him.

"Oh my lord," said Peter, when he straightened up and looked around the room. "We've cut their communication lines and they're without leadership. Well, rats, looks like they might have a hive mentality. What we see here are the worker bees. I wonder where we'll find the source of their intelligence. It isn't with them as individuals."

"I am not sure I understand you," said Someisa. "Do you mean these things don't think for themselves?"

"That's exactly what I mean."

"Could that be why they are wanting souls? They want autonomy?" asked Reisander.

"I don't know." Peter scratched his head and looked around at all the metal men who were wandering around aimlessly, poking at buttons here and there, and muttering about needing assistance. "Didn't you say there were tall metal men as well?"

"Yes," answered Someisa."The short ones seemed to have been serving the taller ones. The short ones never appeared in my dreams. My time here is the first I have seen of the short metal men. They are the only ones to have asked me if I needed assistance or offered me oil. The tall metal men ran the machines and attached metal ropes to Grandma Tea and to me. The tall ones are also the ones who seemed in charge, gave commands, and wanted to know how to remove our souls."

"Looks like they sacrificed these little guys in the rush to leave here," commented Peter. "I'd like to have our techs check them out. Reisander, would you and Someisa see if you can get the robots out the door where my techs can take them back to home base? We may learn something of value from these little guys."

Reisander nodded in assent and approached one of the aimlessly wandering metal men. It moved to get out of his way. He tried another and the same thing happened. "You try gal," he said to Someisa.

She tried, and the same thing happened. She ran after one and it dodged out of the way before she could get close enough to touch it. "I have an idea," she said.

Turning to the nearest little metal man, she asked, "Do you need assistance?"

"Assistance," it replied.

Assistance is outside. Please follow me for assistance." She led the way out the door and, one by one, the little metal men followed her out the door.

"Well, I'll be," said Peter. He followed the last metal man out the door and called for help from his techs.

As if he waited for them to call, a tech arrived seconds later. Someisa said to the metal men, "This one will give you assistance. Please follow him."

"Uh, Someisa, we don't have the resources to carry all of these little robots to our camp. I don't know how we would keep them with us even if we did. We need to know of a way to immobilize them for ease of transportation."

"How about just taking one?" suggested Reisander, who had just immerged from the building in time to hear Peter's comments. "Someisa, you seem to have some influence on these things. Do you think you can talk just one of them to go with, uh," Turning to the tech who had just arrived, he said, "I'm sorry. I don't know your name. By the way, folks call me Reisander, and this gal is Someisa."

"Bill," said the tech, reaching out to take Reisander's hand. Not knowing what to do with it, but following the tech's lead, Reisander put his hand in Bill's and Bill shook it.

"Nice to meet cha," said Bill while letting go of Reisander's hand. "Now, young lady, see what cha can do to get one of these little guys to allow me to examine it. I need to know how to turn it off. Not only will it make it easier to transport, but also prevent the other robots from tracing it to our home world."

Glancing at Reisander, who nodded his approval, Someisa said to the nearest little metal man, "This unit offers you assistance. Please let him look you over."

Peter laughed as he knew the metal men did not understand the word please. He stopped his merriment when he saw the little robot approach Bill and wait for what he assumed to be further instructions from him.

Bill examined the little robot carefully. "Peter," he said. "Come over here and take a look at this."

The two men bent over the metal man, examining something at the back of its head. Bill reached down and pulled on a small lever. Nothing happened that Someisa noticed. In her efforts to see what they were looking at, she moved closer and accidentally stepped on a button atop the little metal man's foot. It immediately went rigid, all movement stopped.

"What did you do?" said Peter.

"I didn't do anything."

"What did you do, young lady?" said Bill. The two men turned to Someisa.

"I don't know. I wanted to see what you were looking at and accidentally stepped on the metal man's foot," said Someisa.

Both men turned their attention to the metal man's foot. Reisander moved in to take a closer look, too. He spotted the little button on top of the robot's foot and pointed it out to the two other men. It wasn't very obvious, more of a small flat disc. Kanshisha nodded her approval. As far as any of them could tell, the little metal man was out of commission.

"We'll know back at camp whether or not this one is transmitting and/or receiving signals. If it's clean, we'll come back for the others. If not, we'll find a way to stop its transmissions and then decide what to do with the rest of them. Good work, young lady," said Bill. He bent to pick up the little metal man. "It's a lot heavier than it looks. I'll have to get a hand truck to move it."

He poked a button on the side of a little hand-held device and spoke into it, "Hey, Jimmy Boy, I got a little robot here I want to examine in the shop to see what makes it tick. The thing's too heavy for me to lift on my own. Would you mind bringing a hand truck down here and help me get the thing back to camp?"

Someisa couldn't hear the response, as it was too soft for her to make out the words. A few minutes later, another tech appeared beside Kanshisha with a piece of equipment that had a handle, a flat area, and two wheels at the bottom. Bill and Jimmy Boy maneuvered the robot onto the hand truck, stepped away from the group, and disappeared with the little metal man.

"Shuckey darn, but you people come and go fast," exclaimed Someisa, wondering if they teleported or had some other way of moving quickly from place to place. Teleportation was rare among her people. It involved great concentration at a level few people could do.

"Watch your language," warned Reisander.

Someisa looked at him in surprise as the word she used was a common form of exclamation, although not considered a very nice one.

"We'll talk later," he growled.

Peter was trying not to laugh as he watched the two Cheschenaki exchange angry glances. Kanshisha coughed to hide a chuckle.

To change the subject, Reisander turned to Peter and asked, "What should we do with the rest of these?"

"Well," said Peter, "We could have a foot stomping party and store them here. There is other stuff in here we need to examine as well. You and I together could lift one and carry it outside where there is more light. We're short on techs and I know the ones at the camp are going to be busy examining the one sent back with Jimmy Boy. You up for it?"

Peter walked toward a metal man intending to step on the button on its foot. It backed away and moved to the far side of the group of metal men. "I think we're going to need the help of the young lady again," he said.

Someisa spoke to the little metal man nearest her and asked if it needed assistance. It hesitated and turned to look at Peter. "It's all right. He will put you to sleep, but do you no harm," she said.

"Need assistance," said the little metal man. Someisa thought the little thing looked lost and forlorn even though she knew that was impossible.

Chapter Forty-Seven

Just when everything seems hunky-dory, the whole world changes.

O nce all the little metal men had been put to sleep, Reisander asked for a meeting with Someisa, the dragons, and Peter to take place on the eastern side of the grounds, far away from any possible listening ears that might belong to machines and robots. Once all were assembled, Reisander said, "This has all been too easy. I doubt anything left behind by the metal men will be of much value to us."

Peter interrupted, "You are right. Most of what we have found is normal stuff found in most any metal men's outpost. Lots of wires, what you call metal ropes or strings, and random pieces of metal that tell us nothing. Two of the buildings here are completely empty."

Seeing a quizzical look on Reisander's face, he added, "The equipment lining the wall where the planes were stored disappeared in a flurry of dust and sand a little while ago. The one housing the robots may contain some items of interest, but I think the little robots are the only things left behind that give us any clues. Our techs are hoping to tap into the computer systems of the little guys and gain some insight."

"That's what's bothering me," said Reisander. "Why did the little metal men get left behind? Are they studying us through them and we not know it? There is something going on that we are missing and if we don't find it soon, I fear for our safety. Someisa, you seem to have the best rapport with the little guys. What do you sense?"

'I'll trance and give you a report in a few minutes." Someisa grounded and centered herself, and placed her consciousness in front of the window of her mind. She found Soonak waiting for her.

"Been busy, haven't you," said the cat dryly.

"I am glad you are here. Have you been following our conversation about the situation here?"

The cat began purring, something Someisa rarely heard the cat do. "Let's look in on the sleeping small metal men. I am sorry to say you have put them to sleep, but not turned off their mechanisms. They are following every move you make. The one taken back to the tech camp is fully functional and only appears to be asleep. Somehow, the tall metal men have a way of controlling them to allow information to be passed on with no outward sign something is going on. Come out of your trance long enough to warn Peter and then come back to me."

Someisa did as she was told, and soon returned to her vantage point in front of the window of her mind. Soonak was still purring. "What do we look for now?" she asked the cat.

"Pull up the inside of the building housing the small metal men on your window. What do you see?"

"Is it my imagination, or are there fewer of them than when we first saw them there?"

"Good noticing. Now, look for a portal or some other means of transporting them out of there. Obviously, they are doing it one at a time, so it must be small."

Someisa surveyed the room and found nothing. Focusing her attention, she went over the entire room again, bit by bit. At first, nothing appeared. The inside of the building was dusty and dry. The dust seemed to form narrow pathways around the metal men, but nothing else. Away from them, the dust spread out in random patterns. Some of the dust seemed to be caught in a small gust of wind swirling in a small circle inside the interior of the building. Thinking that a bit odd and even though it was a very small thing to Someisa, she brought it up to Soonak. "The only thing I can see, that is a little out of place, is the way the dust swirls around the metal men and is random everywhere else."

"Bingo. What does the dust hide?" said Soonak.

"The swirling dust makes the images blurry and hard to see. There are other things in here besides the metal men. I saw them randomly pushing at buttons and turning knobs on things when we first entered the building. Our focus has been on the metal men, not what else is in here."

"A mistake," observed the cat. "But right now I am more interested in the swirling blurry dust." Someisa watched the cat enter the building and carefully walk around, avoiding the swirling dust. Just to the right of her, the dust rose up, swirled around a metal man, and disappeared with it. "Someisa, summon Peter at once."

Someisa came out of her trance and yelled for Peter. The two men took off running for the building housing the metal men. By the time they arrived, two more had disappeared. Avoiding the moving dust, Peter and Reisander pulled another metal man out of the building.

"It is transmitting," warned Someisa. "The foot button makes them immobile, but doesn't stop communication with the tall metal men. What do we do now?"

Peter reached for his hand held communicator and poked the side of it. "Hey Jimmy Boy, is that robot still with you?"

"Yeah, why?" came the words out of the device.

"It's probably transmitting. The foot button makes them immobile, but doesn't stop communication. Throw a blanket or something over it so it doesn't transmit pictures. See if you can find a mic. It's bound to be very small, like a needle puncture."

"Gotcha. I'll report back anything else we find. We weren't looking for mics and cameras just yet. Will do now."

Peter re-entered the building and began observing the dust. He pushed a narrow line of dust around with his foot forming a break in the line and sat back to watch what happened. The dust slowly meandered back together, forming a connection.

"I think this stuff is a lot more than just dust," he said.

Reisander, who had been watching him, nodded in agreement. "Someisa, stay outside," he commanded. "Peter and I are going to see if we can mess up their portal system here. We need you to keep watch with Kanshisha and Everonius.

"Everonius flew off somewhere."

"Where's Kanshisha?"

"She's flying over the dead lands, scouting."

"See if you can bring her back here."

"Will do."

Chapter Forty-Eight

Keep It Simple Sweetie.

S omeisa scanned the horizon to the west, looking for Kanshisha. Not seeing the dragon, she went to the window of her mind. Finding the dragon beyond a few hills, she made contact and told her what Reisander and Peter were doing.

"This land is changing," said Kanshisha. I am seeing more varieties of plant life here and lots of insects. The lizards are everywhere. They seem to be a merry bunch. They remind me of river otters."

Someisa never heard her. One minute she was looking at Kanshisha and the next she was standing beside Grandma Tea's body in a building she didn't recognize. A large metal man stood in front of her.

"What do you want with us?" she said. Her knees were shaking, and it was hard for Someisa to focus her mind on anything. It was as if she had just come through a portal. Then it occurred to her, she probably had.

"We want your souls," it said.

"We can't give them to you. It doesn't work that way. You have here a unit, as you call it, that is now defective. All units on this planet will become defective if you treat them the way you did this one." Someisa glared at the metal man. "A soul is a thought form made up of energy in the form of light rather than an actual physical thing, as in a person, place, or thing. This one's soul has left its body."

The metal man was quiet for a while. "Then you are of no use to us," said the metal man.

"That's true. We can't help you." Something about the metal man made Someisa feel threatened. She couldn't say why, but she became very frightened. Before she could think of something else to say, she found herself back in the desert in the shade of a building with Grandma Tea's body beside her.

She looked around to summon help. Kanshisha poked her enormous head around the corner. "Oh, there you are," the dragon exclaimed. "I was wondering what had happened to you. One minute you are talking to me and the next you are here."

Someisa told her what had happened and the threat she felt. "I think we need to get out of here. This place isn't safe," she concluded.

"Hurry! Get up on my back," commanded Kanshisha.

Someisa did as she was told. Kanshisha carefully picked up The Eldest Grandmother's body and rose above the buildings. The movement hurt in the areas of her broken ribs, but she ignored the pain. "We have had a warning," the dragon bellowed down to those on the ground. "Leave the premises immediately, no matter how important you feel the work you are doing is for you. Leave!"

Kanshisha flew very high to where the air became cold and it was hard to get a full breath. As they flew, to Someisa's relief, she saw all the men below leave the buildings and head toward the hole that marked where the barrier had been. They all jumped into the hole. The last one had barely made it when the entire installation of the metal man disappeared in a brilliant flash of light.

Kanshisha flew over to the camp set up by the dragons for the off-worlders. A box was waiting for Esther's body. The box was lined with fine linens in all the colors of the rainbow. Kanshisha very carefully lowered the body into the box. A man helped place a perforated lid over the top. Someisa's eyes filled with tears as she watched the proceedings.

"I miss her so much," she said to Kanshisha.

"We all do, dear," the dragon answered. "But life goes on and so must we. Come, Peter and Reisander have arrived. Let's see what they have to say."

Kanshisha had a little trouble turning around. There wasn't much space. Vehicles and equipment lay scattered all over. Kanshisha had to pick her way carefully to avoid stepping on anything. Added to her troubles were men and women scurrying around. "Let's go see what's happening down below," she said to Someisa.

The two of them met Peter and Reisander making their way to the encampment. They turned to see the remains of the metal men compound. There wasn't much to see. The buildings, metal ropes and strings, metal poles, equipment, and some of the nearby plants were completely gone. Even the flat stone like surface had disappeared. With the barrier down, some men wearing protective white suits approached from down below, in vehicles Someisa had never seen before. They seemed to move forward or backward all on their own. She was so fascinated by them she missed hearing Reisander's command to come away, and he had to repeat it.

"What's with you, gal,? Didn't you hear me?" he said. "Let's get some lunch and when we get the all clear, we can go down and see what's left."

Someisa turned away reluctantly. "I've never seen people carriers move all by themselves like that. What makes them go?"

Reisander and Peter laughed. "You'll be seeing a lot more of that kind of stuff before we get this metal men business settled. For now, let's eat while the grub's hot," said Peter.

Chapter Forty-Nine

We all have ability. The difference is in how we use it.

"What is that wonderful smell?" asked Someisa. A terrific aroma found its way out of a nearby tent. The inside was filled with men and women happily eating their noonday meal. The three of them grabbed some trays and loaded up. Not wanting to share small talk with others right then, they found a quiet table in the back of the room.

A tech entered the tent, saw where Peter was sitting, and strode over to talk with him. He took Peter aside, and they talked for several minutes. The look on their faces showed both alarm and sorrow. Preparing herself for some bad news, Someisa ate her savory stew quickly, feeling she might not have time later. She noticed Reisander was doing the same.

Peter finished his conversation and walked back to their table. He sat down and stared straight ahead for a few minutes. The others waited quietly for him to compose his thoughts and tell them what had happened.

"It seems that when the robots blew up their compound here, they also blew up all their other installations. Our guys didn't have somebody like your Someisa here, to warn them and several of our guys got killed and some of yours, too." Peter sighed and stirred his stew, but didn't eat any of it.

"I'm so sorry, Peter," said Someisa.

"Anything we can do?" asked Reisander.

"Put the word out for all folks to stay away from these robots and their installations. There may be some we don't know about. If anyone happens upon one, tell them to leave the scene and report it to their elder grandmothers or some other leader that can get in touch with us. You folks are too innocent to handle these things."

Reisander frowned, but said nothing. Someisa was about to say something, but Reisander kicked her under the table. She stayed quiet.

Some dust had found its way under the edge of the tent and circled around the chattering diners. A bit of it brushed over the top of Someisa's foot. Thinking the sensation was odd, she looked down. Dust was snaking its way around the tent, weaving in and out of tables and chairs. Every once in a while, it seemed to pause as if listening to what was being said at a particular table.

An alarm went off in Someisa's head. "I heard you," she said out loud, even though the message was meant for Soonak. Both men looked at her in puzzlement. She held a finger to her lips and with the other pointed to the ground.

Reisander frowned at her. He was about to say something, but her expression stopped him. He looked at the floor. At first, he saw nothing unusual except a little dust swirling around. In desert country, that was normal. It took him a fleeting second to remember that swirling dust inside a tent was not normal.

Peter started talking about what they planned to do with the metal men they had captured. Reisander grabbed his arm and pointed down to the floor.

Peter nodded his head and said, "These spuds are mighty tasty. Think I'll get me some more."

He stood up and, as he did so, he scraped away some dust by moving his chair across the line. The action created a break in the dust for a moment.

Then it swirled to reform a connection. Peter scraped it again, this time making the break much bigger. A puff of wind entered the tent through an open flap at the entrance. No one else noticed it, but the three watched its progress as it slowly swirled around the tent, moving lightweight fabrics and papers as it went. It came to rest at the break and reformed the connection.

Peter stepped over the stream of dust and beckoned to a couple of other techs. Looking back, he nodded to Reisander and Someisa, waving them over to him as he went out of the tent. They gathered in a rocky area away from sand and dust.

"I hope this is important," groused Reisander. "I am leaving behind a delightful piece of apple pie that had my name on it."

Ignoring Reisander's comment, Peter said, "Someisa, you seem to be the more observant one around here. I want you and Reisander to go round to the outside of the tent from where we were sitting and see if you can follow this freaky dust. Once you find where it's coming from, come get me and we'll take it from there."

Reisander led the way around the tent. "I know these tech guys are pretty smart and know their way around their machinery, but they don't have your ability to communicate with offworlders, especially the metal men. I can track better than you, and make less noise while doing it. Follow me and stay in my footsteps or as close to them as you can.

Someisa nodded. They followed alongside of the dust trail a considerable distance. Most of the time, unless the dust was moving, Someisa couldn't tell it from the sand on the desert floor. At first, she thought it was her imagination. Now that they were in the open and away from people and machinery smells, she noticed the dust gave off a slight metallic odor. Without thinking, she reached down and picked up a handful of the dust.

"What are you doing, gal?" cried Reisander in alarm.

Indignant at his outburst, she said, "I'm smelling the dust. A metallic odor is still with us out here in the middle of nowhere and I wanted to know if it came from the dust."

"Do you want to breathe in any of that stuff? Swallow some accidentally?"

"Well, no."

"Then put it down and use some of your water to wash your hands. Dang it all, gal. I thought you had more sense than that."

Someisa did as she was told, glaring at him the whole time. Once finished, she asked, "Did you notice the metallic smell?"

"No. I didn't. My concentration was on the ground. I am glad you did. Now that you have brought it to my attention, I do smell a slight metallic tinge near the dust. It's the same color as the desert floor, but it seems a little denser than sand. I don't like that we can smell it. That means we're breathing it in, and I don't think that is in our best good, to put it mildly. Get hold of Soonak. See if she can come join us."

Someisa did the ground and center thing and called for Soonak. After a few seconds, the cat showed up in Someisa's mind.

"I'm a little busy right now. Can this wait?" asked Soonak.

"I don't know." Someisa shared with her power animal about smelling the metallic odor to the dust. "Reisander would like you to come be with us while we follow the trail of dust."

"Stay where you are. I don't want the two of you wandering around, following metallic dust without me there. Give me a few minutes."

Reisander led Someisa away from the dust to wait for Soonak. To his disgust, some of the dust followed them. "I don't like this," he said. "This dust obviously has some intelligence either in it, or guiding it. I don't like it. Not at all."

He thought for a while. "What we need is water," he said. "The metal men have no use for it that we know of. We need some kind of barrier to keep that stuff away from us."

"There's a little depression over there with some dry brush around it," said Someisa, pointing to the southwest of where they were standing. "Let's dig there and see if we can find water."

"Might work if we had something to dig with."

Just then, Soonak showed up. "Where's the trail of dust?" She asked.

Someisa tried unsuccessfully not to giggle. "You're standing in it."

The black panther looked down at the dust swirling around her paws. "Disgusting stuff," she said as she shook most of it off her fur.

Someisa noticed the cat refrained from licking it off.

The cat gave a sigh and said, "Let's see where this leads us. We might have to create a good rain and thunderstorm."

Puzzled, Someisa followed Soonak and Reisander as they made their way around rocks and cacti, keeping the dust always in sight. Not that it took much effort because if they veered away from the dust, some of it would wind its way over to them.

A quarter of a mile from the tech camp, they found a square metal box half buried in the sand. The trail of the dust ended there.

"I have an idea of a way to break the line of dust," said Someisa.

"Out with it, gal."

"If we break the line, the metal men will know we have found their box, if they don't already know," said Soonak.

"What's your idea, gal?"

"Well, it's something a man can do. Women don't have the right equipment."

Reisander's face broke into a big grin. "You're a genius, gal."

Even Soonak had a big, toothy grin on her face. "Let me converse with some of my people and the dragons, and we'll decide what to do." The cat was quiet for some time. "Help is one the way. Everonius is still at the tech camp. Once he's here, we'll make the final decision about wetting down the dust. Drink some water, Reisander."

Someisa handed him her water bottle. Reisander drank all the water the two of them had.

"I told Everonius to bring water," said Soonak. "I don't want the two of you going without in this heat."

It was hot. The sun was at mid afternoon and beaming down on them. To Someisa's surprise, she could see the tops of some thunderclouds peaking over the mountains to the southwest of where they stood. The rangers, with the help of the dragons, had created a snowstorm as a way of defeating the Kewoyuspans. She wondered if they were planning something like that now. Probably not snow, but maybe a good hard rain.

Before she could ask about it, Everonius arrived. "Okay, Reisander," he said. "Do your thing as close to that box as you can get."

Someisa turned her back to Reisander while he 'watered' the ground all around the box. He ran out of urine before he could finish. Everonius indicated a large container of water tied to his back. Using some of that water, Reisander completed the task.

Even though it was hot and dry, steam rose where urine hit the dust. No new dust moved to reconnect the line. Where there was only water, dust moved around it and tried to reconnect. However, once the line of liquids completely encircled the box, the line of dust stopped moving.

Peter arrived driving a vehicle. He parked it several feet away from where they all stood. "I see you successfully broke the connection. How'd you do it?"

"It was the little lady's idea," said Everonius and explained how it was done.

Someisa blushed at Everonius' talk about male anatomy being a handy tool for the job.

Peter grinned. "Never would have thought of it myself. Interesting how the dust reacted to the urine, though. Might be the acid in it," he mused.

"I've a truck coming. We're going to shovel all this stuff up and isolate it. Don't want you folks around while we're doing it. Everybody involved will wear masks to avoid breathing any of the stuff."

Someisa was staring at the dust while Peter was talking. "Look," she cried. "I think you are going to be too late."

The top of the box had opened, a little wind picked up dust, and all of it was pouring into the box. Everonius placed his foot over the lid and forced it closed. All but a handful of dust had returned to the box.

"Well, at least we have the box," said Peter.

Before Reisander could stop her, Someisa walked over to the box and reached down to scoop up the little of the remaining dust with her hand-kerchief. She heard Soonak cry, "Run, Someisa!" Putting the dust in her pocket, she turned and ran away from the box. Not soon enough. A few seconds later, the box disappeared in a flash of hot, white light. Someisa fell when it hit her and the flash burned her back and the bottom of her exposed feet as she hit the ground. Fortunately, she had her back to the flash, and it didn't blind her. The blast didn't project very far. The others were far enough away to feel the heat and receive the equivalent of a mild sunburn where skin was exposed.

Frustrated, she sat up, not yet feeling pain in her feet. "I'm getting tired of this flashy business. Just when we get to where we can learn something about the metal men, they flash the stuff and it all disappears. It's not fair." She tried to stand up and the pain from the burn damage to her feet flared. "Ow!" she cried, promptly sitting down again, only to find her bottom hurt, too.

The soles of her moccasins had completely burnt away, exposing blistered feet. Parts of the back of her tunic were also missing, revealing more blisters on her back and bottom.

Reisander was the first to reach her. "Send for Gobha," he said.

"Our medics have salves for that," called Peter when he saw Someisa's back.

"Get him over here," said the ranger. "Our healers aren't here right now and we'd appreciate any help your guys can do for the gal."

A young woman approached and asked, "How may I help you?"

Someisa was in too much pain to answer. Tears rolled down her cheeks from the agonizing sensation and she yearned for her mother's comfort, both personally and professionally.

Just then, a lizard popped up. The young woman tried to shoo it away. "These pesky things are all over the place. We've had to shoot a couple of them for getting into our equipment. Good riddance, I say. Hey, get that thing away from the girl's feet!" She pulled out a weapon and aimed it at the lizard.

"No!" commanded Reisander. Before the woman could react, the ranger had the weapon out of her hand. "Never do that again! Violence against sentient beings is forbidden on this planet, and these lizards are sentient! Leave us!"

Not sure she understood everything Reisander said, but knowing she was not welcome, the woman left.

The lizard began gently licking one of Someisa's feet. Two more approached, carrying leaves. Once the lizard finished licking Someisa's foot, it moved on to the other one. A lizard began wrapping her foot with the leaves, using saliva to hold the leaves together. A dozen more lizards showed up, all carrying leaves. Two of them started licking her back. The first one dropped back to let the new ones through. They made a cape of leaves to protect the girl's back and bottom and wrapped the other foot with leaves.

Someisa quit crying and heaved a great sigh. Although the pain had not completely disappeared, she felt a wonderful sense of relief.

"I am sorry about the deaths of your lizard friends," said Peter to Reisander. "I don't know what to do to make amends. Do you?"

"I don't know either," said Reisander. "We'll have to ask them."

Everonius came over to see what was going on. The first lizard trilled to the lead dragon, who answered him with a guttural trill that the lizard seemed to understand.

"The lizards have their own way of taking care of their dead. They thank you for stopping the killing of their kind. Their quick forgiveness is a valuable lesson for us."

"These ones have come to help the girl. One of them saw what had happened and sent out a call to all the nearby lizards to heal her. They have also sent out a message for all lizards to leave the offworlders' equipment alone. So, it looks like they have taken care of that situation. How are you doing, little lady?"

"I still hurt a bit, but I feel so much better. I don't think I can walk, though. Thank you for asking."

"I have called for Kanshisha. She has a gift for you and will be at the camp in a few minutes. She can carry you around until we find a conveyance for you."

Someisa wanted to know what a conveyance was, but the dragon left before she could open her mouth.

Reisander threw Someisa over his shoulder and carried her back to the techs' camp. Peter followed him. The little lizards faded into the desert before Someisa could thank them.

"Sorry you're uncomfortable, gal," said Reisander. "It's the only way I can carry you without further injuring your back."

For Someisa, it was a long way back.

When they reached the camp, Reisander asked Peter if there was some place where he could put Someisa. "I think she'll be more comfortable lying on her stomach," the ranger said.

"Of course," answered Peter, and led the way to the medics' tent. There Reisander gently laid Someisa on her stomach. "How you doing, gal?"

"There's something in my pocket that is making lying on my stomach uncomfortable." She rolled on her side and pulled out her handkerchief full of dust. She gave it to Peter. "I snatched this bit of dust just before the flash and put it in my pocket. My body must have saved it from the flash. I assume you'll know what to do with it?" she said with a mischievous grin.

"Thank you, Someisa. You have no idea how important it is for us to be studying these nanoparticles." To her surprise, he bent over and kissed her cheek. He left, carrying her heavy handkerchief.

"I think you made a hit with him," said Reisander, smiling. "I'm glad you did. I was concerned he might take offense at my displeasure over the killing of some lizards. He'll make sure it doesn't happen again and that the little creatures are treated with respect from now on."

"I'm glad to hear that. What the lizards did has made me sleepy," said Someisa. "I'd like to take a nap."

Chapter Fifty

When in doubt, tell the truth.

H aving been called to a meeting and annoyed at being disturbed from a pleasant nap, Soonak considered staying where she was. However, Everonius mentioned the meeting might concern Someisa, which meant the cat had to go. Wanting to stay invisible, she settled herself in an out-of-the-way spot to avoid being stepped on. With her eyes half closed, but still alert, and her ears cocked forward, she watched silently, a feline presence known only to Everonius and Reisander.

***

Shortly after Someisa fell asleep, Everonius called Reisander to a gathering, along with some offworlders. The ranger grabbed a mug of fresh tea and headed for a small knoll half a mile from the offworlders compound. Wind kept the top of the knoll free of debris and created a comfortable landing place for a dragon. The view was clear in all directions, making it easy for Reisander to keep watch. To his knowledge, no robot activity occurred in this area. Moving sand would be easy to spot. He would notice uninvited listeners and see to their removal if needed. Of course, Soonak was there, and he counted on her to alert him of anything unseen or menacing. The dragon began the meeting.

"Thank you all for being here and helping us deal with this unusual situation."

Reisander nearly choked on his tea at that comment. The dragon gave him a dark look.

"Doragon and Dragonis, both dragon guardians of this planet, scoured the planet looking for active signs of robot habitation. Some sort of blast, like we experienced here, has swept all the known sites clean. We suspect that is the method they used to clear the cave that stored the metal man's body.

It is not the sites that concern us or the robots working there. It is the observation of Seefar concerning a single metal man in a meadow. This one is of a different shape from the others and seems to think for itself. Unfortunately, other than that one sighting, we have no further information about this thing and it concerns us greatly.

"At first, we thought the metal men were using portals to move about, but according to Seefar, these metal men can slip in and out of dimensions at will. What we originally thought were portals, we now know are merely places where they changed dimensions, sometimes leaving a temporary blur behind them as they did so. That made us think they were using portals.

The slipping between dimensions can occur anywhere and is not limited to the physical places portals require. We do something similar when we teleport. Most of us can only teleport to areas we know well to avoid landing in the middle of a piece of furniture or under water. The way these metal men slip dimensions, I don't think they are concerned about obstacles. They must have a way of seeing where they are going before they move."

One of the offworlders interrupted at this point. "Who is this Seefar? How was he able to see this one robot? I don't get it."

"Don't worry about it Fergus. I'll explain it to you later," said Peter. "Please excuse the interruption, Everonius. Some of our guys, although great techies, are new to this quadrant of the galaxy and with this emergency, we didn't have time to train them about the use of proper etiquette."

"Point taken," was the dragon's acknowledgement. "Does anyone from your contingent have anything to add, Peter?"

"Not that I know of. You have summed it up well. We have not encountered the robot Seefar observed on any other planets. This concerns us. It means there is a change in the ranks of the robots. It seems the big boys are arriving."

"We have called for more dragons to help us," said Everonius. "We expect three to arrive next week."

***

A breeze blew some sand through the area while they were talking. Soonak took note and frowned. Breathing deeply, she detected a slight hint of metal. However, the sand scattered without leaving a trail. It worried her and she sent a message to Reisander.

Chapter Fifty-One

Gratitude helps us see what is there instead of what isn't.

S omeisa woke feeling stiff and sore. Her feet hurt and her back complained during the lightest of movements. Someisa had no memory of being moved to a bed situated in a space surrounded by draperies to give her privacy. A medic came in to check on her. The lady smiled and said, "You have some visitors wanting to see you." And then she left.

Three lizards poked their heads into the room where Someisa lay. They all carried fresh leaves. She grinned when she saw them and beckoned them to her. They scampered over to her and climbed up onto her bed. One of them began removing the dried out leaves surrounding her feet.

Someisa surveyed her feet and found they were healing nicely and at a faster rate than she expected.

Zoenka entered the room, while the lizards were at work licking the few remaining blisters on her daughter's feet, buttocks, and back. One lizard scampered over to her and accepted a pat on its head. It trilled in appreciation and returned to work on Someisa. One by one, the other two lizards came over to the lead healer of the Cheschenaki nation and exchanged greetings.

"I see you have met my little friends," said Someisa.

"Yes. They are quite the amazing creatures. How are you feeling?"

"Better than I expected, but still painful in the worst burn areas. I think these little friends saved my skin and possibly my life."

Zoenka laughed. "You weren't burned that badly. It will be a week or two before you can walk again or sleep on your back. Otherwise you're doing just fine."

"Why are you here, Mother? Did you come just for me? How long have I been out of it?"

"Well, in part, you were a good excuse for me to come and meet the tech medics, as they call themselves. You have been asleep for over thirty-six hours. We've awakened you a few times to get you to drink some water, which you probably don't remember."

A tech medic entered the room. "Here is the tea you requested, Mistress Zoenka."

"Thank you, Sally. Now that she is awake, let me introduce you to my daughter, Someisa. And Someisa, this is Sally, one of the lead medics in this group. We have been sharing a lot with each other. It's been great fun. Together, we have studied what the lizards are doing. Sally actually talked one of them into spitting into a vial so we could analyze their saliva. Good things will come of this."

The two younger women nodded to each other. "I'd like to stay and chat, but other duties await. I hope to see you again before you go home, Someisa. It's nice to meet you."

Before Someisa could say anything, Sally waved farewell, and disappeared behind the tent flap.

"When do I get to go home?"

"As soon as Everonius is free to fly the two of us home. Kanshisha can fly, but her ribs need to heal completely before she can carry anyone that great a distance. You need rest to heal those burns. Your lizard friends volunteered to go with us, but I fear our climate would not be good for them. Finish your tea. It's getting cold."

Someisa had forgotten about the tea and promptly took a sip. She made a face, as it was quite bitter. "Why do the remedies always taste so bad?"

"It's to discourage people from drinking or eating too much of a plant with healing properties. Most remedies are best in very small doses, but can cause harm if one ingests too much."

"Don't worry. I'll drink as little of this stuff as I can get away with."

Mother and daughter laughed.

Reisander entered the room. "You packed up and ready to leave, gal?" he said.

Both women laughed again. "She just woke up, Reisander," said Zoenka.

"Good," he said, "Because Everonius can take you home now and he is ready to leave. He's anxious to get going before someone thinks of something for him to do that he doesn't want to do."

There was more laughter. Someisa's pack stood in a corner. Zoenka pointed it out to Reisander and said," I think all of Someisa's things are in that pack. I have a few things scattered in the medics' tent. It will take me a few minutes to get them. During that time, I assume my daughter has a few personal needs she must take care of before a long trip."

Reisander grinned and picked up Someisa's pack. "I'll be back in ten minutes to carry my foghlamach to her ride." He winked at Someisa and left.

Chapter Fifty-Two

Courage. Kindness. Friendship. Character. These are qualities that define us and propel us, on occasion, to greatness.

A large group of people had gathered to see Someisa and her mother off. Kanshisha flew in to say good-by. The two dragons took up so much space, the farewells were removed to an empty space set aside for dragons a short distance away. Someisa noticed Soonak lying under a group of dried shrubs. She blended well enough with the shadows given off by the plants that others failed to notice her. In her mind, Someisa could hear the cat purring.

Reisander set Someisa down on a stool with a cushion on it. Kanshisha approached her carefully and Someisa reached up to hug the dragon's nose. It hurt her back, but the girl didn't care.

"It's time," said Kanshisha in a soft voice only Someisa could hear.

"Time for what?"

"You have earned The Orange Stone."

Reaching in under her arm, the dragon pulled out a bright orange crystal and turned to the people standing around. She held up the stone for all to see. It glittered in the sunlight, dazzling the eyes of many people there.

More offworlders stopped what they were doing and joined the small crowd watching the proceedings. It was not yet the warmest part of the day, but was still hot enough for everyone to break out into a sweat. The aroma of warm bodies perfumed the air. Nobody cared.

"Most of you are new to our ways," said Kanshisha. "When a child comes of age to go through a ceremony called the Wasaru, the candidate learns about their life purpose and field of study. A colorful crystal represents each course of study. The seven colors of the rainbow stand for each course, and so there are seven colored crystals from which a Wasaru candidate must choose. The child cannot see the stones. They are kept in a basket held a little over the child's head while they reach into the basket and draw out a stone.

"Someisa didn't draw a colored stone. Instead, she drew a white stone. White is the combination of all colors. This means she is to study herself, and all the colors the other stones represent. It is a long and arduous path she has set for herself. She has already earned the red stone. This time, she is being presented with an orange crystal. I imagine some of you are wondering what this stone requires.

"Most people who draw the orange stone end up working in the arts, as creativity and beauty are big parts of that stone's field of study. But Someisa must also learn more about herself. The hardest things for her to accept are the responsibilities of the bearer of the white stone. Among these are receiving help from others, not always an easy thing to do. Accepting what she asks for can be difficult, especially when she realizes it isn't what she really wanted, but being nice about it, and thanking the giver.

"A big lesson for her, concerned seeking independence from outside influences. This means searching her heart for what is true for her and ignoring beliefs belonging to others. Sometimes, beliefs formed in childhood, or carried forth from another lifetime, are to the detriment of the seeker and must be studied and then set aside as inappropriate for a personal life path.

She is still seeking to understand that giving to herself is the same as giving to others, as we are all connected. It is within the council's decision that she has sufficiently learned enough to carry her on to the next stone."

"Someisa, may I have your white stone?"

Fumbling with the string around her neck, Someisa drew out from beneath her tunic a white stone with one red facet.

Kanshisha took the necklace holding the stone and held it up for all to see. Then she pushed the orange crystal into the white stone and an orange facet appeared in the white stone next to the red one.

A gasp arose from the audience. This was magic they didn't understand. Muttering found its way through the little crowd. Kanshisha ignored it and placed the new stone around her foghlamach's neck. Someisa held the stone for a minute, gazing into its depths, and put it back under her tunic.

Peter began to clap his hands, and soon everyone joined him. They recognized something special had just happened, even though most of them didn't know what it was.. Some people cheered the flummoxed girl. Such a greeting embarrassed her.

"Come child," said Kanshisha. "It is time to take you home. I am healed enough that I can carry you on my back. Your mother will ride with Everonius. He will also carry The Eldest Grandmother's body. Preparations for her end-of-life ceremony are under way."

Reisander lifted Someisa up onto Kanshisha's back. Zoenka climbed up on Everonius's back. Everonius grabbed the strap that held the box containing Esther's body with his feet. After a quick wave from Someisa to Reisander, the dragons took off.

Reisander wandered over to where Soonak stood watching. "Well", he said. "I don't think this metal man business is over yet. They may have left the planet, but I don't think they are done with us."

"Too true," said the black panther.

Epilogue

The fog people came, knowing a special event was about to take place. They gathered quietly and watched.

A man stood with his back to a shimmering mist. Friends formed a large ring in front him. The friends came in all sizes and shapes. Some called forth happy greetings, as it had been many lifetimes since they had renewed their acquaintance. Others reminded him he was never alone and that what he was about to experience would be shared by all. One approached him to perform a spiritual hug. He felt the warmth of great love envelop him. At that moment, all worries, stress, tiredness, and bodily aches and pains disappeared. It was as though he were in the arms of a mother cradling her newborn infant with love and affection. He relaxed in the sensation and enjoyed it for some time.

There was no hurry. His friends joined in the spiritual hug. Love flowed through all of them. A feeling of all is right with life and spirit invaded them and they relished the moment.

It was time. He gave a nod of his head, and everyone released their hold on him. He turned and stepped into the shimmering mist. A moment later, he found himself in a lush land filled with the smell of dampness and growing things. He could sense all the plant and animal life that surrounded him. He loved it all.

Looking forward, he saw a robot standing in front of him. The man raised his hand in greeting. The robot raised his arm and pointed an appendage at the man. A flash of light flew from the appendage and entered the forehead of the man.

Surprised to find a robot performing the deed, the man twisted from the blast and fell on his back. The odor of damp foliage filled his nose as he took his last breath.

And then the party began.